Curse of the Caribbean

Where Evil Still Lurks

A Lou Gault Thriller

Dave McKeon

Editing/Formatting: Paula F. Howard, AHAPublishers.com

Cover Design: Bob Hurley

ISBN: 9798992488128

PRINTED IN THE UNITED STATES OF AMERICA

For Sandy Always

"Not everything is as it seems, and not everything that seems . . . is."

Jose Saramago

1

When Antonio Sanchez passed through the prison gates, no one searched him, the bribe had taken care of that. He used an alias, but guards already knew who he was. The guards even knew why he was there. They knew what was going to happen, and they understood the role each of them would play. Cartel money spoke their language. And the cartels owned everybody.

By age nineteen, Sanchez had already sold his soul to the devil. He made his bones as an assassin early in life. Even back then, those in the cartel feared him. The only allegiance he had in life was to himself. Sanchez was a cold-blooded killer. He liked killing people, and didn't care where it happened. He had killed people at weddings, in churches, at soccer games; he even killed a mark after sitting next to the man for hours on a train.

Though his services came with a hefty price tag, the cartels favored Sanchez's work above all other killers. They used him for three reasons: he didn't care who the mark was, he could track down anybody, and he never failed.

Yet, this kill would be unique, even for him. This time, he was bribing his way *into* prison to kill a man who had foolishly tried to double cross the cartels. And this kill would happen within hours of his arrival.

Once Sanchez walked into prison, he was not processed before being placed in a cell. He was also the last prisoner the guards escorted to the cafeteria for the noontime meal. He had never met the man he was about to kill, nor had he ever seen a picture, but that didn't matter, Sanchez would recognize the mark when he saw him.

The moment Sanchez entered the cafeteria, his eyes scanned the room: Guards standing near the doors all wore green, a long line of inmates snaking around the tables all wore orange.

To the untrained eye, there was nothing to distinguish one inmate from another. Their haircuts were the same - short. Everyone's ill-fitting prison jumpsuit had the same baggy wrinkled look. Every prisoner wore white socks and the same single strapped blue Nike sandals. But his was not, an untrained eye.

One by one, Sanchez scrutinized the expressions on faces. The nameless ones were all similar: blank, submissive expressions; eyes all cast downward to divert attention. That is, all but one, a man who caught his attention. Even from the very end of the line, Sanchez could tell this one man was different from the rest. This man stood out because his mannerisms were unique.

Sanchez's eyes locked onto the man. He had to be sure because the bribe would only give him one chance. He had to be sure this was the mark.

EVEN THOUGH ARMED prison guards surrounded the prisoner, he knew he wasn't safe. He knew there was a price on his head and his anxious demeanor gave him away. Unlike the complacency of others around him, his eyes darted from left to right. His weight shifted nervously from foot to foot. He held the metal lunch tray up around his chest, as if it were a shield that could protect him.

As Sanchez worked his way up the line, he revealed nothing about his intent. Dispensing cigarette after cigarette so those in front of him would let him pass, it wasn't long before he stood directly behind the mark.

The assassin was quick.

At first the mark thought the sensation in his side was just a muscle twitch. But by the time his hand reached back to massage himself, a stiletto had penetrated deep into his right side, slicing his kidney in half and severing the renal artery. There was no recovery from such a wound. Yet, to be sure, Sanchez pushed on the blade and twisted it in a wide arc, scrambling the mark's interior even further.

When Sanchez withdrew the blade, the mark's upper body arched backward. He took a single breath before releasing the tight grip he had on the tray. Then as the man's life began to ebb away, he sank to his knees.

An eerie hush fell over the room.

The sound of the metal tray striking the terracotta floor broke the silence. As if in unison, the line of prisoners all took a step backward, leaving Sanchez standing next to the man on the floor, gasping for breath. Sanchez still held a wet blade in his hand.

The first guard to approach, nodded before holding out his hand. Sanchez understood the gesture and handed over his knife. As he was led away, he heard whispers of *"El carnicero."* Sanchez smiled. He didn't care that he was known as 'The Butcher.'

SANCHEZ WAS PLACED in solitary confinement. He knew that would happen once he had fulfilled the contract. He also knew he was safe, that cartel money would free him, and that he would be left alone.

Neither the absence of light nor the pungent smell of urine bothered him. He had been in cells before; they were all the same. As he sat on the dirt floor, he pulled his knees up close to his chest and leaned back against the cold adobe wall. After wrapping his arms around his legs, he closed his eyes and allowed his mind to reimagine the kill. A curse escaped his lips as he again imagined vengeance on the stepfather who had molested him as a child.

NOT EVEN ONE day passed before the door to Sanchez's cell opened. Harsh light from the hallway flooded the dark "hole" he had been confined in.

The guard stood at the open door, momentarily staring at Sanchez. Like the assassin, this guard only served himself. He had willingly accepted the bribe to free this man. But he was nervous. The guard had just come on duty and was slightly unsure about the role he was about to play, but the cartel money offered had been more than he made in a month. Like the other guards, he knew what had gone down was the work of this man, the ruthless one, the one they called *"El carnicero."* This killer was an enigma, no one really knew where he came from or who he was, not even his birth name.

Instinctively the guard raised a single finger to his lips. Once he was satisfied the corridor was empty, the guard beckoned the assassin forward with a hand gesture, and whispered, "Follow me."

As soon as Sanchez emerged from the cell, the guard headed down the corridor. Whenever they came to an intersection, the guard paused and checked the coast was clear. Each time they came to a gate, the guard held his breath, hoping the code he entered would work. When they reached the service gate at the outer wall, the guard whispered, "Carlos will meet you."

"Who?"

"Carlos."

"Where?"

"In the *piazza*."

As Sanchez watched the guard punch in the code for the gate, the guard whispered once again. "Hold out your hand."

When Sanchez felt the familiar knife handle in his palm, he smiled.

"*Gracias!*"

"*Si,*" The guard responded.

As Sanchez passed through the gate, the guard lowered his head and made the sign of the cross.

IT WAS EARLY in the morning hours when Sanchez left prison, the time of day when shadows still teased the eyes just before darkness yielded to a new day.

El carnicero had never been to this village before. But it didn't matter, every piazza was alike. At one end there would be a church with a bell tower, the opposite end would be open. The sides of the square would have archways for merchants. There would be a fountain in the middle. The roofs would be terracotta, the walls a chalky white, bleached by the sun.

Sanchez knew it was the cartels who had freed him, and he was thankful for that. But he was a cautious man; caution had saved him more than once. He had no fear, yet he would remain in the shadows until whoever this Carlos was would eventually show himself.

For the moment he rested. His back pressed against the cool adobe wall he had chosen, waiting, listening, alert for even the faintest sound. His nerves were on edge, but he told himself to stay calm. His senses were alert. He fought to ignore the trickle of sweat working its way through the stubble on his cheek. His eyes shifted from left to right, searching for even the slightest movement in the shadows.

Even at this early hour, the air was heavy. Soon it would turn into another sweltering day. The piazza was quiet, but the eastern sky was turning indigo and would shortly be pushed aside by the pink, red, orange, then blue of a new day. With the light, pigeons would reappear. Later the subtle sounds from the marketplace would fill the square. Yet, for now, the only discernible sound was the trickling of water in the fountain, slowly dribbling from its upper tiers to those below.

When the light began edging out the darkness, Sanchez realized the wall he had chosen faced east. His eyes scanned the piazza for movement. He began to regret the wall he had chosen.

Should I stay or should I move, he wondered. *Now is the time to move, before the shadows disappear.*

Just as he was about to move, a noise captured his attention. It was subtle, but he froze when he heard it.

Was that the wind?

When he heard it a second time, he recognized it as wings fluttering at the far end of the piazza. A smile came to his face.

Something, or someone, has disturbed the pigeons that nest near the church. He remained still, listening. A quarter of a minute passed, then a half minute.

They've quieted down. Whatever it was, is gone.

Minutes passed. He strained to hear even the slightest sound. His mind racing, he wondered what had caused the birds to stir.

It could have been the one who opens the church, or the one who comes to ring the bells who disturbed them. Sanchez took a breath. *Or maybe it was someone else, maybe it was this 'Carlos.'* Sanchez let out a soft sigh as he pressed his back against the wall.

Moments passed. Despite the coming light, Sanchez stayed where he was, listening for footsteps. His senses told him someone else was in the piazza, but where? His mind raced.

Who was this, Carlos? Was he a killer, like himself? Had he, Sanchez, somehow unknowingly crossed the cartels? Had his usefulness to them finally run its course? Why was this Carlos being sent to meet him?

His eyes darted back and forth, searching for even the slightest movement. He saw nothing. More time passed.

Then, he heard it. Someone close to him had cleared his throat. He froze.

Sanchez readied the switchblade as he whispered, "The church is not open yet. Have you come to pray?"

"No . . . I am Carlos."

Sanchez tensed upon hearing the name Carlos. "It is strange, I did not hear you approach."

"I was here before you came."

Sanchez turned toward the direction of the voice, not sure

what to think. *If he was already here and sent to kill me, I would already be dead.*

Finally, his mind cleared. "Why do the cartels want us to meet?"

"Come, we will eat, then we will talk."

2

The name "Carlos" was well-known among upper echelons of the cartels. He was only a soldier and worked for a handler, but his status was well above rank-and-file.

Often, he was given extra latitude because he was very careful and calculated the odds extremely well. Frequently, he was trusted and given a free hand to run small operations. He was a simple man and never asked for much; he knew his place and accepted it.

However, as subservient, and unpretentious as Carlos appeared to others, his life was driven by a personal vendetta. The irony that he needed permission from the cartels before he could fulfill his quest, was not lost on him. He also waited years before petitioning his handler for the next step in his plan, and only after first planning and choosing the very words he would use. Carlos knew money and influence were two things that would sway his handler, and he aligned the plan to feed directly into his handler's insatiable desires.

The man who controlled Carlos' life didn't need approval from anyone. Yet, he selfishly brought Carlos' plan before his peers, knowing its sheer brilliance would elevate his own stature.

Upon hearing the plan, even without any mention of Carlos' name, the others suggested Carlos should be the one to lead this new, illicit venture.

Once Carlos' handler was satisfied that his own peers were onboard, he blessed the second part of Carlos' plan: that Carlos would partner with Antonio Sanchez, the assassin known as "El carnicero."

CARLOS KNEW of Sanchez by reputation only; he had never met the one they called The Butcher. When he had asked for a photo of Sanchez and where he might be located, Carlos received a grainy image pulled off a security camera, the name of the prison where Sanchez would be, and sufficient cash to bribe the guards.

In and out of prison many times himself, Carlos knew the guards on the last shift would be the hungriest and easiest to bribe. All he had to do was listen for word that a prisoner had been killed inside the prison. After that, the bribes would take care of the rest. Cartel money spoke loudly, and Carlos had been listening.

WHEN THE TWO men left the piazza together, Carlos led the way as they passed through the narrow dirt streets of the town. Sanchez deliberately walked a few steps behind, hoping to learn a little about Carlos from his gait.

Carlos was taller than most and had a long stride, which

caused Sanchez to quicken his pace. He also walked with purpose and seemingly without the least bit of concern. There wasn't much else Sanchez could learn about him.

As they walked, the light increased, as did the heaviness of the dank air. It was still early when they reached the restaurant at the top of a hill. The outdoor tables were still being prepared. Carlos turned to look at Sanchez. "Choose a table for us. I will let them know we are here."

Sanchez scanned the dining patio and took a seat where his back would be against the wall. His view of the road coming up from the town would be unobstructed.

When Carlos returned, he pulled out the chair directly across from Sanchez. "You could have chosen any table, Antonio, no one will bother us here."

"You know that?"

As Carlos waved his hand across the empty patio he said, "Can't you see? All the tables have been spoken for."

Sanchez eyes scanned the empty patio, as a young girl placed "reserved" signs on each table. A waiter hurried toward them.

"*Buenos dias!*"

Carlos kept his eyes on Antonio Sanchez, as he said, "Alejandro, if you would be so kind, bring us both a café solo . . . and tell Elena to make a special breakfast for us."

Hmmm, Sanchez thought. *So, they know you are here.*

Alejandro bowed his head in obvious respect, "*Si señor* Carlos." Carlos waited for the waiter to depart before speaking.

"Relax, Antonio, no one will bother us here. You are my guest. I am the only one who knows who you are."

Sanchez paused for a moment. "Perhaps, but I am a cautious man."

"And that is why you are still alive, no?"

Sanchez smiled at the acknowledgment. "I am also curious. Tell me, why do we meet?"

Carlos sat back in his chair. "We will talk about that later. This is the hour to enjoy the beauty that surrounds us and listen to the birds. They will only sing to us early when it is cool."

Both men quietly studied the other's facial expression, each trying to read the other's thoughts. Neither was successful.

Either this one is trying to play me, Sanchez thought, *or he is far more patient than I am.*

WHEN THE FOOD that Elena had prepared finally arrived, both men were impressed. The Spanish omelet covered over half the brightly colored plate. The egg was cooked to perfection, filled with vegetables and cheeses. Large Chorizo sausages, sautéed onions, and thick slices of rustic bread, toasted to a crispness that only comes from the open flame, filled the remainder of the plate. The tangy light green salsa that accompanied the dish paired well with the subtle seasonings Elena had used.

When they were only half through their meal, Sanchez set down his fork. "Tell me now, why has the cartel decided we should enjoy a meal together?"

Carlos smiled, brought his napkin to his face, and cleared his throat. "They want us to work together, that is all." He took another mouthful.

"Doing what? If it is drugs, I have no interest. Only the stupid ones handle drugs. Let them get caught, moving the drugs."

As Carlos continued eating, he said, "It has nothing do to with drugs."

"Then what is it?"

Again, Carlos raised his napkin to his face as he swallowed

the food in his mouth. Then, nonchalantly placing the napkin on his lap, leaned forward and whispered. "They want us to become *corsairs*."

When Carlos saw the uncertainty on Sanchez's face, he continued. "Corsairs . . . you know, pirates. They want us to be pirates. They want us to sail the seas together and capture boats for them."

Sanchez leaned back and crossed his arms as he mused for a moment.

"You used a different word first, it wasn't 'pirate,' what was it?"

Carlos set down his knife and fork, leaned forward and made a magnanimous gesture with his arms. "Corsairs . . . the French invented the word. They gave it to the privateers, *for nothing*, just for doing their bidding."

"So, there is no difference?"

Carlos picked up his knife and fork and went back to eating. As he sliced a large piece of sausage in half, he spoke again.

"Ah, but there *is* a difference, a corsair and a pirate are *not* the same. A pirate, unlike a corsair, owes allegiance to no one. But to be a corsair, that is different.

"To be a corsair, one must be authorized by the one who governs them, to carry out the deeds they will do. Therefore, the cartels are authorizing us to be corsairs! But if you prefer the word 'pirate,' then call yourself that."

Sanchez nodded but remained silent. He had only gone to sea once, as a young boy. Finally, he said, "To capture what kind of boats . . . fishing boats?"

"No, not those, the fishermen need those. The cartels want the expensive ones, the big ones . . . the yachts."

"Why?"

Carlos held up two fingers. "Two reasons: they need more mules to carry drugs, and there is a market for the big boats."

Sanchez shook his head. "Ha, so it *is* about drugs. I told you; I want nothing to do with drugs. They know what I do."

"Trust me, what you and I will do has nothing to do with drugs."

Sanchez shook his head again. "No, I have better things to do than slither around the docks at night, like a thief, stealing boats."

"It will not be like that. We will overtake the boats, once they are at sea."

Sanchez hesitated. "And what happens to those onboard?"

Carlos shrugged his shoulders. "That, my friend, is where you come in. That will be up to you. The cartel does not care what happens to them, only that they disappear."

Sanchez thought for a moment.

"So, you and I do all the work, and take all the risk, eh? What's in it for us?"

Carlos clapped his hands together. "Money! Lots and lots of money. When they sell the boats we bring to them, a third of the profit will go to us."

Sanchez took another moment to reflect. As he lifted his cup of coffee to take a sip, he paused. "Do you trust them?"

Carlos expected the question. But before he would answer, he picked up a thick slice of toast and began buttering it. "Are you asking me if I trust my handler, the one who oversees me?"

Sanchez waited for Carlos to look up. As he stared straight into Carlos' eyes, he nodded.

Carlos didn't hesitate. "I do."

When Carlos finished buttering the toast, he picked up his coffee and smiled. "I trust 'The Chameleon' with my very life, *amigo.*"

Sanchez was intrigued. He had heard of the powerful one called The Chameleon, but he needed to know if this was merely a clever idea, or if Carlos had an actual plan.

"So, how do you propose we do this?"

"We need to be discreet, otherwise, we attract unnecessary attention. The boats we take must always sail from different harbors, never from the same port twice in a row. We'll move from island to island. Nothing can be the same, no favorite marinas, no favorite types of boats, they must all be different. If there is no pattern to recognize, the authorities will believe the yachts were swallowed up by the sea."

Sanchez envisioned Carlos' plan.

"Why do you want to be like a gypsy?"

"For the same reason the frog does not drink all of the water in which it lives."

Sanchez smiled at the wisdom. "So, how do we board these boats?"

"The yachts are always looking to take on crews. Once we reach the open water as part of the crew, we will take over the boat."

"So, we do all of this at sea?"

Carlos nodded his head slowly, "Yes."

"Then what?"

"Once you get rid of the people on board, I will take the boat to Bimini."

Sanchez knew the island of Bimini all too well. He furrowed his brow. "Bimini? Have you been to Bimini? There is no market for boats on Bimini. There is *nothing* on Bimini. It is nothing but a shit hole."

Carlos smiled as he leaned forward. "And that is why it was easy for the cartels to gain control of an entire harbor, no?"

Carlos took another sip of coffee. "They have everything worked out."

Sanchez smirked. "Those boats will sit in Bimini forever."

"Perhaps if they stayed there, but the cartel has another plan. Once they are refurbished . . . they will load them with drugs and take the boats to Miami, some to Havana. Once they are at their new destinations, they will sell the mules and the drugs."

"Then what, we wait in Bimini for another boat? The boats you talk about don't go to Bimini."

"No, you and I will fly to a different island and do it all over again."

"Just like that?"

"*Si*. . . just like that."

Sanchez let out a sigh. "I know nothing of boats."

Carlos smiled. "I have worked on many boats in my life. Do you cook?"

Sanchez shrugged his shoulders.

"Some."

"Good, then you will be the cook, I will be the mate."

"That's all?"

"No, you will do the killing, which is why the cartels have chosen you." What Carlos said was true, but it was only half-true. The rest of the plan, Carlos would keep to himself.

The grin growing on Sanchez's face was both chilling and telling.

"So, you are in?"

Sanchez pursed his lips and nodded.

Carlos cleared his throat. "There is one last thing you must know. They have made one thing clear to me: Should we get caught or exposed, we are on our own . . . we will be dead to them."

3

Nineteen hundred miles directly north, Lou Gault stood on his porch staring out at the frozen landscape before him. Eyes scanned the horizon for anything unfamiliar, anything that looked different, anything out of place, anything that might threaten the environment, or those he cared about. He saw nothing out of the ordinary.

Gault was not a complicated man. He loved his family, was proud of his Abenaki heritage, and would protect what was his. His demeanor was calm, tolerant; yet the spirit of a warrior dwelled deep inside him.

Unlike the warm, gentle breezes of the Caribbean, the air he was breathing in central New Brunswick was frigid this time of year. Gusty winds were sending columns of snow swirling down the frozen valley. The windchill was keeping the temperature from reaching up into double digits. Other than the antics of a few crows on the huge ice-covered lake, all else was still.

Winter at *Havre de Poisson* was a quiet time, like every year at the elite sportsmen's resort Gault operated with his family. Once Lou was satisfied nothing looked out of place in the valley, he touched the talisman he wore around his neck, and turned his wiry six-foot-two-inch frame around to enter his home.

Lou Gault was the epitome of the rugged quintessential outdoorsman to many people. When it came to survival in the out-of-doors, or relying upon one's instincts, Gault was the unquestionable master of his own fate. From an early age, he had learned to draw on the resourcefulness inherent to his mixed French, Canadian, and Abenaki bloodlines.

The resort he ran, and its forty-five square miles surrounding a huge glacial lake, was inherited from his grandfather shortly after he returned from the Afghan wars. Lou had served two years on the front, as a commando in Canada's elite Joint Task Force Two unit. Although over a decade had passed, he continued to keep his hair short and his face clean shaven. He lead a peaceful life now, far from the carnage of war.

This land was all that remained of the once vast ancestral home of an eastern group of Abenaki, known now as Grey Elk's Band. The sacred talisman Gault wore around his neck was the one every chieftain of his band had worn from the beginning of time.

The start of Gault's season was still months away. Yet, he is already waitlisting avid sportsmen, who are willing to jockey their calendars, should a coveted opening materialize.

Aside from phenomenal fishing and hunting opportunities that Gault's resort offered, he, himself, was the reason many sportsmen returned to the resort year after year. Unlike his competitors, Gault willingly shared his knowledge with others. His fishing clinics were legendary. The tracking and wilderness survival program he offered to hunters in the fall was ground-breaking. It was largely because of Gault that his resort always appeared several times a year as a featured article in Canada's leading outdoor magazines. For many sportsmen, a week at Havre de Poisson was akin to making a pilgrimage to Mecca.

WHEN LOU'S WIFE, Kate O'Grady-Gault, heard the man in her life come indoors, she looked up from her laptop.

"Is it any warmer out there Lou?"

"Nope, not a bit."

Kate shook her head, inhaled deeply, and let out a sigh.

I am so totally done with this cold, she thought. *This trip to the Caribbean can't come soon enough.*

Conversely, the frigid winters of central New Brunswick mattered little to Lou. In fact, he looked forward to the quiet, peaceful serenity that came with winter. Like Mother Nature, he used the season to rest, rejuvenate, and reflect upon everything while the valley slept. As every season has its purpose and challenges, so did winter.

Now, Lou looked across the room at his wife, his thoughts returning to the present. "Kate, would you like me to start lunch?"

"No, I'll get to it in a moment. I just need to save what I've been doing."

Lou kicked off his boots as he continued to look across the room at the love of his life, the mother of his twins. By any man's standards, Kate was a keeper. She stood five foot-six, had shimmering chestnut brown hair, beautiful hazel green eyes, and an alluring smile. She still exercised regularly, had an hour-glass figure, was as smart as a whip, and functionally independent.

But in Lou's mind, her biggest plus was being a true partner to him in every conceivable way.

They'd met over a decade earlier, when INTERPOL dispatched Kate O'Grady, then a young lieutenant in the Irish Ministry of Defense, over to Canada. Her assignment was straight forward: coordinate the Canadian Mounties' efforts with MI6 and shut down an international smuggling ring.

The Mounties had been so impressed with O'Grady's skills that when the assignment was over, they made her an offer she couldn't refuse. For the past nine years she's led the Mounties Major Crime Unit in New Brunswick. She decided to maintain her "wee cottage" in Ireland, to keep her independence. But New Brunswick had truly become her home.

AS LOU ARRANGED his boots on the rubber mat next to the door, he glanced over at his wife. "Did that Captain Nisbett fella ever get back to you?"

"No, but I found the answer to what I was looking for on his website."

"And the question was. . .?"

As Kate walked to the kitchen, she said, "I wanted to know if it was best we bring soft sided luggage onto the boat."

"I thought Koby told you to do that."

"That she did, but there's not a wee bit of shame in being sure."

Lou loved the odd Irish phrases his wife sometimes used and the dulcet tone of her light brogue. But he was surprised Kate hadn't taken Koby's word on the luggage.

Koby Callahan, his cousin Jake's wife, had spent the early part of her adult life on small ships, living out of a suitcase and dealing with tight quarters as she traversed the globe on oceanographic expeditions.

After a long, reflective pause, Lou said, "So, we're all set then."

"Well, not exactly. There's a new wrinkle now, around when the four of us meet up in Barbados."

As Lou pulled a chair out from the table, he tilted his head to one side. "I thought we were getting together with Jake and Koby when we get off that charter boat."

Kate let out a sigh as she opened the refrigerator. "Well, that was the plan, but it's not anymore."

Lou waited for Kate to elaborate. When she didn't, he said, "Okay, so . . . what's the plan now?"

"Well, we're not quite sure, yet . . . we're still working on it."

Lou squinted his eyes. *How the hell does something as simple as hooking up with my cousin Jake and his wife in Barbados become complicated?*

"So, what's going on?" he finally asked. "Is Koby now having second thoughts about attending the Oceanographic Conference in Barbados?"

"Oh no, she's planning on going to that."

"So, what's changed?"

Kate hesitated before saying anything. Then, she looked up at Lou. "Koby's been asked to stay on for a post conference meeting."

"And?"

"And now Jake doesn't want to fly down until Koby's finished with all her meetings."

"I can see his point in that."

"Right. So, we're trying to work it out."

Lou didn't respond.

The trip was a month away. At some point, they'd all connect in Barbados and toast each other with drinks decorated with tiny little umbrellas.

What's to figure? he wondered.

As Kate walked over to the table with the silverware, her body shivered slightly, as if she had a chill. "I hope the twins will mind your cousin while we're away. I can't believe Laughing Gull agreed to take them for two whole weeks."

"They're not babies, Kate, they're going on seven. Laughing Gull is looking forward to having them. She's hoping their study habits will have a positive influence on her own kids."

"Still, she's a saint to be watching the both of them while we're away."

"Oh, our two will earn their keep, you can be sure of that," he said. "She's lined up daily chores for them, and you know how that will sit."

Laughing Gull was first cousin to both Lou and Jake, the only close relative they had, who lived across the lake in the village of Grey Elk. Her husband, Tall Tree, also grew up with Lou and Jake and was their closest male friend in the village.

Laughing Gull, wise in the ways of the Abenaki, had stood up during a recent special ceremony, and agreed to mentor the Gault children so they would understand what it meant to *"walk the red road."*

Now, as Kate placed silverware on the table in front of her husband, her upper body shuddered again.

"Kate, if you're cold, I'll adjust the pellet stove."

"No, it's not that, I'm fine. It's just . . . "

When Kate didn't complete her sentence, Lou waited, then broke the silence. "Okay, I'll bite. What's going on?"

"Nothing."

Lou picked up on the dismissive inflection in Kate's voice and waited for her to continue. When she didn't, he spoke up.

"Well, it's not nothing, Kate, it's obviously something. So, what's up?"

"Well, it's that damn nightmare, again, about being on a boat. Last night, I had it again. The wind was howling like a banshee."

"Kate, there wasn't any wind last night."

"I'm talking about it in my *dream*, Lou!"

Lou closed his eyes, and touched the talisman he wore around his neck, hoping to push away a vivid flashback of the ordeal they had both experienced when she was kidnapped eight years earlier. Their memories were from different perspectives, but still, they were frighteningly real. Even though it was rare for Kate to relive the nightmare, it still haunted her upon occasion.

Lou still regretted his faux pas of letting the love of his life travel over to Ireland solo, all those years ago. It had been a bad lapse in judgement on his part and he had vowed never to let it happen again.

Now, after Kate arranged the silverware on the table, she walked back to the kitchen area and glanced out the window at the frozen lake.

"Won't it be grand to just sit in the warm sun without a worry or a bother at all? I wish we were there in the Caribbean right now."

"Be careful what you wish for Kate, things don't always turn out the way you hope."

"It'll be fine. I've exchanged enough emails with Captain Nisbett to know we can trust him to do the right thing."

With that, Lou pushed his chair back, walked over to his wife, and wrapped his arms around her from behind. Kate twisted around in his grasp and looked up at her husband.

"Lou, I just want this to be the best trip ever. No drama, no problems, just flip flops, warm weather, and our toes wiggling in the sand."

"Me, too, and with a little luck, Kate, that's exactly what it'll be."

IT WAS beyond ironic that Lou used the word "luck." Unbeknownst to him, the peaceful life he chose to live was about to come crashing down, again.

Luck wouldn't just influence the drama about to unfold . . . it would be the deciding factor on whether they returned at all.

Life or death for them was about to become a toss of the coin.

4

The yacht that Lou and Kate planned to sail on in the Caribbean was currently tied to a swing anchor in Nassau Harbor. Captain Nisbett had just dropped off passengers from his last charter and now had more than a few days to kill before he needed to be in Saint Kitts to pick up his next group.

During tourist season, Barbados was Nisbett's home port, but Barbados was quite a distance south of Saint Kitts. With the rising cost of running a boat, Nisbett planned to conserve fuel and remain in Nassau until time to set sail for Saint Kitts. He would have done that except for one thing . . . money.

So, when an unexpected opportunity came his way to ferry two couples over to Turks and Caicos, Nisbett upped anchor and headed his sixty-two-foot yacht into deep blue water. It wasn't often he had the chance to pick up extra cash, but if he had time and the price was right, he always took it.

As Nisbett cleared the outer harbor buoys, the two well-dressed couples who had just come aboard were raising their glasses and toasting one another on the aft deck.

The name of Nisbett's yacht was the *Marlin Sea*. Soon it would be a name on many lips.

AT THE VERY moment Nisbett was pulling out of Nassau Harbor, Antonio Sanchez was standing on the aft deck of a different yacht entering a secluded cove 130 miles northwest among the small islands of Bimini.

Sanchez was surprised at how easily he and his partner, Carlos, had passed themselves off as real sailors. In a matter of months, the two privateers had successfully commandeered five large yachts. None of the thefts had raised any suspicions since there was nothing to connect the disappearances.

Each yacht had a different registry along with different hull and length designs. Additionally, they had each sailed from different ports. The only similarity: Each vessel had sent out a *mayday* message just before their radios went silent. Carlos was the one who sent out all the mayday messages, giving false coordinates many miles from the true locations of each yacht that he and Sanchez commandeered.

In the Caribbean, if search and rescue resources failed to locate any survivors, or even debris, within a week, the vessels were officially recorded as "lost at sea."

As for the death of anyone missing aboard such vessels, that was quite a different matter. In the absence of a body, a presumptive death hearing was always required before any judgement was made by a court. Lately, however, a few more hearings than usual were taking place . . . The Butcher had been busy.

PREVIOUSLY, Sanchez had always liked the freedom of operating solo, but Carlos had worked hard at building the level of trust necessary to truly be a team. From the outset, they'd each had separate and distinct roles: Carlos was the sailor and planner. He, and he alone, was responsible for safely piloting the stolen yacht to Bimini and selecting the next Caribbean harbor as their target. Sanchez's role was straight forward. He was responsible for dispatching anyone onboard.

In the beginning, the unsuspecting victims were slaughtered indiscriminately and without mercy. People died wherever Sanchez found them. The salons and staterooms of the first two vessels they brought to Bimini were splattered with blood from the carnage. Only after the cartels rebuked Sanchez for all the additional cleanup required, did he become more selective about where and how his victims would meet their Maker.

As always, once the two pirates delivered any *prize* they'd captured to Bimini, little time was wasted before they boarded one of the cartel's many Gulfstream G280's and were flown to their next destination. This trip was no different.

The next harbor Carlos targeted was San Juan, Puerto Rico.

CARLOS HAD STAYED true to the original plan he shared with Sanchez. Yet, despite his best efforts to stay under the radar, they were becoming victims of their own success. Unbeknownst to them, their freewheeling lifestyle had created a firestorm, the likes of which the Caribbean had not seen since the golden age of piracy.

Once again, the adage of even the best-laid plans having unforeseen consequences would prove to be a true.

The folly in Carlos's plan was twofold: He never gave the slightest consideration to understanding who owned the yachts;

and secondly, he naively assumed the only sustained inquiry over the loss of a vessel would come from insurance investigators following a procedure by route. But when they selected two private yachts belonging to Britain's royal family, it eventually brought attention to their little ploy.

As if commandeering high profile private yachts didn't attract enough attention, when they took the royals' yachts, they had unwittingly brought Britain's prime minister into the picture. Months before the twosome hijacked those vessels, Britain's prime minister had gone out on a fragile limb and personally persuaded the royals to loan two of their finest yachts to Britain's Secret Intelligence Service. It had been MI6's desire to use the yachts as a "get-away perk" in recognition of senior members who had demonstrated exemplary service to the crown.

But when two MI6 deputy chiefs, their families, the ships' crews, and the very yachts themselves were subsequently all lost at sea, every imaginable bell and whistle inside MI6 headquarters and at Number 10 Downing Street went off.

In the absence of a logical explanation for both devastating losses, the prime minister was forced to act. In short order a select group of undercover MI6 operatives were secretly deployed to the Caribbean.

CAPTAIN JIM NISBETT wasn't more than four hours out of Nassau Harbor when the playful bantering and sense of joy that had permeated the very essence of the aft deck seemed to cease. All four of Nisbett's passengers were either on their hands and knees retching violently or leaning over the side vomiting.

Sea sickness wasn't anything new for Nisbett's crew, they'd dealt with it numerous times before. In short order, his first mate was hosing down the deck and Miguel, the cook, was passing out barf bags, hand towels, wet wipes, and Dramamine.

Occasionally, Nisbett would glance down from the bridge to check on things, but this crew had been with him for years and had everything under control. As he shifted in his seat, he shook his head, thinking, *folks those damn little umbrella drinks don't mix well with rough water.* But, if Jim Nisbett had taken the time to give it any more thought, he would have realized something else was going on. The waters of the Caribbean weren't rough that day. In fact, as far as the eye could see, the Caribbean was damn near as flat as a mill pond.

The *Marlin Sea* was still hours east of Turks and Caicos when Nisbett's first mate came up the ladder to the bridge.

"Boss, des folks, dey ain't doin' so good, mon."

Nisbett kept his eyes on the horizon and took a deep breath. "They'll be fine once we get 'em back on dry land."

"Dey don't look like dey's sick from da sea, Boss. Dey's in *bad* shape."

That's when Nisbett turned his head slightly toward his mate, tilted his head, and became concerned.

"How so?"

"Dey's wheezin', mon. Dey got da chills an' soiled themselves. Ain't but one of 'em got any energy. I ain't seen nobody like this afore. Dey's bad sick, mon."

Nisbett was an old salt, if he erred, it was on the side of caution. Instead of keeping course for Cockburn Harbor on Caicos, he changed his coordinates slightly and headed for Grand Turk. All captains who frequented these waters knew the smaller of the two islands had the better medical facility. Nisbett was a little over a half hour out of Grand Turk when he radioed ahead requesting medical transport.

As soon as the *Marlin Sea* docked, emergency responders off-loaded all four of his passengers and shuttled them over to the hospital on Grand Turk.

THE TRIP from Nassau had taken about ten hours. Nisbett still had sufficient time to reach Saint Kitts, reprovision, and board his next charter, and he was anxious to move out. He knew there would be a wait at the refueling station, but before he left the harbor, he needed to deliver the belongings of his sick passengers over to the hospital.

Nisbett's first mate gave him a hand transferring the luggage into a taxi, then also traveled with his boss to the hospital. When they arrived, Nisbett explained why they were there and who he wanted to see. The receptionist nodded and asked them to take a seat.

Close to an hour later, they were still waiting. Nisbett took out his wallet and handed his first mate a twenty and a credit card. "This is taking a helluva lot longer than I expected. Here, take this and get back to the boat, refuel, and make sure everything else is ready. When I get back, we gotta haul ass and get down to Saint Kitts."

"Damn good thing we gets paid up front, hey, Boss?"

Nisbett nodded. "Ya got that one right."

"No tip for me this time though, hey, Boss?"

"Ah, don't worry about that. I'll make you and Miguel whole later."

"You's a good bossman, Boss."

"All right, get going. We need to make up for lost time. The last thing I need is for word to get around that people were waiting on me in Saint Kitts."

A FULL HOUR and a half passed before Nisbett learned that all four of his former passengers were in quarantine. The diagnosis was a highly contagious, unpredictable beta version of the Covid virus. All four of his passengers were on respirators and going nowhere. What the hospital staff didn't tell Jim Nisbett was that he might need to be placed in quarantine too. They would test him, first.

Fortunately for Nisbett, his test came back negative, and he and the *Marlin Sea* were free to leave for Saint Kitts.

ANYONE WHO KNEW Nisbett would say that he was wedded to the sea. He had a few girlfriends, but for years, there wasn't anyone special in his life. His parents were both dead and they were the only relatives he knew about. His crew was his family now, and he generously compensated them above the usual rate. In return, his crew was extremely loyal, required little supervision, and went well beyond what a ship's captain could expect from the hired hands.

THE WATERS of the Caribbean remained calm, and the *Marlin Sea* made excellent time. It was well after dark when Nisbett's first mate came up to the bridge.

"Boss, I got bad news."

"What's up?"

"It's Miguel, he ain't doing good, mon."

Hours earlier, they had left Turks and Caicos and were now just off the northern coast of Puerto Rico. Close to land, the boat traffic had noticeably picked up and Nisbett's eyes and focus was on what loomed ahead. As his eyes scanned the water for running lights, he absentmindedly said, "Tell me more."

"He's coughing up blood, mon. He been leaning over da side, too. He got what dem others have."

Nisbett paused. Finally, he asked, "How 'bout you . . . doing okay?"

When his first mate didn't respond, Nisbett picked up a flashlight from the bridge and fixed it on the face of his first mate.

"Shit, man, you're white as a friggin' ghost!"

"I knows. I ain't feeling so good neither, Boss."

Nisbett turned off the flashlight.

"Crap."

"But, Miguel, he got it worse den me boss, he's real bad."

Nisbett shot a glance at his first mate again, shook his head and continued scanning the water around him for lights. "All right, get below, and tell Miguel to hang in there. I'm gonna pull into San Juan. I gotta get you guys checked out."

5

W hen the flight originating in Bimini received clearance to land in San Juan, it began to descend. The change in cabin pressure woke Carlos. He was tired from the long haul from Bimini and had slept soundly during the five-hour flight to Puerto Rico.

Now awake, his bladder told him it was time to get up. Just as he slid open the door to the cramped onboard toilet, he heard the pilot's voice.

"Fasten your seatbelts and prepare for landing."

JIM NISBETT HAD JUST ENTERED the San Juan harbor 'no wake' zone when the sleek jet passed directly overhead. Nisbett barely glanced up at the underbelly of the jet. He was concerned about his crew's health and wanted to tie up at a dock as quickly as possible. He had been to San Juan Harbor enough times to know there was only one marina he trusted - Mullin's Dock.

San Juan had long been a sleepy inlet with only a few wharfs. Then, almost overnight the cruise ship industry had transformed it into the bustling upscale harbor it was now.

That being said, only a few of the original old waterfront bars had managed to hang on, like the one run by Skip Johnson. His place had a rather checkered past, making it a popular hangout with local dock workers.

Even Johnson, himself, was somewhat of a mystery. He came from somewhere in the mainland when he was in his forties. How he came to own the place was anybody's guess. Some believed he won the bar in a high stakes poker game. Others said the place was a front for the cartels.

Mullin's Dock was only a short distance from Johnson's. It, too, had a checkered past. There was a time when this old part of the dock was the envy of the harbor. But the original owner lacked the necessary capital to continue operating and went belly-up. The second owner acquired the dock at auction and turned it into a hub for distributing drugs. It was a sting operation conducted by the Drug Enforcement Administration that led to the arrest and conviction of that owner.

The current owner had renamed the wharf Mullin's Dock and repurposed the old run-down structure located at its far end. Like any number of waterfront buildings, the exterior of the shack had weathered to grey. The only thing even close to being new about the building was a sign over the door in bold letters that read: *OFFICE*.

Nisbett had radioed ahead and EMTs were waiting at Mullin's Dock to transport his crew to the hospital.

Only after Nisbett had his crew en route to medical care, and his sixty-two-foot yacht securely tied up, did he step ashore. But before he headed off to the hospital he hesitated.

Do I walk over to that run-down shack at the far end of the dock now, or later? Nisbett stared at the shack for a full half minute. The light inside was on, someone was there.

Nah, he thought, *the Marlin Sea is safe; the rest can wait.*

AN HOUR LATER, Nisbett stood in the waiting room, lips pursed, listening to the resident physician on duty who had just finished examining his crew.

"Sir, both men have tested positive for a new version of the Covid virus. Standard protocol, and this hospital's policy, requires they be placed in quarantine."

"For how long Doc?"

"Hard to say, five, six, maybe seven days, it varies. We just don't know enough about this genetic strain, yet, to know anymore."

"Come on Doc, can't ya just give 'em a pill, or something? I gotta get down to Saint Kitts."

But before the doc would even let Nisbett leave, he was led to an examination room, and for the second time that day, he tested negative for the virus.

NISBETT WAS in a lousy mood when he left the hospital. With his crew in quarantine and his next charter expecting to meet him in Saint Kitts, he had to make a choice: either forfeit his next two lucrative charters to another captain or temporarily take on a new crew.

In the past, whenever a member of his crew needed time off, Nisbett had backfilled with one of the locals who hung around his off season home port. But that port was hours away on the island of Josh van Dyke, the smallest of the main British Virgin Islands.

While he could have traveled solo back to Josh van Dyke, that would have further delayed his arrival in Saint Kitts. The business savvy thing to do was bite the bullet and take on a temporary crew in San Juan.

Besides, the charter money was already sitting in his bank account, and he didn't want to just hand it over to another captain. No, better to face reality. The final decision would depend on the man who owned the wharf where he had tied up.

TOM MULLIN OWNED Mullin's Dock. Like Jim Nisbett, Mullin had grown up on the island of Josh van Dyke. They had gone to school together and upon graduation, both had chosen to spend their life at sea.

Going to sea was a common career choice for the men on the smaller islands. And once the allure of the sea was in their veins, it never left. Eventually the two men had each saved enough money to become charter boat captains.

In many ways, Tom Mullin was no different from his friend Nisbett. When they were growing up, all the two ever talked about was running a boat and going to sea. But when a broken down, abandoned wharf in San Juan harbor went up for sale, the savvier businessman of the two seafarers, saw a way off the water and out of the life he had chosen, and he took it.

Mullin sold everything he owned at that time with the belief the grass was greener in the other fella's yard. He eventually made a go of it, but also learned the grass really wasn't any greener, it was just different grass, with different challenges.

LEAVING THE HOSPITAL, Nisbett returned to his boat, noticing the lights were still on inside the gray weathered shack on Mullin's Dock. At that hour, it could only mean one thing: his buddy was burning the midnight oil.

As Nisbett opened the door, a little bell announced his presence.

Tom Mullin was on the phone, but looked up, smiled, and pointed at a wooden chair opposite his desk. Like most things inside the disheveled shack, the chair had seen better days.

Mullin was the same age and height as Nisbett. But Mullin was more athletic and did his best to stay in shape. However, like Nisbett, Mullin's hairline was receding which made him very careful about exposing his scalp to the extreme UV rays known to be stronger in the islands due to so many cloudless skies.

As Nisbett waited for his friend to finish the phone call, Jim's eyes wandered around. It had been a while since he was last here, and nothing seemed changed. The same faded pictures adorned the walls; the floor needed to be swept; the waste basket was overflowing; the nicotine film from tobacco smoke still marred the windows.

Hanging on a coat rack was Mullin's trophy memorabilia: a Boston Red Sox baseball cap personally autographed by Luis Tiant. The now sweat-stained, shapeless, bleached out cap should have been a keepsake and never worn, but Mullin wasn't a sentimentalist.

He noticed one thing different, though, the ash tray that was always full of butts was missing. Nisbett took a deep sniff and realized the room no longer smelled like stale smoke.

So, maybe, he's finally kicked the habit, Nisbett thought.

After a few minutes, Tom made a motion with his hand

indicating whoever was on the other end was long-winded. But, finally he said, "All right, listen, I gotta go. You want dock space? Money talks and bullshit walks. So, gimmie a call when you're ready to pony up."

As he hung up, he looked at his friend. "Well, you're certainly a sight for sore eyes. Gonna be here a while? I got a shipment going over to Kingston. There's an easy grand in it for you if you want it."

When Nisbett didn't respond, Tom shuffled a few papers, saying, "Going once, going twice. Want in, or not?"

"I'll pass."

Mullin dismissed his friend's refusal with a shrug. "So, to what do I owe this pleasure?"

"I'm in a bind."

"Police?"

"Nah, I need to take on a couple of guys, that's all. I can't believe it but my friggin' crew just got quarantined. I need to find a crew and haul ass down to Saint Kitts."

"Pickings are slim, Jim."

Nisbett smiled at the pun. "I only need 'em for a week . . . well, maybe two."

Tom nodded his head, "Not a problem, I got a guy I can call."

"Whoa, I was hoping you could lend me a couple of *your* people."

"Not a chance in hell of that happening, Skipper. You want me to make the call?"

Jim sighed and positioned his hands behind his head, fingers locked together, as he leaned back and closed his eyes to think.

Mullin extended his fist, his thumb horizontal, waiting for a reply. When Jim didn't say anything, he called out, "Jim, open your eyes. Yay or nay? Do I make the call for you, or not?"

Nisbett opened his eyes and took a deep breath. "Make the damn call."

WHEN IT CAME to any administrative process, Mullin was still very much *old school*. The next thing he did was push aside a stack of papers and pull a Rolodex closer that was overflowing with business cards. "This'll just take a minute. I got a guy who owes me a big one."

Nisbett didn't even attempt to follow the phone conversation his friend was having. Finally, Tom cupped one hand over the receiver.

"What kinda crew you need?"

"A first mate and a cook."

"Max, tell your guy that my guy needs a first mate and a cook . . . and good ones! This is a friend of mine. We go back a long way. I don't wanna find out he sailed outta here with a couple of shoemakers. You know what I'm talking about, right?"

Whoever was on the other end, asked Tom something else. "Yeah, now!" Mullin paused a few seconds before saying, "Yeah, he's in a hurry. He needs to get down to Saint Martin."

Jim waved his hand.

"Tom, Saint Kitts! Not Saint Martin."

"Strike Saint Martin. He's going to Saint Kitts."

After another pause, Tom continued. "So, you know for certain these guys are good?" After a slight pause, "Who cares if they just flew in, send 'em over. Yeah, he's here now. Yeah, a cook and a first mate, that's what he's looking for."

Tom gave Nisbett the thumbs up sign.

"Okay, thanks. Tell 'em it's the *Marlin Sea*. It's tied up at my wharf. Okay? Okay, listen, I gotta go, we'll talk later. Ciao!"

Nisbett folded his hands across his stomach and waited for his friend to fill in the blanks.

"Okay, they're gonna send a couple guys over. It sounds like they just flew in. They'll meet you at the wharf."

"Have they worked on boats before?"

"Hey, Jim, I don't know, I guess, but . . . come on, man, you're a beggar. Beggars can't be choosey, you know that."

Nisbett let out a groan.

"Come on, connect the dots on this, Jim. These guys are looking for work on a boat. What's that tell ya? They've worked on boats before. Am I right? Am I right?"

Nisbett nodded.

"Hey Tom, look, I'm appreciative as hell for all this, I am, but I gotta run. I gotta take my own crew's personal stuff over to the hospital before I shove off."

Mullin stood up as he smiled, his hand outstretched. "All right, go on, get the hell outta here."

When they shook hands, Nisbett held on to his friend's hand for just a second longer. "We'll grab a beer when I get back."

"The hell we will! You're coming over to the house for dinner."

Jim smiled. "Think you can talk Kathie into cooking up a batch of her conch fritters?"

"Ha! All I gotta say is, 'Nisbett's coming for dinner.'"

Nisbett nodded once. "Tell her I said 'hello.' I'll be back once my next two charters are done. Shouldn't be more than a fortnight."

"Stay safe my friend," Tom said in farewell.

BY THE TIME Nisbett and his new crew pulled out of San Juan Harbor, dawn was only a few hours away. He wasn't thrilled about never having heard the names of the boats his new cook and first mate said they'd worked on. But he was less thrilled with the prospect of forfeiting a couple of very profitable, prepaid charters.

Hmm, my new cook looks a little pale to have worked on boats. Nisbett thought. *But maybe he stayed in the galley a lot.*

But, he was very impressed when he noticed the cook had a line in the water and was pulling in fish before they cleared the second buoy heading out.

Glancing back a couple of times, Nisbett watched the cook dress and fillet the fish. Even with only the stern light, there wasn't a doubt in Nisbett's mind that his new cook could handle a knife.

WITH ABOUT FIVE hours to make up, the course Nesbitt punched into his autopilot was risky, but if the tides were in his favor, he'd make up all the time he needed, and then some. He'd sailed in these Caribbean waters since he was a kid and knew every reef, shoal, channel, and harbor along the way, like the back of his hand.

Now, Nisbett checked the tide schedule one last time. The trickiest part would be the shallows going over the Big Sandy Shoal. Once beyond the shoals, it was a straight shot down Deadman's Cut to Adler's Narrows.

If the tide was right, he'd make it through the narrows, take Colvin's pass, and head straight across open water to Saint Kitts.

Things are going okay for a change, he thought.

IN REALITY, if Nisbett had stuck to his original plan and stayed in Nassau, the trip to Saint Kitts would have been a breeze. His crew wouldn't have gotten sick, and he never would have pulled into San Juan Harbor. But all those things did happen.

It was only when he took on the temporary crew that his rendezvous with destiny changed. As they left San Juan Harbor, Captain Jim Nisbett had no idea it would be the final run he'd ever make at the helm of the *Marlin Sea*.

6

Nisbett had both throttles set full forward as his sleek, sixty-two-foot yacht deadheaded from San Juan to Saint Kitts, still two full days from their destination.

Fortunately, the Caribbean had remained calm, and the wooden hull sliced through the water so smoothly it barely seemed to disturb the surface. The *Marlin Sea* was as seaworthy as they came, but it was the mahogany trim and spacious salons topside that always caught everyone's attention.

All was quiet aboard ship.

Nisbett was aloft on the bridge; Antonio Sanchez, his new cook, was in the galley; and Carlos, his new mate, was sitting in Nisbett's stateroom reading the ship's log. While the unsuspected pirates knew they were heading to pick up a charter, they weren't sure yet how they planned to play their game this time.

The cartels had never set any expectations on timing nor when any captured yacht had to be in Bimini. It was accepted that whenever they got there, they got there. Once they had taken over each of their previously captured vessels, and Sanchez had dispatched everyone onboard, the long trip to Bimini had always proven to be boring.

But this new prize, the *Marlin Sea*, was a beauty. For some time, Carlos had been toying with the idea of playacting as "Captain." Now, the more Carlos thought about the idea, the more he liked it. The only thing he still needed was to persuade Sanchez to buy into his little charade.

WHEN CARLOS FINISHED READING the ship's log, he joined Sanchez in the galley. What he didn't immediately catch was the fact that Sanchez was aching to plunge his blade into Captain Nisbett. He needed *the rush* that always came with sticking his blade into someone's flesh. It had almost become an obsession.

At first Sanchez thought Carlos' idea was foolish. In the end, they reached a deal: For a larger piece of the prize, Sanchez agreed to go along with Carlos' fantasy plan to masquerade as a captain. He would still play the cook.

Carlos had two plans centering on the masquerade. But he only shared one with Sanchez. The other one would have to wait.

THREE HOURS HAD PASSED since the *Marlin Sea* left San Juan when Sanchez decided he didn't want to wait any longer and made his move.

At first Nisbett thought the sensation he felt in his side was an itch. By the time his hand reached back to scratch the area, the stiletto's blade was deep inside his right torso. As always, the knife severed the right kidney in half and cut the renal artery.

This time, Sanchez smirked as he jiggled the blade, scrambling the insides of Nisbett's lower abdomen even further than usual.

When Nisbett slumped forward, Sanchez withdrew his blade, wiped it clean on Nisbett's shirt, and motioned to Carlos that he could begin playing Captain.

Carlos, himself, was not a killer. He had stayed back and watched from a distance. But now that they controlled the yacht, he helped Sanchez carry the *Marlin Sea*'s former captain aft.

When they reached the stern, Sanchez was ready to toss the body overboard. "On the count of three," he said, but Carlos shook his head.

"No, we'll dump him later."

"Why?"

"We're too close to land."

"So?"

"So, do you want a *floater* to wash up somewhere? We'll push him over once we're in deeper blue water." Carlos looked over the stern and handed Sanchez a rope. "Here, tie him to the swim platform."

Normally at this point, Carlos would have sent out a fake mayday message with incorrect coordinates. Instead, he disconnected the ship's radio. Today, he would play Captain for a while.

HOURS PASSED before either man gave another thought to the body tied to the aft swim platform and Sanchez waited until early dawn before he returned to it. He figured they were now far enough away from land that the risk of another boat coming across Nisbett's body floating in the open water was nil.

But when he leaned over the transom to untie Nisbett, the

last thing he expected to see were four dorsal fins in their wake. Nisbett's right hand had apparently been dangling in the water and his blood had left a trail in the water just like a chum bucket. How long the sea dogs had been following in their wake was anyone's guess. The fingers of Nisbett's right hand were missing, but the rest of his body was intact.

Then, just as Sanchez attempted to untie Nisbett and roll him into the water, a bull shark came forward and grabbed Nisbett's entire right arm. One tug from the shark was enough to drag the body completely off the swim platform.

Nisbett's body was now in the water, but he was still tethered to the stern. The erratic twisting and turning of his body in the wake incited the sharks. In an instant, another shark came forward and Nisbett's right foot was gone.

The wake behind the boat suddenly turned a frothy pink as a complete feeding frenzy unfolded before Sanchez, totally mesmerizing him. Nisbett's body was literally disappearing, piece by piece, before his very eyes.

Suddenly, a great white exploded from the depths. Startled, Sanchez jumped back. The huge powerful jaws of the monster shark closed around Nisbett's body and severed him in half. In the frenzy that followed, the rope snapped and whatever remained of Nisbett's body, sank to a watery grave. Sanchez stood there with a grin on his face, wishing he had someone else to feed to the sharks. He had loved it.

NOW THAT CARLOS was controlling the *Marlin Sea,* he again opened the captain's log. He saw that Nisbett's next charter was just a two-day trip out of Saint Kitts; after that, the boat would head to Barbados for a week-long charter out of that port.

This was the sixth vessel the two modern-day corsairs had

seized. By now, they had become "old hands" at the game of pirating and the newness and sense of adventure of their work had worn off. Carlos had begun to accept the routine more readily than Sanchez who was an adrenalin addict. Sanchez thrived on the rush he felt when watching someone die. But now he had the sharks to play with, and it began giving him ideas.

When the *Marlin Sea* docked in Saint Kitts, Sanchez headed off to reprovision the galley, and Carlos donned the captain's hat which Nisbett had always worn, now ready to welcome their next "guests."

TIVERTON WAS the surname of the English couple who came aboard the *Marlin Sea* in Saint Kitts. They were seasoned cruisers and had sailed the British Cunard ships for decades.

Sir Edmund Tiverton was a Cambridge man, a member of the English gentry and a retired MI6 department head. Tiverton and his wife, Rose, relished the extravagant high-end Cunard experience, especially their impeccable afternoon tea served with freshly baked scones, finger sandwiches, and other delectable sweets. They adored being fawned over with the over-the-top attentiveness of the British staff who catered to their every annoying, eccentric whim. The level of service they received made every sailing trip a delightful experience for them.

Edmund Tiverton had one child. Like his father, the younger Tiverton had also chosen a career in public service. He, too, was a Cambridge man and had quickly worked his way up the MI6 ladder. The younger Tiverton had been among the very first group of senior MI6 staff members to receive the newly introduced Caribbean yachting perk.

Not long after his parents listened to their son rave about the intimacy and delightful level of service he had received aboard the small yacht than the elder Tiverton decided to give up the "big boats" and give a-go at *yachting*.

Their trip on the *Marlin Sea* would be their first, and unfortunately, also their last.

EACH TIME CARLOS had come aboard the vessels they had commandeered, he had paid close attention to how every captain had welcomed their passengers. When Edmund Tiverton and his wife stepped aboard the *Marlin Sea* in Saint Kitts, Carlos turned on the charm and played the game of gracious captain to the hilt.

Had it not been for Edmund Tiverton's quirky personality, he and his wife might have survived the yachting adventure they were embarking upon. But Tiverton and his wife were high-maintenance travelers. To say Edmund Tiverton was demanding was an understatement. Tiverton's style and behavior just naturally annoyed people.

Growing up, his words and actions regularly pissed off his peers. As a child, nary a day passed when he didn't return from the playground with a bloodied nose. As the years passed, his mother thought he might outgrow his self-centered approach to life, but it never happened. The only thing that changed were the people around him who, eventually, ignored his character flaws. For that reason, Tiverton never gave a thought to changing his social behavior.

THROUGHOUT THE FIRST day on the water, Sanchez tolerated Tiverton's boorish behavior and played his role as cook extremely well. He even turned down their beds that first evening, and humorously (for him) placed a mint on their pillows. Later that night, he picked up the shoes Tiverton had left outside his stateroom and actually polished them.

The following morning, when Edmund Tiverton decided to take Sanchez *to school* on precisely *how* he wanted his eggs prepared (with freshly ground *white* pepper, not *black* pepper) and from which side to correctly serve food, Sanchez lost it.

Tiverton was enraged at Sanchez's foul-mouthed push back. He threw his cloth napkin down on the table, cleared his throat, and stood up.

"You, sir, are an insufferable *fool*, and I dare say, an *idiot!* This foul outburst in front of my wife is a disgrace! Your captain shall hear of this!"

When Edmund Tiverton stormed out of the galley, Antonio Sanchez was close on his heels. Sanchez was so incensed, he barely waited for Tiverton to reach the aft deck before the stiletto quietly put an end to the man's life.

Just the night before, Sanchez had dreamt about using both Tivertons as live bait for the sharks. However, at this moment, he was so enraged, that he merely pushed Edmund Tiverton over the side of the yacht and into the sea.

When Sanchez returned to the galley, Lady Tiverton was placing her teacup carefully down on its saucer. As she pointed to the pot of tea on the table, she said, "You may pour me another cup of tea now, and you may take my plate."

Sanchez stared at her. After a brief pause, he snarled, "Pick up your own plate." A surprised look appeared on Rose Tiverton's face.

"I beg your pardon?"

Sanchez lowered his voice, but it was still sinister as he repeated his words: "I said . . . pick up your own plate."

Rose Tiverton was completely flustered and paused to catch her breath before managing to say, "Why are you talking this way?"

Sanchez leaned close into the woman's face and whispered, "Because breakfast has been moved to the stern."

When she didn't react, he yelled: "Move your ass!"

Aghast, she asked, "Is my husband aware of this?"

"No," Sanchez snarled, "He went for a swim . . . now move!"

If the next thing that happened wasn't so macabre, it might have been a comedic scene in a melodrama.

As Sanchez hovered over Rose Tiverton, she fluttered her eyelids as if bewildered, then began fanning herself rapidly with her own hand. Finally, she took hold of her plate, stood up, and walked to the aft deck, waiting there as if she expected a table to be set up.

Instead of carrying up a table, Sanchez emerged from the galley with a rope in hand.

"Put your arms up."

"I'll do no such thing! Where is my husband? I demand to know where he is!"

The indignant response didn't land well with Sanchez. Before Rose Tiverton knew what was happening, she was tied up, thrown overboard, and trailing six feet behind in the wake of the boat.

As she flailed her arms and gasped for breath, her body bounced around in the water like a fishing lure.

Completely devoid of empathy, Sanchez had lost the thrill of merely sticking someone with a knife and scrambling their insides. Now, he wanted more and had been wondering if using *live bait* would make a difference with the sharks. This was his chance to find out.

It turned out not to matter at all to the sharks whether

Tiverton's wife was alive or dead. The murderous scavengers devoured her the same way they did Nisbett's body, one bite at a time.

WHEN THE TIVERTONS failed to return to Saint Kitts, the mysterious disappearance of a retired, former MI6 department head quickly made the rounds in MI6 headquarters, adding fuel to the fire about strange happenings.

The following day, the MI6 station chief assigned to the Caribbean hosted an early morning breakfast to debrief the operatives who had covertly arrived in the Caribbean. As an independent sovereign democratic state, St. Kitts was aligned under the British Commonwealth as a Constitutional Monarchy. That being said, local authorities in Saint Kitts were not informed of MI6's clandestine operation being put into place, nor were officials on any of the other island in the Caribbean.

FOR DAYS, the body of Sir Edmund Tiverton floated in the warm Caribbean waters before washing ashore on the island of Montserrat. Bodily gases had inflated the corpse and kept it afloat like a balloon until it reached the pristine sands of Rendezvous Beach. The torso was still largely intact, but the eyes, ears, lips, and other delicate body parts were gone.

Once Montserrat's Royal Police Service learned that a body had washed ashore, they went about the tedious task of identification. All neighboring islands were alerted that *a floater* had been found. Ultimately, after some time, authorities identified Tiverton from his dental records.

Decades earlier, Edmund Tiverton and his wife had taken out sizable whole life insurance policies, the accumulated monies were intended to fund the cost of their grandchildren's education. The younger Tiverton was quite anxious to receive the funds. However, due to questions surrounding the death of Sir Edmund, and the absence of Mrs. Tiverton's body, the distribution of funds would not occur until a thorough investigation on the cause of death had been performed. That was going to take a while.

7

It took a few attempts before Kate O'Grady-Gault and Koby Callahan, Jake's wife, finally ironed out final details about when they, and their husbands, could all meet up in Barbados. The plan was straightforward: both wives and Lou would first fly down together. Jake would arrive on the final day of the extra post conference meetings that Koby had agreed to attend.

After Kate had rearranged their itinerary several times, she heard a plane coming up the valley. It was a full day before they were to leave, and she held her breath.

Mother of God, don't tell me I gave them the wrong date? We don't leave until tomorrow!

Lou walked over to the door and put on his coat. "That's Jake. I'll be right back."

Kate tilted her head. "That's Jake? He's never back this early. I hope nothing's the matter."

"Nah, he's fine. He's dropping off the package I had Amazon

overnight us." Before Kate could say another word, Lou was out the door. Kate took a breath and relaxed.

Saints be praised. The last thing we needed do is to start off on the wrong foot.

WITHIN MINUTES, Lou returned carrying two large cardboard boxes. When he didn't offer any explanation, Kate's curiosity got the best of her.

"So, what was so urgent?"

"I bought you a little something."

"Did you, now?"

With that, Lou lifted a light tan, soft sided, hand rubbed Italian leather grip out of a box and presented it to his wife. "I thought you might like to travel in style."

Kate's eyes opened wide. "I don't know that I've ever seen the likes of such a beautiful thing!"

"Well, I bought three; one's a carry-on. I had them put your initials on the two for you."

As Kate ran her hand across the smooth leather, she beamed. "Will you just look at how grand it is. The very color and the stitching brings back memories of one my own father had. Now, *he* was a traveler, if ever there was one. He always said to me, the one thing that will serve you well and bring you luck is a good set of luggage."

"Did he say what kind of luck?"

"Now, don't be saying that . . . it was *good* luck."

Lou smiled at his wife and blew her a kiss. "Well, here's to good luck, Kate."

With that, Kate put the grip aside, lifted herself up on her tiptoes and kissed the love of her life with all the passion of an amorous young bride on her wedding night. When they finally came up for air, Lou held his wife out at arm's length and just looked at her.

"What?"

"I can't believe how much it turns me on just to be your man!"

Kate went up on her tiptoes again and gave her husband a peck on the cheek. "Well, hold on to that thought until tonight."

"Kate, we're alone. The twins are across the lake at school."

"I know where they are, but we don't have time for anything now. I'll be jumping onto a zoom call with my Major Crime Unit in twenty minutes."

"Twenty minutes? Kate, that's more than enough time for 'a quickie.'"

"Lou, right hand up to God, I love you with every ounce of passion in my Irish heart. But, if you think for one minute, the colleen you married will go on a zoom call with her hair looking like she's just had a romp in the hay . . . you've got another think coming!"

Lou laughed at how quickly he'd been rebuffed, "Whoa, Kate, it was only a suggestion. Don't get your Irish up."

Kate took a step back and placed her hands on her hips. "Well, don't you be forgetting, not everyone under this roof has the luxury of working a *seasonal* job."

Lou thought twice about objecting to her inference, but he'd been married long enough to know when to just let things go.

When Lou didn't say anything, Kate broke the silence. "Now, if you're looking for something to do, and you have a mind for it, you can transfer what's in our old grips to the new ones. Everything else we're taking is on the bed in the spare room."

When Lou didn't move, Kate continued. "And there's no better time than the present to get things done that need to be done."

I wonder how many times the twins have heard that one? He chuckled.

As Lou moved toward the spare room, he called back over his shoulder, "I hope you're bringing that sexy nightgown that belongs to your cousin."

Kate rolled her eyes. "It's not a nightgown, it's a negligée. But to answer your question . . . yes, I am."

Lou pumped the air with a fist. "So, what time is Smyth Air picking the three of us up tomorrow."

"They'll be here bright and early, at first light."

"And Jake's coming down when?"

"Nine days later."

THE FOLLOWING MORNING, everyone in camp gathered at the lodge well before dawn. Angelo, the resident chef at the resort, had insisted on hosting a special *Bon Voyage* breakfast for his friends.

The goodbyes between all four parents and their youngsters had happened the previous night. The younger generation was actually eager to stay with Lou and Jake's cousin, Laughing Gull, across the lake in the Abenaki village. It meant they'd be among their friends.

The village was only a few miles north of the huge glacial lake. Lou and Jake had both begun their lives there, and the cousins had a strong connection. When the parents of both boys died in a small plane accident, their paternal grandfather, Grey Elk, had taken the orphans in, and Havre de Poisson had become their home. He had raised his grandsons like they were his own, and they grew up as brothers. Taught the ways of the forest, both boys had flourished. Grey Elk prepared them for life and gave them the skills and values they would need.

But it would be up to each of them to decide whether they would "walk the red road" in the village or live in the outside world.

THE FOLLOWING MORNING, the sun had barely appeared in the sky when a plane entered the western end of the valley. Hearing the twin engines, Lou looked out the front window of the lodge. The needle on the thermometer was still pointing at ten and he smiled.

Kate's right, even a short respite from this damn cold will do us good.

"Jake, you ready?" he asked his cousin.

"Putting on my jacket now, cuz."

As they walked down to meet the plane, Lou said, "I wish we were all going down together, Jake."

"I do, too, but I'll be damned if I'm gonna sit around, twiddling my thumbs day after day, while Koby's in a conference, and you and Kate are off somewhere enjoying life on a boat."

"You could come aboard with us, there's still room."

"Yeah, and be a third wheel? No thank you."

"So, we'll see you in Barbados a couple of days after Kate and I get back from sailing around the Caribbean."

"That's the plan."

Within minutes, the landing skis on the incoming plane touched down and the pilot taxied across the frozen lake. Earlier, Lou and his cousin had cleared a foot path down to the dock and secured a couple of ratchet straps to the tie down rings. They liked to be ready, especially during the winter season.

As it turned out, Jake and the Smyth Air pilot were good

friends. Once the Twin Otter was secured, Lou headed up to the lodge while Jake jawed with his buddy.

WHEN LOU RETURNED to the lodge, Kate and Koby had already said their goodbyes to Chef Angelo and his wife, Alesandra.

"Gather your things, ladies, there's a plane waiting on us. As soon as I say my goodbyes, we're outta here.

In short order, the plane was nothing more than a distant spec in the sky.

The DHC-3 de Havilland Twin Otter was a reliable craft, but as Jake had warned, the heater inside the cabin left a lot to be desired. The temperature on the ground was barely registering ten, at nine thousand feet up, the outside air temperature was close to twenty below zero. This time of year, Smyth Air wisely outfitted each passenger area with buffalo robes.

When the trio landed in Grand Falls, they boarded an Air Canada flight to Halifax. From Halifax they flew to Boston. After a short delay, they boarded a direct flight to Bridgetown, Barbados.

NINE HOURS OF TRAVEL LATER, they cleared customs in Barbados and loaded their luggage into a taxi. When they finally came to a stop under the portico of the Hilton Hotel, Koby turned to Kate. "It just dawned on me, we only have the rest of today before the two of you sail away to explore the Caribbean and I'm stuck in a conference."

"I was thinking the same thing," Kate said. "Let's change into something quick and meet down at the pool."

Koby smiled. "Yeah."

Having overheard the conversation in the back seat. Lou said nothing. When the women started getting out of the taxi, Kate reached forward and tapped him on the shoulder. "Lou, are you game?"

"No, I'm good. I think I'll mosey on down to the wharf. Maybe check and see if the *Marlin Sea* is in port. I'll be back in time for dinner."

AS HE LEFT the hotel lobby, Lou grabbed a map of the island and set out for the docks. The weather in Bridgetown was exactly the opposite of the cold valley he'd left behind. The streets of Barbados were alive with people. It was warm. Brightly colored awnings hung from the storefronts that lined the streets, the sounds of motor scooters, reggae music and people talking filled the air.

Wow, he thought. *Maybe we should do this every year.*

As he approached the wharf area, he couldn't help but notice a brightly colored kiosk directly under an oversized sign advertising excursions on charter boats. As he approached the kiosk, a woman dressed in traditional island attire stood up, leaned over the counter, and smiled at him.

Lou hadn't intended to stop, but he did. "Could you tell me where I might find a boat called the *Marlin Sea*?"

The woman behind the counter nodded her head. "Oh, you want to book a char-ta, huh? Char-ta woman take good care of you. I give you *best* deal on island."

Lou shook his head. "I already have one. We board tomorrow. I'm just asking if you know where the *Marlin Sea* pulls in?"

"Ahhhh, dat's a good boat, mon."

Seconds passed as the woman's eyes gave Lou's entire body the once over. Then, without the slightest hesitation or modesty, the woman leaned even further over the counter, divulging every bit of cleavage she had to offer and pointed to her right.

"Char-ta boats . . . all on wharf two . . . go there . . . you see."

Lou nodded and walked away, the pronunciation of the word *char-ta* lingering in his thoughts.

Fifteen slips down the wharf, a sixty-two-foot, well-appointed sleek yacht sat high in the water.

When Lou saw the name on the stern, he stopped and called out.

"Ahoy, the *Marlin Sea!*" No immediate reply.

After a few seconds, he called again.

"Hello, is anyone aboard the *Marlin Sea?*"

Lou's ears picked up a soft voice coming from behind him. "Ain't nobody on dat boat, mon."

Lou turned around to see who had spoken. Except for a disheveled, homeless-looking man on a bench under a huge poinciana tree, Lou was alone. He scanned the area a second time, then settled in on the homeless man.

"Did you just say something?"

When Lou first arrived, he had noticed the man on the bench but dismissed him. After a moment, the man responded with a shrug and a slight nod. Surprised, Lou tilted his head and took an even closer look at him.

Something isn't right, something doesn't seem to fit, he thought, *but it isn't obvious. Is it his hands? Is it the way he's sitting? What is it?*

The man needed a shave; his hair was disheveled, his clothing looked soiled, yet his eyes lacked the emptiness of someone afflicted with *island fever,* a colloquial term for psychological distress in the tropics.

Lou stared at the man for more than a moment. Finally, he

asked a question. "You wouldn't by chance know when they'll be back?"

The man diverted his eyes and looked far down the wharf. "Soon, mon, soon."

"How soon?"

Instead of responding, the man began swaying back and forth, in a rhythmic motion, almost as if music had suddenly filled his head.

"Dunno. Up to dem, mon," he finally said.

Lou smiled at the response. "Can you tell me how long ago they came in?"

Instead of answering Lou's question, the homeless man turned sideways and stretched out on the bench, his back facing Lou. The conversation was obviously over.

As Lou turned to walk away, Lou thought he heard a whisper.

"Be careful, mon."

8

The following morning, Koby accompanied Lou and Kate down to the dock area, to see them off. "Don't forget Kate, ask the captain what time he thinks you'll be back and send me a text."

"I will."

"Okay, I gotta run, otherwise, I'll miss the opening conference ceremony. As she hurried off, she called over her shoulder, "Don't forget, text me when you'll be coming back!"

As Kate waved goodbye, a movement on Lou's left caught his attention. Turning, he saw the same homeless man he'd spoken to the previous day sitting on a nearby bench.

That's odd, I don't recall seeing him there a minute ago when we arrived.

Lou stared long at the lone man. Like the previous day, on the surface, he had all the earmarks of being homeless, but there was something off, it was subtle, but definitely odd. The longer Lou looked at him, the more he had doubts.

What is it that doesn't fit? It's . . . something.

"Come on Lou, let's go aboard."

When he heard Kate's voice, whatever thoughts were running through his mind were dismissed.

AS KATE STEPPED aboard the beautiful yacht, Carlos greeted her with a warm smile. "Welcome aboard the *Marlin Sea*, ma'am, I'm Captain Jim Nisbett."

Kate did a double take. *Hmm, except for that captain's hat, you don't look at all like the pictures on your website.*

"Good morning, Captain, thank you," was all she replied.

Once introductions were made, Kate asked a simple question. "I need to let a friend know when we'll be coming back. At approximately what time will we be returning to Barbados, Captain?"

Kate didn't expect she would need to rephrase her simple question several times before receiving his vague response, but she did. Never one to be shy about asking questions, nor letting go if something was unanswered, Kate turned to the man she believed to be Captain Nisbett as they proceeded to their stateroom.

"Were there any issues with my responses to your online pre-boarding questionnaire?" Based on numerous email exchanges she'd had with the man, Kate expected a direct, no-nonsense answer. When he waffled, again, Kate was surprised.

I wonder if he's read anything I've sent.

When they reached the door to their quarters, Kate turned and asked one more question. "We'd like to do a little snorkeling in Saint Lucia today. I hope that's in the plan. I did request we do that."

This time, Carlos avoided her question entirely, feigning an urgency to depart on schedule. Before Kate could say another word, her captain was hurrying aloft to the bridge.

Literally left standing at the doorway to their stateroom, Kate stared after him in amazement. *What in God's good name is going on? I'm beginning to wonder about this man.*

In the short time Kate had been onboard, her intuition was screaming, *Stop, rethink!* However, instead of listening to the caution flags going off in her head, as she usually would, this time she dismissed them. It was the beginning of her long-awaited holiday escape from the brutal Canadian cold. So, in her mind, nothing, not even a quirky, uncommunicative boat captain was going to derail it.

SANCHEZ WAS in good spirits as he stood on the dock, ready to release the tie lines. He liked the looks of the woman who had just come aboard asking question after question. He smiled to himself, his thoughts entertaining him.

This one is feisty. It will be fun watching her play with the sharks.

UP ON THE BRIDGE, Carlos was reflecting on his interaction with their previous passengers, the Tivertons. He felt he had pulled off his masquerade as a captain very well. But he was not nearly as confident playing the role of Nisbett this time. This "Kate" had asked far too many questions, ones he had not been prepared to answer.

By any measure, Carlos was an unscrupulous scoundrel, but he wasn't a killer. He had no qualms about stealing the shirt off anyone's back, even if they were in it. Yet, strangely, confrontation had always been his Achille's Heel. Unless trapped, he shied away from it especially because his improvisational skills were also well below par. Those two weaknesses made it difficult for him to stay in character, especially when dealing with a strong, independent personality like Kate O'Grady-Gault.

Misgivings about his ability to pull off the masquerade a second time was not the only thought racing through Carlos' head.

This one reminds me of my sister, Maria. She was always asking questions, too, always looking for answers. I loved her very much. He closed his eyes and inhaled deeply. *Maybe this one is sweet like my Maria.*

Now Carlos' thoughts were conflicted. He knew what would happen once Sanchez tired of playacting. He knew there could be no witnesses when they delivered this prize to Bimini. When he opened his eyes, he took another deep breath.

Maybe there is another way.

BY THE TIME the *Marlin Sea* pulled away from the wharf, Kate had changed into a modest bikini and had stretched out on one of the lounge chairs on the aft deck. The sun was warm, and she breathed a sigh of relief while soaking up the rays. Lou lay beside her, deciding whether to close his eyes and drift off to sleep, or crack open the paperback he'd bought at the airport.

Carlos was on the bridge maintaining a respectable distance behind a large sport fisherman boat also heading out of the harbor. Sanchez was busy in the galley, periodically casting a lecherous glance over at Kate. It had been a while since Sanchez had been with a woman, and now, he planned to change that.

As time passed, Carlos' self-confidence continued to erode. It bothered him that his latest attempt to masquerade as Nisbett wasn't going as well as it had the first time. It bothered him that the woman Sanchez would soon kill, reminded him of his sister.

No more than thirty minutes out of Barbados, Carlos climbed down from the bridge, pulled Sanchez aside, and tried talking him into a different plan.

Sanchez shook his head in disagreement; he wanted no part of anything Carlos suggested. "No, we stick to my plan. Once I feed the man to the sharks, I will have my way with his woman. Then I will watch her swim with the sharks."

THE WARM SUN INVIGORATED KATE. She had been nestling in the soft lounge cushions on the aft deck for hours before turning to Lou. "I'd love to know if we're going straight to Saint Lucia, or if we're stopping off somewhere along the way to snorkel."

"Then go ask your captain. He's sitting right up on the bridge."

"I asked him before, but he gave me some cockamamie answer."

"Then ask him again."

Kate was a little put out that Lou wasn't catching on that she wanted *him* to go and ask. When he didn't move, she finally got up and climbed the short ladder to the bridge.

"Captain Nisbett, how much longer will it be before we stop to do a little snorkeling?"

Between the roar of the diesel engine and the wind, conversation on the bridge was challenging. Carlos knew his guest had asked a question but wasn't quite sure what it was. He turned slightly toward Kate and leaned backwards.

"What did you say?"

Kate cupped her hands around her mouth and repeated her question. "When will we stop to snorkel?"

Carlos smiled this time and nodded that he understood. "Soon! Don't worry, be happy. There are many islands in the Caribbean." With that, he looked away.

Again, the response was far too non-committal for Kate. She decided to press harder. "Captain! What's the name of the island where we'll stop to snorkel?"

Carlos looked back nervously. Finally, he called out: "*Perdido.*"

Kate tilted her head, pondering the name. "I've never heard of that island. Is it a large one?"

This one is just like my sister, he thought. *Muchas preguntas, always asking questions.* Carlos let out a sigh. *I don't like playing this game with her.*

When Carlos didn't respond, Kate pressed yet again. "Is it a *big* island or a *small* island?"

Finally, Carlos shrugged his shoulders. "The Caribbean is home to many islands; some are big, some are small, many are uninhabited. But don't worry . . . be happy, every island is a paradise. You will see."

"Is it far?"

Carlos merely shook his head and pointed toward the distant horizon, then he looked away. The conversation was over.

Kate returned to the aft deck where Lou was relaxing. "We're snorkeling at some island called 'Perdido.' I hope it isn't crowded."

He looked up at his wife and hesitated for a moment. "Kate, did you ever take Spanish in school?"

"What, as a language? I'm Catholic, remember? Catholics take *Latin*, although I did sneak in a year of French."

"Do you know what the word 'perdido' translates to in English?"

"Well, no, not exactly. But Spanish and French are both

romance languages, and similar, so I guess it means something like 'missing,' or 'mislaid,' or something like that."

"It means '*lost*,' Kate."

She closed her eyes and thought about the word. Then she opened them again and nodded once. "Good, then hopefully, it won't be too crowded."

Lou laughed. "Kate, I think that'll depend on how close it is to Saint Lucia, not on the island's name."

As he closed his own eyes, Lou missed an important marker. Had he looked up at the position of the sun, he might have realized they were not heading north toward Saint Lucia, but actually southwest toward the remote, uninhabited islands dotting the waters between Saint Vincent and the Grenadines.

FROM THE MOMENT they had cleared the harbor in Barbados, Carlos had opened the engine wide. There was a light chop on the water, but the sleek wave-piercing bow of the *Marlin Sea* had sliced through the deep blue water with ease.

They were close to three hours out of Barbados when Carlos turned toward the aft deck and waved to capture the attention of his passengers. As he pointed to a chain of islands on the horizon, he shouted, "Perdido, straight ahead!" The wind carried his voice.

Lou nodded and both he and Kate returned to their stateroom to stow their personal items. As they passed by the galley, they didn't notice what Sanchez was busy getting ready. It was the chum bucket he would soon lower over the side.

AS SOON AS Kate was ready, she was out the door, heading aft.

Lou was close behind her but stopped to remove the Abenaki talisman he wore around his neck.

Better leave this here, he thought, *wouldn't want to lose it in the water.* His first instinct was to place the scared artifact inside his luggage. But rather than keep Kate waiting while he pulled his bag out from under the bed, he just hung it on the edge of a photo affixed to the wall.

IN THIS PART of the Caribbean, water was nearing high tide. Carlos knew this from the different wave action in the shallower water. Clouds of foam spewed high into the air as waves relentlessly pounded against the protective barriers which had built up over thousands of years. Even from a distance, he could see waves crashing up and over the jagged reefs surrounding the land.

Some of the islands were nothing more than small spits of earth, sparsely sprinkled with palm trees; others were merely barren tracks of sun-bleached sand. But the island Carlos was heading toward was large enough to have a mountain in its center surrounded by deep, dense foliage.

By the time Lou reappeared on deck, Carlos had positioned the boat just off the reef protecting the large island. Noise from the waves pounding up against the reef made it difficult to hear one another speak.

Carlos cupped his hands around his mouth and shouted from the bridge, "This is as close as I dare go. It's rough here, but don't worry, once you are in the water, you will have some great snorkeling."

Lou and Kate both nodded and began putting on the blue and yellow notched swim fins Nisbett kept in the aft storage locker for all his guests.

"This is going to be grand, Lou!" Kate called out. "This is exactly what I wished for! There's not another soul on the beach. We'll have the whole island to ourselves."

As Lou looked out at the desolate shoreline, he nodded. "It does looks that way." But another thought echoed in his mind: *Be careful what you wish for.*

9

The longitudinal line known as the Tropic of Cancer crosses the western hemisphere in the Caribbean. Once Carlos had the boat in somewhat of a stationary position, the heat from the sun felt almost as intense as at the equator.

While Kate was happy to be away from the cold, now she was anxious to escape the heat. Wearing her flippers and headgear, she was ready to enter the water even before Lou had finished adjusting his blue and yellow flippers.

What neither of them noticed was Sanchez working his way toward the bow with a bucket in hand. Inside was a bloody mess of chum.

With the boat being drawn toward the reef on the incoming tide, Carlos was at the wheel with his hands full manipulating the twin levers and maintaining a safe distance from the jagged barrier. He was also contending with deep swells between waves as his eyes fell upon Sanchez lurching his way along the boat's railing.

Once Lou finished adjusting his flippers, he stood up, grabbed onto a stanchion to steady himself and joined his wife on the starboard side.

"Kate, this is rough. The leeward side of the island would be calmer."

She shook her head. "No, this is fine. The water in the lagoon is calm. We'll just ride a wave over the top of the reef. It'll be grand!"

Lou nodded and extended his left arm out in a gentlemanly gesture toward the water. "Women and children first."

In her mind, Kate dismissed his subtle reference to a phrase famously connected to the warning, *"Abandon Ship,"* as she fitted the snorkel in her mouth and prepared to enter the churning sea.

AS THE INCOMING tide kept drawing the boat ever closer to the reef, Carlos seemed to get the hang of it and was skillfully maneuvering the twin screws to maintain a safe distance from the looming rock barrier.

Meanwhile, Sanchez lowered the chum bucket into the water. No one noticed the blood leaking from it, but its scent was already drifting away from the boat in an ever-widening arc.

But Carlos seemed anxious as he watched the two separate scenes: the reef and Sanchez. He turned toward the aft deck and shouted. "Please, get in the water! This is as close as I can get. Once you are in the water, I will move further out. Signal when you want me to come back to pick you up."

Lou nodded that he understood and gave Carlos a thumbs up.

When Kate heard Carlos, she turned to look at him and

missed seeing a long dark shadow pass under the boat. She entered the water no more than seven yards from the reef. Then after three quick kicks, a huge incoming wave easily lifted her over the reef and into the calmer lagoon.

As soon as Kate was in the water, Carlos positioned the wooden hull a little further away from the reef and waited for Lou to go over the side.

NEVER ONE TO GO ANYWHERE WITHOUT his knife, Lou touched the steel on his weighted dive belt one last time. Then, just before going over the side, he noticed a speargun attached to the bulkhead below the gunwales and grabbed it.

I've never tried one of these things. Maybe I'll do a little fishing.

As Lou entered the water, a shark had already picked up the scent from the bloody chum line. Nor was it just any shark, it was a mature bull shark, an aggressive predator who often attacked without provocation and was capable of swimming twenty-five miles an hour in spurts.

When Lou entered the water, the shark was no more than seventy-five feet behind the boat. It hadn't sensed any disturbance when Lou entered the water because of the constant sound of the waves crashing against the reef. But now it turned around and was slowly heading back toward him.

The first wave that came at Lou could easily have lifted him over the sharp, jagged coral, but he wasn't ready for it. He kicked back a few yards from the reef, switched into a prone position facing it, and waited for the next one.

This time, Lou's movement near the water's surface attracted the shark's attention. It had already driven off a smaller reef shark, but now the territorial beast sensed it had another adversary to deal with. Blood in the water had already heightened the shark's senses and in a frenzied motion, it quickly zeroed in on this new intruder.

Lou was lying prone on the surface, not more than ten yards off the reef waiting for the next wave to carry him safely over the top of the coral and into the lagoon when, without warning, the reef shark reappeared from the depths where the bull had chased it earlier. With lightning speed, the apex predator diverted its course away from Lou and headed for the reef shark, who quickly turned and disappeared back into the shadowy depths.

Meanwhile, a second wave that would have taken Lou over the reef reached him, but his body had turned slightly sideways and, again, he wasn't ready. Now he decided to kick back and wait for yet another wave.

After chasing off the smaller reef shark again, the nine-foot monster turned on a dime and circled under the ship's hull. The maneater was now less than twenty yards from Lou and had the swimmer in sight. But when the strong odor of blood oozing from the nearby chum bucket momentarily distracted the beast, he hesitated.

With a single flip of its tail, it turned in a heartbeat, and the fish traveled under the ship to where the chum bucket was floating. With menacing jaws opened, its lips receded, exposing row upon row of pointed, razor-sharp teeth. In a second, the monster's jaws came together with a force exceeding 475 pounds and severed the bucket in two. Then, with a flip of its tail the bull reversed direction.

Completely unaware he was being hunted, Lou lay flat on the water's surface. He turned his head to gauge how close the next wave was and its approach. The shark was below and the fifteen-inch dorsal fin of the man-eater had yet to break the surface.

Having passed on a couple of waves, Lou was finally prepared for the massive swell that was now behind him. When the wave hit, Lou kicked his legs with every ounce of strength he had, hoping the added thrust would help propel him over the jagged edges of the reef. At the exact moment Lou kicked forward, the shark shot out from under the boat. Lou was halfway over the reef when he felt an unmistakable tug on his right leg.

I must have snagged my swim fin on the sharp corral, he thought.

Once its intended prey had escaped to the opposite side of the reef, the 400-pound killing machine turned on a dime with a swirl of its tail and made its way back to the chum line, giving up its pursuit.

As the waves continued to pound the rock, a piece of blue and yellow rubber, the size of a grapefruit, slowly descended to the bottom of the sea.

INSIDE THE LAGOON, the water was smooth and crystal clear. The sun's rays created a shimmering mosaic-like image on the white sandy bottom. As Lou propelled himself forward, he scattered a small school of brightly colored parrotfish. When he broke the surface, he saw Kate. She was standing close to the shore, looking out toward the sea, one hand shielding her eyes, the other waving over her head.

I can see ya' Kate, he thought, *ya' don't need to wave. It's not like we're on a crowded beach.*

Taking a breath, he lowered his face into the water and snorkeled a distance along the reef. The microscopic organisms and various forms of algae on the reef blended into a curious kaleidoscope of color. As Lou moved forward, a never-ending assortment of brightly colored fish scurried ahead, darting left and right. Some sought safety among the crevices in the reef, only to instantly reappear after a current occupant repelled them.

After traveling a distance, Lou stopped, *I must be about even to where Kate is now*. With that, he turned his body and kicked toward shore.

As soon as the sandy bottom came up beneath him, he stood up, spit out the mouthpiece and pushed the face mask up onto his forehead. "Kate that reef is just teaming with fish."

Kate ignored Lou's comment. "I hope Captain Nisbett is planning to come back for us."

Lou slowly made his way toward shore. "He said he would stay a little further out until we signaled."

"Well, he's pretty far out there now."

Lou reached down to undo the straps on his flippers and saw the torn toe. "Hmmm...I guess I left a piece of my flipper out on the reef." Once his feet were free of the huge swim fins, he turned around and faced the open water. "When these waves die down, he'll come in closer."

Kate glanced at the speargun Lou had in his left hand. "Are you planning on doing a little fishing?"

Lou smiled as he lifted the speargun up to chest level. "Yes, as a matter of fact, I thought I'd make points with the cook by bringing him something. He's gotta know how to prepare whatever's in these waters."

"That cook gives me the creeps."

Lou reached down with his free hand to grab his flippers. As he headed toward the beach, he dismissed Kate's comment. "You're imagining things."

"No, I'm serious. Did you see the way he kept looking at me?"

"Nooo, I didn't." Lou shook his head. "Whaddya talking about?"

"I swear, the way he looked at me, it felt like he was undressing me."

Lou smiled, looking at his bikini-clad wife. "Well, you look good, but he's harmless. You just gave him a thrill parading around in that teeny bikini."

"I did no such thing!"

Lou smiled at Kate's rebuke. As amorous as she was with him, she reacted to his tease exactly the way he expected his Irish Catholic wife would. He also missed the exasperated expression on her face as he again examined the damage to his right flipper.

"Do you feel like doing a little more snorkeling, or do you want to just head over to Saint Lucia?"

Kate shielded her eyes with her hand and looked beyond the reef. "Lou, I'm beginning to wonder if that boat is ever going to stop."

Lou looked up and saw her concern. Then he looked out to sea.

"He *is* quite a way out, I'll give ya' that. But he said to just give him a wave and he'd come back. Do you wanna go back?"

"Yes," she said. "That's who I was waving at when you came over the reef."

Kate started waving her arm over her head in a wide circle. "The water is hitting the reef hard, Lou. Do you think he can see us over the spray? I'll move further back on shore and keep signaling him."

As Lou watched Kate move further back from the water, his eyes caught a glimpse of movement near the tree line. His eyes zeroed in on the location but when he didn't see it a second time, he dismissed it as his imagination.

No, we're alone on this island.

10

When Carlos pulled away from the reef, he never intended to look back. Pushing the twin throttles full forward, he headed the boat out to sea. The only thing on his mind now was their fourteen hundred nautical mile trek to Bimini. Cruising speed for the sleek yacht averaged twenty knots in calm waters. Barring unfavorable conditions, he figured they would reach Bimini in a little over seventy hours with their latest prize, the *Marlin Sea*.

Deadheading to Bimini was the part neither man relished in the entire operation. But Sanchez tolerated it because of the twisted excitement he always got from killing the people onboard. This time, however, it hadn't happened, and he was furious when he realized Carlos had made a unilateral decision with this couple, denying him the fun he had planned. As they sailed away from the island, the two of them argued.

SOMEHOW, Carlos had grown uncomfortable playing "Captain" with this woman who asked too many questions he couldn't answer. But the true reason he had let them go was because of the uncanny similarity between the woman and his beloved sister whom he had lost in childhood. His sister's death still haunted him along with a great sadness for not being able to save her. This anguish still lingered in his heart. However, in some bizarre twist, denying Sanchez his usual murderous role had given Carlos a great satisfaction. It almost felt like Carlos had done what he had been unable to do decades ago – finally save his sister from death.

Now, the only way Carlos was able to appease Sanchez was to give him his entire share of money for this prize, along with a commitment to return to their old ways of operating on their next captured boat.

For Sanchez, it took a while before his anger subsided after this betrayal. He had been looking forward to enjoying this woman before the sharks had a chance. It was the reason he was maddest of all.

AS THE *MARLIN Sea* sailed further away, Kate kept frantically waving her right arm. "Lou, do something . . . we need to attract their attention!"

When Lou saw how far the boat had traveled and its definitive wake, he let out a snort.

"Kate, I don't think a friggin' bonfire would bring that boat back."

"Lou, don't even think that!"

But Lou didn't respond.

When Kate finally sensed the *Marlin Sea* still wasn't turning around, she began jumping up in the air, waving both arms.

"What is the matter with that man? Why isn't he turning around?"

Again, Lou didn't respond. His eyes were like narrow slits as he watched the *Marlin Sea*, head toward the horizon along with their luggage and his sacred talisman.

"Lou, will you *please* start waving your arms? He probably can't see me over the spray from the waves hitting the reef. I'm going to move farther back."

For the moment, Lou remained where he was, deep in thought.

As soon as Kate moved further away from the water's edge, she turned and shielded her eyes with one hand. Then she noticed Lou still wasn't waving his arms, and became exasperated.

"Lou . . . for God's sake, we need to *do* something! Wave your arms. Maybe he'll see us, if we're both waving our arms."

"Kate, that boat is not coming back." Lou's voice was close to a whisper. She ignored Lou's comment.

"He *has* to come back!"

Then she cupped both hands around her mouth, raised herself up on her tiptoes and yelled as loud as she could.

"Captain Nisbett, come back! We need you to come back! Captain Nisbett!" Mere seconds went by before Kate turned to her husband.

"Lou, he's not turning. Why isn't he turning? He can't just leave us here!"

The edge of Lou's right hand rested against his forehead, shielding his eyes from the sun. "Kate, it looks like that's exactly what he's doing."

She began jumping and waving her arms again. Then she stopped.

"Jesus, Mary, and Joseph, I don't even want to think about

that possibility for one second! That is *not* what is happening here."

Lou let out a frustrated sigh. "It looks like it to me."

Kate turned to her husband. "Lou, for God's sake, this is the twenty-first century, not the eighteenth. Charter boat captains don't go around marooning people on deserted islands."

Lou continued to stare after the distant boat. "Well, it sure as hell looks like that's what he intends on doing."

Kate closed her eyes. "Lou, that can't be it. Maybe there's something wrong with the rudder and he can't turn around."

"Kate, if that was the case, he'd have backed off on that engine long ago and thrown the hook."

As Kate began half-heartedly waving her arms, again, she said, "Lou, be honest, you don't really think he's leaving us here on purpose, do you?"

Lou nodded his head twice. "It sure as hell looks that way."

Kate's shoulders sagged. "Why? Why in heaven's name would he do such a thing?"

Lou subconsciously twisted the sole of his right foot into the sand, as if he were squashing a bug. "I'm not sure Kate." After a slight pause, he continued, "But, when I catch up with that son-of-a-bitch, I'll ask him."

"Lou, everything we brought with us is on that boat! Our luggage, our cell phones, our passports, our money, *everything*!" She let out a long sigh as she brought her hand up to her forehead, shielding her eyes from the sun's glare. "Lou, he *has* to turn around!"

Lou heard the tone of his wife's lament, but he was already deep in thought. He had left an item onboard the *Marlin Sea* that he had pledged to safeguard. The sacred talisman wasn't his to lose. Like the ancestral lands of the Abenaki, that relic belonged to his people, he was merely this generation's custodian.

Kate let out an exasperated sigh after waving her arms a few more times.

"Damn it, damn it, damn it. I had concerns about that man before we even pulled away from the dock. I should have followed my gut, but no, I stupidly dismissed every red flag."

Kate paused, took a deep breath, then pursed her lips and let out another sigh.

"I exchanged numerous emails with him. He wanted to know where we wanted to go, did we snorkel or did we scuba, what foods we liked, what our favorite wine was, were there any dietary restrictions, did we have any medical issues. Yet, when we came aboard, he acted like a completely different man. It was like he hadn't read a single thing I'd sent him." Without knowing it, Kate had hit upon the truth.

In the distance, far to the left, the sky had changed from light blue to an ugly shade of purple. A squall was approaching. When Lou heard the distant thunder, he walked over to where Kate was standing.

"Let's go. We need to find a place to stay dry."

"Lou, we can't leave. We need to flag him down!"

"Kate, he's not coming back. Let's go."

As they walked toward the line of palm trees, hidden eyes were observing everything and quickly withdrew from the underbrush before disappearing into the shadows.

MEANWHILE, back in Barbados, Koby Callahan stood up and applauded enthusiastically as the chair of the Oceanographic Conference introduced Dan Shively, her longtime friend and colleague, as the next speaker.

Shively's accomplishments in the fields of oceanography and archaeology were world renowned. His research was revered among his peers. Many considered Shively to be the world's current, preeminent explorer. Shively and his research ship, *Magnavox II*, had become as legendary as Jacques Cousteau and the *Calypso*.

As the tall, stately looking explorer took the stage, the words *"Lost City"* boldly appeared on the gigantic screen directly behind him. A hush fell over the crowd as Shively cleared his throat and began to speak.

"What you are about to see are underwater structures unlike anything we typically expect to find on the ocean floor."

Without saying another word, Shively clicked forward to his first slide. The huge screen was instantly filled with images of geometric shapes, arranged in an orderly manner akin to urban developments.

"This picture was taken just north of the Grenadines, near the southern outer islands of Saint Vincent. The age and origin of what you see behind me is still uncertain and undoubtedly, will remain a topic of conversation for some time."

Shively's words and the grainy sonar image sparked a flood of excited murmurs among the audience.

"These images are at a depth close to one hundred and twenty meters. Obviously, the only way we were able to explore a site at this depth was robotically. Most interesting, is the fact that some of the rocks we brought up were volcanic. That, of course, suggests the possibility that what you see on the screen behind me, at some point in time, was above water. Volcanos are prevalent in the area. There is an active volcano on the island of Saint Vincent, and there's an inactive volcano on one of the uninhabited outer islands in the immediate vicinity."

Shively paused to let his words sink in.

"In this next slide, you'll see what appears to be a row of

pyramids. It's difficult to estimate the size of the structures, and I apologize for the graininess of these slides."

Deviating from his intended talk, Shively turned to someone standing off stage in the wings. "Is it possible to dim the house lights a little further?" As if on cue, the lights went down. "Thank you, that may make it easier for you to see more of the details."

Shively waited a few moments before clicking to the next slide.

"This picture is interesting. As you can see, the structures appear to extend off into the distance. Take note of the area in the forefront and left side, we believe those straight lines may be roads. If that is the case, this clearly indicates that at some point in time, a highly advanced, intelligent civilization existed in the Caribbean. Now, even during the most recent Ice Age, nothing on this screen would have been above sea level, which leads us to speculate further on how long ago all of this might have sunken into the ocean."

When an audience member shouted out a question, Shively politely responded.

"Please, hold that thought. I'll take questions momentarily." As the next slide appeared, Shively continued. "Given the existence of volcanic rock at the site, we may be looking at a caldera larger than the one in Santorini. It's difficult to get a sense from these pictures, but this image covers an area approximately three miles across. If a volcano were involved, and I'm not saying it was, more than likely it would have been a super volcano, similar in nature to the one under Yellowstone National Park in the States.

At that point, someone in the audience shouted, *"Atlantis!"*

Shively smiled. "Atlantis, so let it be written, so let it be done!"

Once the laughter settled down Shively continued. "Throughout history, humanity has constructed remarkable structures which continue to perplex modern scholars. Examination of these accomplishments does raise the question of whether our ancestors' possessed technologies which have long since fallen into obscurity."

As Dan Shively clicked forward to the next image, he turned to look at the huge screen behind him.

"This next picture is a closeup of the pyramids. I'll zoom in a little. Again, it's grainy, but if you look closely, you'll notice these pyramids are like the ancient Myan structures on the Yucatan Peninsula and in Guatemala. They are not smooth and pointed like the great pyramids along the Nile.

"Interestingly, and I add this only as a side note, there is a local legend among a small group of islanders in the region, that a culture near here vanished into the sea. I imagine all of this may lend more credence to Plato's claims about Atlantis."

Ironically at the very moment Shively's audience was erupting into a firestorm of questions, a tropical storm was moving rapidly into the exact area of the Caribbean about which he was talking.

"KATE, let's get off the beach and find higher ground before this thing hits." Lou's voice was commanding and she complied.

Beyond the tree line, the island was littered with fallen palm fronds and other natural debris. The stranded couple hadn't gone twenty yards before Lou heard something and sensed movement in the underbrush. As he continued walking, his right hand instinctively moved to the knife on the dive belt around his waist. At first, the only sound was the wind and rustling of palm trees. But when he heard the sound again, he raised his hand, signaling "stop." Waiting a few seconds, he then moved slowly toward the area from where he believed the sound had come. Using the business end of the speargun in his hands, he slowly parted the underbrush.

"Well, what do we have here?"

Kate was tentative, but curious. "What is it?"

"Take a look see."

At first, the only thing Kate saw was the brown decaying debris which was everywhere.

"What is it?"

"Look to the right, on the ground."

Kate's eyes again scanned the area. "Lou, I honestly don't see anything."

Lou used the tip of the speargun to poke at a mound and a motionless bird opened its eyes.

"My God, it was sitting right there, and I never even saw it!"

Lou moved the brush back a little further, so Kate had a better view.

"Lou, it looks just like the domestic hens Chef Angelo raises back home. How did she get here?"

"Well, not all by herself, that's for damn sure. She's a descendant of a breeding pair someone left here years ago."

"Do you think she's sitting on eggs?"

"Definitely, otherwise she would have scampered away."

Kate shrugged her shoulders. "Well, if all we can find to eat are raw eggs, I suppose we can risk salmonella."

Lou only half-listened to Kate's comment. A different disturbance among the debris had caught his attention. Thinking he knew what it was, but not being positive, he'd hold his thoughts until he was sure.

"Let's keep going Kate."

THEY HADN'T TRAVELED MORE than a hundred yards, when Lou raised his hand again. Here, the appearance of the floor under the dense canopy was completely different. The lower halves of bushes were stripped of leaves, and there were gouges on the stems. The ground was as clean as if someone had taken a broom to it. Aside from a couple of broken coconut shells, there wasn't a single piece of debris on the ground. Lou continued to hold up his hand as he scanned the area searching for telltale signs.

Finally, Kate whispered, "What do you make of it?"

Lou was deep in thought, his eyes continuously scanning the area.

When Lou didn't say anything, Kate broke the silence again, this time whispering a different thought.

"It's higher ground here, and except for one or two coconut shells, it's clear of debris. We could camp here."

Lou shook his head. "Maybe, but there's a reason the ground is bare."

Lou scanned the area a few more minutes before turning to his wife. "Kate, take a look and tell me what you see."

Kate knew her husband had seen something. His eyesight rivaled that of the raven, nothing went undetected. Among all the creatures who dwelt in the forest, the eyesight of the raven was unparalleled. The quizzical bird also often used its claws to uncover whatever was hidden from view. As a young warrior, the Abenaki elders had named him *Raven Claw* because of his prowess in reading signs along a trail.

Once she left Ireland and relocated to New Brunswick, Kate had learned about the forest, but she was far from the skilled tracker and outdoorsman her husband was.

Now, when Kate didn't say anything, Lou asked, "Do you see any holes in the ground?"

Kate took another careful look. "I see one. No, wait . . . now I see two."

"Look again, there are more than a couple. This is a colony."

"A colony of *what*?"

"Coconut crabs."

"What kind of crabs?"

"They're also known as land crabs. They're big fellas. I doubt you'd be happy camping here, they come out to feed at night."

Kate shook her head. "Lou, how do you know all this stuff?"

"Survival training. We covered this kinda stuff in commando school."

"I thought you fought in the desert, not the tropics, when you were on active duty."

Lou nodded. "They prepared us for every environment, not just Afghanistan."

"Do you think these things are edible?"

"Yeah, they don't look very appetizing, but they taste like Maine lobster."

She smiled. *Well, that's interesting, there's actually something that doesn't taste like chicken.*

Then she tapped Lou on the shoulder.

"I think we can move on."

Kate wasn't squeamish about much, but she pointed to two humongous claws that had just emerged from one of the holes.

As they circled around the colony of crabs, the sky darkened, and an icy rain came crashing down. Even the thick canopy of leaves offered little protection against the onslaught.

"So much for staying dry, Kate. Let's keep going. Hopefully we'll find some fresh water."

WHEN THE STORM QUICKLY PASSED, the brief respite from stagnant humid air ended as well. The further inland they traveled, the muggier and buggier it became. When they reached a marsh, Lou stopped and held up his hand.

"Do you hear that?"

Kate had been far more conscious about what she was stepping on with her bare feet then listening for sounds. Finally, she whispered, "No, what is it?"

"There's a plane out there somewhere, it doesn't sound like it's too far away. Listen."

Kate squinted as she tilted her head. "Don't you think it's early for them to be out looking for us?"

"They're not out looking for us. We won't show up as missing until we fail to return to Barbados. But the good news is, if there's one plane, there'll be others."

Lou looked upward, as if he was trying to locate the plane.

"Come on, we need to go back to the lagoon. We wouldn't have a chance in hell of signaling a plane underneath this canopy. When we get back to the beach, we'll collect some coconuts and spell out SOS"

Kate swatted at a couple of insects buzzing around her head. Her arms, legs, and shoulders were already spotted with red welts from the venomous little buggers.

"Lead the way. Hopefully, there's enough of a breeze coming off the water to keep these bugs at bay."

"Even if not, we'll have a far better chance of attracting attention out on the beach."

As they worked their way back down the trail, Kate's thoughts never ceased.

Finally, she said, "Lou, what about food? Do you think there's anything on this island besides eggs."

"We can go days without food, Kate. Staying hydrated is our

biggest issue. In fact, let's stop now and drink some of the rainwater that collected on these huge leaves before it evaporates."

As Kate bent over a leaf to sip the water, she pulled back smartly as a small anole lizard scooted off the leaf.

What neither of them noticed was a fresh footprint in the soft earth, inches from Kate's own.

11

Carlos sat alone with his thoughts on the bridge of the *Marlin Sea* after the passengers had been abandoned. Within less then an hour the coast of Saint Vincent came into view. The outer buoy markers for Wallilabou Bay were still a distance away when he glanced at the fuel gauge.

Three quarters of a tank, he thought, *Bimini is still days away and we are traveling at full throttle. If I stop now and top off, I'll have enough fuel to reach Puerto Rico.*

Sanchez was below deck when the *Marlin Sea* began turning course direction and came up on the bridge to investigate. Between the wind and engine noise, it was difficult to hear. Leaning close, he yelled into Carlos' ear.

"How many days before we reach Bimini?"

Carlos recoiled at the unmistakable smell of tequila on Sanchez's breath.

"Three days," he finally answered.

Sanchez scoffed. "Then it's a good thing we're pulling into this port, otherwise, we'd never be able to make it."

Carlos turned his head in surprise and looked at his co-conspirator. "Why do you say that?"

"Because there is not enough tequila on board for you."

"What are you talking about?"

Sanchez smirked. "There's enough for *me* . . . but very little for you, my friend."

When Carlos said nothing, Sanchez continued. "I do not want you to go without, *mi amigo*. So, when we pull into port I will go ashore and get a bottle just for you. It will have your name on it."

Carlos had a taste for tequila, but nowhere near the obsessive level Sanchez had. He shook his head, dismissing Sanchez' drunken words. In the past, whatever they found aboard any vessel they had acquired, they shared equally. Neither man had ever laid claim to something as belonging to him alone.

But Sanchez was long past sobriety. Also, he had not gotten over the feeling that Carlos had cheated him out of his one pleasure in life . . . killing. So Sanchez was taking his frustration out with the tequila, as well as by teasing his partner in crime.

Carlos looked at his watch, but time didn't matter to either of them since they had no schedule. He only wore it because it didn't need to be wound. Whenever they took control of a vessel, they became masters of their own fate. They were free as the seabirds flying overhead. Yet, Carlos was anxious to keep moving.

Finally, he turned to Sanchez. "I just want to refuel. If we're low on tequila, I can wait for mine until we reach Puerto Rico."

But Sanchez shook his head and patted Carlos on the shoulder. "No, my friend, it is not going to work that way. When we pull into Saint Vincent, I will go ashore and return with more nectar of the gods . . . just for you. It is not fair that I have so much, and you have so little."

Carlos knew if Sanchez went ashore, there would be more delay. He shook his head. "No, if there is enough tequila for you, there is no need for us to waste time in Saint Vincent."

Now Sanchez was slurring his words. "My friend, I don't think you understand . . . *your* share of the tequila will be gone before we even pass the island of Martinique."

Carlos could tell from his speech that Sanchez was inebriated. "Antonio, it will be fine. Go back to the galley and enjoy yourself."

Abruptly, Sanchez's demeanor changed from beguiling to anger. "*Señor*, you do not wish to drink with me?"

Carlos could tell where this was going and responded with a soothing tone. "Of course I will drink with you, Antonio. It is just that . . . one of us needs to stay here, at the helm."

"Then we will drink at the wheel, no?" Carlos had no choice but to nod. Sanchez straightened up. "Good, I will bring the bottle here, my friend, then we will drink together, no?

Sanchez was dangerous to be around when he was sober, but when drunk, he was totally unpredictable. Preferring to placate Sanchez, Carlos nodded.

"Yes, my friend, thank you."

WHEN SANCHEZ REAPPEARED ON DECK, he insisted they each down three shots of tequila. After they were finished, he stumbled down the ladder and went below where he polished off what remained in the bottle. By the time Carlos docked, Sanchez had passed out in the forward stateroom.

AS THE *MARLIN Sea* entered the harbor of Wallilabou Bay, Carlos pulled back on the throttles. He didn't plan on being in port long and had decided to tie up at the public pier. The distinctive lines of the *Marlin Sea* were hard to miss. The man on watch in the harbor master's shack in Saint Vincent Harbor made note of her arrival in the log.

WHEN THE BOAT DOCKED, a representative of the harbor master walked over to collect the standard docking fee. The harbor master was religious about collecting fees. He was also religious about taking his *personal* share before anything ever went into the government's coffers. So when the rep wanted a full day's fee for tying up at the public pier, the amount was outrageously usurious, even for this notoriously pricey Caribbean port. But Carlos' argument about the unfairness of having to pay a full day's fee fell upon deaf ears. So when the argument attracted the attention of a nearby constable, he relented. In Saint Vincent, it was all about money.

The local currency in Saint Vincent and the Grenadines was the Eastern Caribbean Dollar. However, when Carlos took out a ward of bills and began counting the dollars out, he heard the rep say, "*Pounds*, not dollars!"

Although Saint Vincent was an independent nation, the reigning monarch of England was still the Head of State. The British pound was not only an accepted alternate currency on the island, it was also considered stronger. The representative could have accepted Caribbean dollars, but the pound's exchange rate gave him an opportunity to skim off a little more for himself.

Carlos reluctantly handed the fee over, in pounds. He looked at the thief standing boldly before him.

It is lucky for you it is not Sanchez you are cheating. If it were, you wouldn't live to see tomorrow, he thought.

Once the fee had been settled, Carlos checked below deck. Seeing his co-conspirator sprawled out in a drunken stupor, he decided to humor Sanchez and replenish the supply of tequila himself.

Carlos slipped into town and bought more tequila. A half hour later, when he returned, Sanchez was still quietly sleeping it off.

WHEN THE *MARLIN Sea* left Saint Vincent Harbor, the same individual who recorded the yacht's arrival, noted the time of its departure. The log reflected the true length of time the ship was in port. The time in the logbook also would be the basis for calculating the amount reported to the government. But the difference between the amount reported and what was collected would never see the light of day.

As the yacht passed beyond the last buoy, Carlos dismissed the incident at the dock and set the auto pilot for Puerto Rico. Confident he had enough fuel now, Carlos was more relaxed. Unlike their previous prizes, no mayday distress message had gone out during this venture. But if all went according to plan, by the time anyone reported the boat missing, it would already be sitting in Bimini, undergoing its transformation.

MILES TO THE SOUTH, the squall had passed beyond the island and Lou and Kate were back at the lagoon. Kate had hoped the *Marlin Sea* would be waiting offshore when they returned, but it wasn't. Lou wasted little time constructing a lean-to style shelter just inside the tree line. Kate busied herself collecting coconut shells of assorted sizes and aligning them to spell out the word *HELP* on the beach.

As soon as Lou was satisfied with the integrity of the three-sided shelter, he walked out to see how Kate was doing. At first, he was going to suggest she rearrange the coconuts to spell out the letters "SOS," but something further up the beach caught his attention. Lost in his own thoughts, it wasn't until Kate's voice distracted him that he returned to his reality.

"Lou, are the letters big enough? There are more than enough coconuts, I could double the size of the letters," As she brushed the sand off her knees, she looked at her husband. "What do you think?"

"It looks fine," he said, not even looking at the coconuts.

As Kate leaned over to widen the half circle of coconuts forming the upper portion of the letter "P," she dug her feet a few inches down into the sand to give her toes a little relief from the blistering heat of it.

"Kate, let's go for a little walk, there's something further down the beach I wanna check out."

"You go ahead, I'm getting off the beach. This sand is way too hot; it's burning the bottom of my feet."

But Lou needed to know far more about the island before he was comfortable leaving Kate alone. "No, I want you to come with me. We can walk along the edge of the water. It will be cooler there. I think I see a break in the reef. I wanna check it out."

Kate turned and held her hand to shield her eyes from the sun's glare. "I think I see it, too. Is that a good thing, or a bad thing?"

"Hopefully it means fresh water is coming into the lagoon."

"You think so?"

Lou nodded. "Yeah, coral won't survive in areas where freshwater mixes with seawater."

"How do you know that?"

"Survival training 101."

Kate raised her eyebrows. "You obviously paid attention in that class."

Yeah, Lou thought, having a flashback to days he'd spent in survival training.

You had to pay attention. If you didn't, you washed out.

As they made their way up the shoreline, a small group of sand pipers scurried ahead of them along the water's edge.

"Lou?"

"What?"

Kate paused a moment before continuing. "Do you think there are any snakes on this island?"

"I don't think so," he lied. "If there are any, they'd be small. Outside of tree frogs, small lizards, and insects there isn't much for them to eat." Lou never deliberately lied, but he needed to confirm his suspicions before saying anything else.

"Well," Kate said, "I hope there's more on this island than just who eats who."

AS THEY CONTINUED along the beach, a natural change in the tree line opposite the opening in the reef became apparent. It wasn't until they crested a slight rise on the beach, that the sun's rays sparkled across the shallow stream of water flowing steadily across the mudflat into the lagoon.

Lou shielded his eyes as he studied the area in front of them. Other than shorebirds gliding overhead, the mudflat and the marshy area beyond seemed to be uninhabited.

"Come on, Kate, let's see where this stream comes from. With luck we might find out something else about this island."

Kate looked at the water flowing around the brightly colored scum which had built up on the mudflat. "Do you think this water is actually safe to drink?"

"Further up it should be. It looks like it has a good flow."

Just before they entered the rainforest, Lou held up his hand again signaling her to stop. There were tracks in the sand indicating something large had recently traveled across the mudflat.

As Lou knelt to study it, Kate whispered, "What is it?"

"A sea turtle."

After a pause, he continued. "Probably came ashore to lay her eggs. See the claw marks in the sand? That's where she dug in to pull herself forward. From the looks of it, she's a decent size. I don't see where she came back, so she's still in there probably covering her eggs."

Kate didn't say anything, but the thought of downing raw turtle eggs didn't particularly excite her. As they passed through the tree line, she looked up at the canopy.

"Do you think we'll find any edible plants?"

"We'll see."

THE STREAM BED WAS SHALLOW, but the flow was steady. As they traveled further into the island the ecosystem changed from palm trees to a lush rainforest.

"Lou, are those bananas?"

"Plantains . . . same family. They're edible raw, but taste better cooked. They're like sweet potatoes. I saw some papayas earlier."

"We should grab some on the way back."

"We will. There were a few ripe ones."

AS THEY CONTINUED FOLLOWING the stream bed, they were gaining altitude. The constant flow of water had worn away the soil, and in many places, the water cascaded over rock. After they had pushed through the undergrowth for a half-hour, the stream bed disappeared.

Kate had been carefully choosing where she placed her bare feet and had not paid close attention to what was ahead. When she realized the stream had disappeared, she was surprised.

"Lou, what happened to the water?"

"It went underground, that's all."

"How?"

"Well, the ground is porous. We've been going uphill for a while now. Somewhere up ahead, it found a fissure in the coral."

"This is coral rock we're standing on?"

"Yes, this was all underwater at one time. I suspect we're on the side of a volcano."

At that, Kate's eyes widened. She looked around. "Do you think it's active?"

Lou shook his head. "No, there's too much vegetation. I think we might sense a little heat from the ground if it was active, especially on our bare feet."

Kate looked at the ground. "If this is a volcano, shouldn't the soil be black?"

"That depends on which side the lava came down. But everything's been covered over by topsoil for a long time. Come on, let's go up a little further."

NOT MORE THAN fifteen minutes passed when Lou raised his hand again, signaling to stop. "Listen, do you hear that?"

In between the sound of birds in the distance, she did hear a noise. "It's faint, but I do hear something. What is it?"

"Let's go see," he said.

So, barefoot and clothed only in a bikini, a bug-bitten Kate followed her barefoot man wearing swim trunks up the side of what might be a volcano, with only one thought: *This is NOT the vacation I wanted.*

12

A full seven days had passed since the real Captain Jim Nisbett sailed out of San Juan while his regular two-man crew was left behind in quarantine. Twice since then, both men had tested negative for the virus and were now scheduled for discharge.

Before Nisbett left, he had willingly provided the hospital with a credit card to cover the men's expenses, along with a note instructing his men to wait for him at Mullin's Dock. Nisbett had also left a small amount of cash for them even though it wasn't much. To conserve what little money they had, and give their legs a stretch, the two men decided to walk the distance to the harbor.

MULLIN'S DOCK was a busy place and this day was no different. There were boatloads of sugar cane coming in, and cases of Island Rum going out. As usual, Tom Mullin was out on his dock pacing back and forth, clipboard in hand, attempting to bring order to everything that was going on.

When Nisbett's men arrived, they waited for Mullin to take a break from the action. But after a while, when it appeared that wasn't going to happen, they approached him.

"Mister Mullin?"

Mullin was busy flipping through page after page on his clipboard, looking for a specific sheet, and responded without even looking up. "Yeah, what is it?"

"Mister Mullin, Capt'n Jim Nisbett said we was to come here and wait for him."

Mullin merely shrugged his shoulders. Then a movement on the dock caught his eye. "No . . . stop! Not those! I told you to leave those crates alone! Those go on the next boat."

Satisfied he had just averted a costly mistake, Mullin pulled a handkerchief from his pocket and pushed up the frayed peak of a sun-bleached Boston Red Sox ball cap he always wore, wiping sweat from his brow. Turning to the men standing next to him, he asked, "What was it you said about Nisbett?"

"He left us a note saying we was to come here and wait for him."

Mullin, still paying more attention to happenings on the dock than the two men standing beside him, said, "He hasn't come back yet."

"Well, he told us to wait here."

Dismissing the comment, Mullin yelled out again. "I said *not* those crates!" Shaking his head again, he cursed. "Damn it, bad help is easy to find."

Nisbett's former cook, Miguel, instantly saw an opportunity to make some cash. "If yur looking for good workers, Cap'n Jim'll tell ya' we's good. We ain't got nothing ta do now but hang 'round and wait."

Finally, Mullin looked at the two men. "Are you the two Nisbett said were quarantined?"

"Yes, sa'."

Mullin looked each man up and down, twice. "All right, you wanna work, go relieve those two knuckleheads over here and start loading the cases with the orange labels onto that boat, *not* the green labels, leave those where they are. Tell the others to come over here."

For the rest of the day, boat after boat lined up at Mullin's Wharf and Nisbett's former crew members worked their tails off. Each time Mullin came out to check on things, he barked out a few more orders and returned to the weatherbeaten shack that doubled as a warehouse and his office.

Nisbett's two men never finished working until after dark. When the last boat pulled away, they walked over to Mullin's office and stood in the doorway.

"We's done now, boss."

Mullin looked up from the stacks of paper piled on his desk and motioned with his hand. "All right, come in, come in, don't just stand there."

Mullin had already fired the two men Nisbett's crew replaced. Now as he leaned back in his chair, he clasped his hands together in front of his chest. "Jim still ain't back yet, and I can use the both of you, if you wanna work tomorrow."

Miguel spoke up first. "We ain't doing nothing else."

"Good, then come back tomorrow – early."

"We needs to find us some place to sleep, least 'til Cap'n Jim come back for us."

Mullin finally woke up to the fact that the two men had been in the hospital until today. "Tell ya what, I'll make a call and arrange for you to bunk over at *Skip Johnson's*. It's just down the street. It's not fancy, but it's clean. You like spicy food?"

Both men nodded.

"Good, you'll like his stuff, just stay away from his homemade *pique*. I can't eat it . . . it's so damn friggin' hot, it burns going in *and* coming out. But if you like hot stuff, go for it."

DAYS PASSED and Nisbett's men continued working tirelessly from sunup to sundown. It had been years since Mullin's dock looked so orderly, and because he wasn't on the dock all day directing traffic, he was getting home earlier. Each night, when the last boat pulled away and the work was finished, Nisbett's men would head over to the watering hole most dock workers in San Juan frequented, Johnson's Bar and Grille.

IT WAS after dark the night the *Marlin Sea* pulled into San Juan harbor. Carlos was tired from sitting on the bridge for as long as he had. He also decided they'd spend the night in San Juan, carouse a little, refuel in the morning, and when they reached Nassau, would kick back and relax a few days before heading on to Bimini.

There were plenty of available swing moorings in the harbor, but Carlos was tired and didn't feel like offloading the dingy from the bow so, he pulled into the first open slip he came to. Sanchez had recovered sufficiently from his tryst with the bottle and stood at the bow, ready with the docking line.

Harbor masters throughout the Caribbean maintained a record of who entered and exited their harbors. And as in Saint Vincent, authorities in San Juan made note of the *Marlin Sea's* arrival.

Sanchez no sooner had the bow line secured and was

walking aft to secure the stern line, when Carlos called down from the bridge.

"Are you hungry?"

"Si, my poor stomach, it is so empty, it aches for food."

"Is your belly ready for some pique? You like pique, yes?"

Sanchez smiled. "Yeah, you know I love pique, man." Sanchez stopped and thought for a moment. "If we are going to have pique, then we need to go to Skip's, he makes *damn good* pique, man!"

Carlos nodded. "Okay, you wanna go there, we'll go there."

"Do you know why I like Johnson's? I tell you why, it's because he uses a lota chili peppers, man. He makes his pique nice and hot. He makes his so spicy it makes you sweat. Am I right, amigo?"

Carlos merely smiled.

The recipe Johnson used to make the traditional bean dish was hotter than any other in San Juan. He used Pequin chili peppers, which were eight times hotter than the jalapeno peppers everyone else used.

Before they left the *Marlin Sea*, Carlos grabbed Nisbett's captain's hat and put it on, for no other reason than he liked it.

ABOUT TWENTY MINUTES LATER, the two modern day privateers arrived at Johnson's Bar and Grille just after Nisbett's two crew members had taken seats. Even if they had arrived at the same time, it wouldn't have mattered, neither party knew the other, or that they all had a connection to Nisbett, albeit very different ones.

Nisbett's crew hailed from the island of Josh van Dyke. Carlos had heard of Josh van Dyke, as had Sanchez, but neither had the slightest idea where it was. Up to this point, the two thieves had spent their entire lives on the island of Puerto Rico.

Like most nights, Johnson's place was busy, and Skip was working behind the bar. When Nisbett's men walked in, there was only one open table, and seats at the far end of the bar. Tired from being on their feet all day, Nisbett's former crew members took the table.

When Carlos and Sanchez walked in, they walked straight to the bar. As soon as Skip saw them, he nodded and pointed at two open seats at the far end. When they walked past the table Nisbett's former crew were sitting at, Miguel took note.

"Look," he whispered, "that one is wearing Captain Nisbett's hat."

"Where?"

"Over there, the one who just sat down at the bar."

The first mate turned to look, then scoffed. "What makes you think that? There are many hats like that one. Even somebody like you could buy one."

Miguel grimaced. "No, I don't think so, look how he wears it. I don't think that captain's hat belongs to him. I think he stole it."

CARLOS HAD FREQUENTED Johnson's place for years. When he sat down at the bar, every barfly he'd ever met raised a glass in salute. As friendly as the reception was at the bar, Carlos had no idea that an unfriendly eye was watching his every move.

At the table, Miguel wasn't ready yet to let go of just whose hat the man was wearing, despite his friend's urging. "I think I will go ask him how he came by his hat."

"Why are you looking for trouble, Miguel? It's just a hat;

forget it." But Miguel pushed his chair back, as if preparing to get up.

"Miguel don't be a fool. Didn't you see how the others greeted him when he sat down? Who do you think they will help, if there's a fight, huh?"

When Miguel didn't say anything, the former first mate placed his hand on Miguel's forearm. "Are you that anxious to taste hospital food again?" At that, Miguel smiled, and pulled his chair back in.

"Be patient. Cap'n Jim will come for us."

AFTER SANCHEZ HAD his fill of pique and both privateers had downed a few cold beers, Carlos reconsidered his plan to stay in port. "Sanchez, I think we should leave tonight."

"Why, there's no rush."

"I just have a feeling. We should go."

Sanchez looked at his watch; it was late. "No, it would be stupid to leave now, my friend. Do you know why?"

Carlos took a swig of his beer before answering. He knew what Sanchez would say, but he asked the question anyway. "No, tell me why."

"Because we don't have enough tequila, if we go now. Bimini is still a long, long way off and the stores here are all closed now."

Carlos motioned for the bartender.

As soon as Skip finished drawing a couple of draughts, he came to the far end of the bar. "Carlos, are you ready for another?"

"No. I have a favor to ask."

Skip took a step back, folded his arms and squinted before saying, "What kind of favor?"

He expected to hear Carlos say he wanted to run a tab, but instead, he heard, "I need to buy a case of tequila."

Skip shrugged his shoulders and smirked. "What brand?"

Carlos looked at Sanchez. "What brand do you want?"

"Jose Cuervo, gold."

Johnson nodded and walked away.

When the pirates returned to the *Marlin Sea*, Carlos went directly to the bridge and Sanchez undid the lines.

THE ROOM NISBETT'S former crew occupied at Johnson's was directly above the bar. They only had a single flight of stairs to navigate, and they lingered at the bar long after the two pirates left. When Miguel climbed the stairs to their room, he stopped to look out the small window facing the harbor. The sky was clear, and the light from the moon glistened across the water. He was about to turn and get ready for bed when the silhouette of a boat heading out of the harbor caught his attention. He did a double-take.

"Hey, come quick, hurry, I see the *Marlin Sea*!"

"Is she coming in?"

"No, she's *leaving*!"

The first mate was already pulling down his bed sheet. Without even walking over to look, he said, "Then don't worry, it isn't the *Marlin Sea*, so go to bed."

"No, I tell you, it's the *Marlin Sea*, but she's heading *out*."

"If the boat is heading out, it's *not* the *Marlin Sea*. Now, be quiet so I can go to sleep."

Miguel held on to the sill and leaned out of the window as far as he could. The moon was almost full, but it still wasn't enough light for him to read the name painted on the ship's stern. As he watched the sixty-two-foot, yacht leave the harbor he said, "I know that's our boat."

"It isn't."

"How do you know? You didn't even come look."

"Cap'n Jim said he would come for us. Now go to bed, it's late."

"It was the *Marlin Sea*. I'd recognize her silhouette anywhere."

The first mate yawned and closed his eyes. "You are mistaken my friend. But, if you don't believe me, go over to the harbor master's tomorrow and look at his log. Then you will see I'm right."

Miguel took one more look out the window, but the ship had passed from sight. *Maybe I will go over to the harbor master's tomorrow.*

13

A magnificent waterfall cascaded off a precipice down into a pool twenty feet below, not more than forty yards beyond the spot where Kate and Lou had stopped to listen, The idyllic scene before them was close to surreal. The water was sending an ever-expanding ring of ripples out across the surface of the water. The sunlight penetrating the sparse canopy of green directly over the pool seemed to dance upon the surface of the water. The pool was close to fifteen feet across. White flowers, resembling orchids, trailed down from limbs of trees whose branches stretched halfway across the water. The underbrush was kept at bay by a wide perimeter of green moss encircling the pool.

Lou's eyes scanned the area, unable to detect even the slightest trace of a trail or path leading to it.

Kate was the first to break silence. As she leaned into Lou, she whispered, "Have you ever seen anything as grand in all your life? This is the most beautiful thing I've ever seen."

Even Lou was amazed at how the light coming through the canopy seemed to transform the setting. "This is unbelievable."

Kate responded again with a whisper. "This can't be real."

Lou draped his arm over Kate's shoulders and pulled her even closer to him. "If this is what paradise looks like, I'm all in."

"Well, there is still that little thing about food."

Lou ignored Kate's practical comment as he gently turned her around and kissed her full on the lips. When she responded, his kisses moved down along her neck. Kate lifted her chin and arched her head back, offering her neck to the man she loved. Slowly Lou worked his lips downward, listening to her sigh as his lips touched the sensuous areas of her neck that always excited her. She turned slightly to open the space between them as Lou's hand found the fullness of her left breast and began gently caressing it.

Moments passed as their foreplay became more passionate. They left reality behind as a desire to satisfy each other's needs increased. Kate moaned softly, her arms slowly caressing her husband's back. As she moved her hands toward Lou's shoulders, she lifted up on her toes and their moist lips came together. Lou pulled Kate's body even closer, now beyond fully aroused. Their arms held each other in a lover's embrace, each anticipating what they knew would come.

As their foreplay continued, the physical magnetism between them grew stronger. Lou felt Kate wiggle in his arms as she slipped out of her bikini top. Lou began pushing his bathing suit down with his free hand, Kate quickly stepped out of the lower half of her bikini. She pulled him toward the ground where they continued.

The moss that formed a wide ring around the edge of the pond was silky against their naked bodies. Hands caressed and tenderly explored the curves and crevices of each other they knew so well. Finally, they submitted to their passions and became one. When that happened, even the sound of the water falling into the idyllic pool faded into obscurity.

LATER, as Lou lay on his back, his eyes scanned the canopy overhead. "This reminds me of an old movie."

Kate was stretched out beside him, her head on his chest, her hand gently resting on his stomach. "And which one would that be?"

"Remember the one Brooke-what's-her-face was in? They survived a plane crash and ended up on some tropical island."

Kate thought for a moment. "Are you talking about 'Blue Lagoon?'"

"Yeah that one."

Kate sat up and reached for the bottom half of her bikini. "Hollywood made that whole thing up, it wasn't real. But this . . . this is our reality, and it's a far cry from a Hallmark movie."

Lou smiled at the reference to Hallmark movies as he looked around. "It's beautiful here, next to this pool, but the canopy is too dense. We'll never be able to flag down a plane from here. I still say we camp near the lagoon."

Kate had completely transitioned back into the present. She let out a sigh. "Okay, but let's gather something to eat on the way back."

"We will, and I'll harvest a few of these gigantic leaves, too."

"You think these rubbery things are actually edible?"

As Lou drew his knife from its sheath, he shook his head. "Hell, no, I'll use these to make a couple of shawls. We'll need to protect ourselves from the sun. I'm not exactly sure where we are, but I know we're a helluva lot closer to the equator than New Brunswick is."

"Lou, I may be Irish, but I do tan . . . eventually."

"Kate, the last thing we need to deal with is skin poisoning from UV rays."

"More Survival 101?"

Lou nodded. "Your shoulders are already red. I saw a couple of Aloe plants earlier. The sap is gooey, but it'll prevent you from blistering up."

AFTER RETURNING to the area that would become their basecamp, Lou wove several huge leaves he had gathered into primitive shawls.

"Kate, try this on, let's see how it fits."

"What is it? It looks like a huge basket with a hole in it."

"That's exactly what it is. The Abenaki have made baskets out of reeds since the dawn of time."

"Now, who would have thought the Abenaki taught their warriors the art of basket making."

"They don't."

Kate kept staring at him, so he continued. "I used to sit next to my cousin, Laughing Gull, when she was learning how to make baskets. I pretended to be making arrows, but all the time I was watching her."

"She's pretty intuitive, didn't she know you were watching her?"

"Not at first. But one day, I saw her make a mistake and told her a reed needed to go in the opposite direction."

"What did she say?"

"At first, she just looked at me. Then she laughed and said I'd make someone a good wife one day." Quickly, he changed subjects. "Listen, I'd like to check out the far side of the island, are you game?"

"Lou, my feet are a little tender from traipsing barefoot around 'Paradise Island.' I'm going to take a pass. Besides, one of us should stay here in case a plane or a ship comes by."

Lou leaned back against the trunk of a palm tree. "Okay, we can go exploring tomorrow." *But I'm not going to be comfortable until I check out this island.*

THAT FIRST NIGHT was spent near the lagoon. While breezes kept insects away, Lou knew, if they were to camp there, he needed a plan to offset their distance from life-giving fresh water in the stream.

The following morning, after a breakfast of papaya and raw eggs they scrimmaged from a fruit tree and a bird's nest, Lou set out to scout the island for a better location. Kate remained near the lagoon on the off chance a plane might appear.

When Lou left, he took the same trail they had traveled the previous day down the beach from their makeshift camp to where the stream entered the lagoon. This time, when he reached the waterfall, he didn't turn back.

As he worked his way through the thick growth, he knew he was traveling uphill and toward the right. As elevation increased, he noted the undergrowth wasn't as dense, and a refreshing breeze lessened humidity. Eventually, he reached the leeward side of the island. So far, the only wildlife he had seen were iguanas and an abundance of colorful birds flitting among the trees.

After pushing his way through more undergrowth, Lou paused when he came upon what appeared to be a game trail, heading down the slope he was on.

Yesterday's heavy rain would have washed any tracks away, he thought. *But let's see where this takes me.*

A little further down the slope, the ground leveled out as underbrush completely disappeared. Scanning the plateau, Lou remained concealed. He was about to write off the clearing as another land crab colony, when something unexpected caught his attention. It wasn't a sound or movement but a shape, a geometrical shape, inconsistent with its surroundings and dead center in the clearing.

As he continued scanning the area, the voice of Grey Elk, his grandfather, flooded his thoughts: *Be patient, when uncertainty appears, the wise watch, and listen.*

Minutes passed as Lou waited on the hillside. Periodically, the wind picked up and palm fronds moved, but that was the only sound or movement he detected.

The shape that caught his attention was a perfect rectangle, something that would never randomly occur in nature. It stood about four feet high and three feet wide. Whether it was a table or an altar, it stood in the exact center of the clearing.

Sensing he was alone, Lou emerged from the brush and walked toward the center of the clearing. As he neared the structure, he realized it wasn't a single piece. Rather, it was constructed from blocks of coral, chiseled into perfect squares. As he examined the flat, weathered surface, he let his imagination flow.

How long has it been since whoever built this came here?

As Lou looked around the clearing, his right hand moved across the top of the edifice. He could tell from touch that the outer edge of the surface wasn't as smooth as the center. When he looked down, he saw the discoloration in the center where fires had scorched the coral rock. Ash from previous fires filled the crevasses, making it smooth to the touch.

This evidence of what had undoubtedly been ritual fires peaked Lou's interest and he became even more curious about the site. His thoughts raced as his hands carefully explored the top of the structure.

Whoever constructed this edifice was a master craftsman. The seams between stones are almost invisible.

Finally, he found what he was looking for, a loose stone on the outer edge. It took every ounce of patience and skill he had to remove the stone from the flat surface. It was loose but the grit between the stones held it in place. Twice he almost had the stone out before losing his grip and seeing it slide back into place.

Eventually, Lou worked the stone out. He suspected something might be hidden underneath and he wasn't disappointed. Beneath the stone was a small chamber containing a leather pouch. The pouch didn't appear ancient, perhaps because the leather had been well oiled.

How long this pouch has been there is anyone's guess.

When Lou unfolded the elaborate layers of leather, he saw what he'd hoped to find, a large piece of flint and iron pyrite.

The ability to make a fire would totally change their lives, maybe even save them. Their diet would no longer consist of raw food.

Finally, he thought, *something other than bad luck.*

Pleased with his find, Lou kept the two items but replaced the leather wrap and the stone before he scouted around the plateau for further signs. The trunks of palm trees surrounding the area each had markings on them, some resembling stars, others looked like the sun, the rest just looked like squiggly parallel lines. Whether they represented bolts of lightning or snakes, was difficult to tell. Lou scanned the area, his thoughts open.

I'm not sure what went on here, but whatever the hell it was, I hope it had nothing to do with consuming human flesh.

Lou's thoughts about cannibalism were not completely unfounded. As a student of history, he knew the Arawak were the original indigenous people to occupy the islands in the Lesser Antilles. But by the time Columbus arrived, the Arawak had been driven away by the more warlike Kalinago, also known as the Caribs. To this day, rumors persisted that the Caribs had certainly practiced cannibalism.

The only other noticeable thing Lou found was a well-used path leading down to the beach.

WHEN HE REACHED THE BEACH, he discovered a few large, weathered poles someone had driven into the sand near the water. Other than that and what he had seen up higher, there was no further evidence that humans had come to the island. How long ago they had, was impossible to tell.

As Lou looked out across the water, he raised a hand to shield his eyes. *I think I can see a few islands on the horizon. But, without binoculars, it may just be my imagination.*

Lou had left Kate alone longer than he had intended and was anxious now to return to camp. As he followed the shoreline around the island, his mind wandered.

We are really off the beaten track. Whoever used that ceremonial site probably doesn't even come here anymore. If they did, the big question is: would they help us, or hinder our escape?

14

For the umpteenth time, Koby shut off her cell phone and let out an exasperated sigh.

"*Augh*, Kate! Why can't I get through to you!"

Six days had passed since Lou and Kate had gone on their mini cruise and Koby had yet to hear even once from her friend. It was completely unlike Kate to disappear like that.

When people started filing back into the conference room, Koby put her cell phone away, but kept thinking about Kate. *Okay, the Caribbean is one big cell phone dead zone, but that shouldn't matter since we're both using satellite phones. Kate must have her phone turned off and doesn't realize it. Well, I don't know where they are, but hopefully, they're off having a good time.*

ON THE DAY Lou and Kate were due back in Barbados, Koby took a taxi over to the wharf area to wait for her friends. Earlier in the week, she had seen them off from there and knew exactly which dock they'd be returning to.

I shouldn't be annoyed, but a little part inside me is downright angry, she thought. *I can't deny it.* Annoyed her friend hadn't called her, Koby knew they had the whole of next week to hang together.

That'll make up for it all.

IN BRIDGETOWN, Barbados, there were four wharfs, each with a different purpose: Larger cruise ships docked at the outermost wharf, another wharf served smaller cruise ships; a commercial wharf served the cargo ships, but the oldest of the wharfs was where fishermen, tour boats, and private yachts tied up.

Only the latter wharf area had wooden benches which also doubled as outdoor advertising.

Koby left the conference a little early to make sure she would be at the dock when the *Marlin Sea* would finally arrive. Although she had been sitting in the conference all week, she took advantage of an open bench in the shade since the sun was directly overhead when she arrived. When a disheveled homeless-looking man sat down at the far end of the same bench, Koby moved a little closer to her end.

She waited for close to an hour for the *Marlin Sea* to pull in while trading emails with fellow conference attendees and scanning various online news apps. Finally, Koby got up and walked over to a brightly colored kiosk advertising charter boat excursions.

When the lone woman behind the counter saw Koby approaching, she stood up and stepped closer to the counter.

Koby gave the woman a courtesy nod before saying anything. "Hi, by any chance would you happen to know what time a boat named the *Marlin Sea* will return to port?"

With her conference name tag still hanging around her neck,

Koby waited for the woman to respond. She had the distinct impression she was getting not only "the once over," but "the twice over" from this woman behind the counter. Finally, the woman cleared her throat.

"You want to book a char-tah?"

"No. No, I'm sorry, not today. No, I'm just here to pick up some friends. They went out on a boat earlier this week."

"Lots of deals this week . . . but dey go fast. Big, big convention on island this week."

"Thanks, but I'm just here waiting for some friends. Can you tell me when the *Marlin Sea* is expected back?"

"Dat Cap'n Jim's boat . . . him good captain."

Koby acknowledged the woman with a slight smile and polite nod. "I'm sure he is. Do you know when he's due back in?"

"You change mind, you come see me." As the attendant's fingers clicked across her keyboard, she said. "Got good deal on sunset cruise this week. You want one? I give you one."

"Maybe next week."

"Uh-huh." The attendant nodded her head as if she had heard every excuse imaginable for not booking a charter cruise. "You say *Marlin Sea*, right?"

"I did."

"Four p.m. Wharf two. 'Dey in now."

"I was just over there. They haven't returned yet."

The attendant smiled. "On island, Missy, everything is 'bout da tides. Tides come in, boats go out. Tides go out, some boats stay out. But Cap'n Jim, him *goooood* cap'n. You set watch by him."

"Thanks, I guess I'll just hang around."

WHEN KOBY RETURNED to the bench she had been sitting on, the homeless-looking man had stretched out and taken over the entire length of wood. She stood looking at him for a moment before she cleared her throat.

"Excuse me, could we please share this bench?"

Without saying a word, the man sat up and extended his arm in a casual gesture indicating: "Be my guest." Koby nodded and returned to where she had been sitting before at the opposite end.

A few minutes passed. Koby had her iPhone out and was scrolling through her emails, when she heard a voice. "You lookin' for Nisbett's boat?"

Curious, Koby looked up. Other than the homeless person at the far end of the bench there wasn't a soul around. She turned her head and looked directly at the man, and without thinking, blurted, "Did you say something?"

"Seen you here with dem' others."

Koby was totally not interested in having a conversation with this person, but she had heard enough stories to not risk making a scene by ignoring him. Nodding her head, she said, "Yes, I was here several days ago."

"Dat weren't Nisbett they went out with."

Koby wasn't sure what his words meant, but had to decide whether to respond, or let the comment drop. Finally, curiosity got the best of her.

"Really?"

"Dat was his boat, but dat weren't 'ole Jim on it."

At this point, Koby decided it was best to disengage, and without a word, she stood up. As she walked away, she took out her iPhone and pulled up the Apple *Find My Network* app. Before the foursome had left New Brunswick, she had placed an *Air Tag* in Kate's luggage. It was a long shot, but, if the tag was able to send out a Bluetooth signal, she might be able to get a read on exactly where her friends were.

Why didn't I think of doing this before? she thought hopefully. But nothing came up.

Enough time had passed that Koby decided to pursue another approach. She had noticed the harbor master's office earlier, and that was exactly where she headed now.

BRIDGETOWN WAS A BUSY PORT, and it wasn't unusual for the harbor master's office to remain open far into the night.

Like every government building on the island, it was painted an obligatory pale yellow with white trim. The windows had plantation shutters, and the doors were open, creating an airy island atmosphere. As soon as she entered the office, a middle-aged man, dressed in a crisp uniform looked up.

"May I help you?"

"I'm in town for the Oceanographic Conference and am wondering if you might be able to reach a ship called the *Marlin Sea* on your Marine VHF radio. It is quite important."

"Is this an emergency?"

Koby hesitated. "Well, no, I wouldn't call it that."

"Then I'm sorry, ma'am, I'm not able to help you."

"Look, I know this is not something you normally do. But I'm asking for your help. My friends are late returning to port."

The man saw the Oceanographic Conference badge Koby still had around her neck. "Is this related to the conference here in Barbados?"

Koby thought for a moment. "Yes, indirectly it is," she lied.

The man took in a breath and let it out slowly. "When were they due in?"

"Four p.m."

The clock on the wall read a little after seven. After looking at the clock and running his hand over the top of his head and down the back of his neck, the man let out another sigh. "You said the *Marlin Sea*?"

"Yes."

"All right, gimmie a second, I'll see if I can reach Nisbett."

Koby thought to herself, *Is there anyone on this island who doesn't know Captain Nisbett?*

After several tries, the man turned off the radio. "Nope, sorry ma'am, Jim's not picking up. Are you sure he was coming back to Bridgetown?"

"Yes, he was dropping off two passengers."

"Well, he's not responding. Either he's still out of range, or his radio is out. Other than that, I don't know what else to tell you, ma'am."

Koby took a breath and slowly let it out. "Okay. Well, I guess I'll just wait until they show up. Thanks for trying." Then, as she turned to leave, she stopped and turned back around. "Tell me, do you know anything about a homeless man who hangs around Wharf Two?"

"Are you talking about the one who's always sitting on a bench?

"Yes."

"Ha, that's Johnny Coconut. He won't bother you. He's a wharf-rat, harmless as they come."

"He seems rather familiar with the *Marlin Sea* and this Captain Jim Nisbett."

Laughing, the man replied, "Well, like I said, he's a wharf-rat, ma'am. Ole Jim's one of the charter captains who gives him his leftover food. That's the only reason he hangs around there. You'll find him on that wharf seven days a week."

"Is he an islander?"

"No, Johnny Coconut's not a *Bim*. He showed up not even a month ago. The constables keep an eye on him."

"What did you just call him? Did you say *Bim*?"

"Yes, Bim. It's slang for anyone born on Barbados. Nobody knows where Johnny Coconut came from."

"Is that his real name?"

The man shook his head. "One day somebody referred to him as Johnny Coconut and it stuck. Like I said, he just showed up one day. Folks like him come and go. He'll move on sooner or later.

As Koby headed out the door, she pulled Jake's phone number up on her iPhone and pressed the call button. After several rings, his voicemail message kicked in. "Hi, this is Jake. You know I wanna talk to you, so leave a message."

Damn it Jake, she thought, *can't you EVER answer your phone?* Frustrated, she ended the call and sent her husband a text.

pls…call…important!

WHEN JAKE'S phone vibrated a second time, he took it out of his pocket. After reading the text, he pressed the call button. "Hey Hon, wussup? I was gonna call you a little later."

"Jake, they didn't show up today."

"Who are we talking about?"

Koby let out a frustrated sigh. "Lou and Kate. They were supposed to be back in Barbados around four p.m. today."

"And?"

"It's now going on eight and they're still not back."

"Well, maybe they're having such a good time they extended a day or two."

Koby paused for a moment. "Hmm, I don't know why I didn't think about that, but it makes perfect sense."

"I'd put money on it."

"Really?"

"Koby, think about it. If they were having a good time and could extend a day or two, why would they come back just to hang around the pool and sip little umbrella drinks? They're out there somewhere having the time of their life communing with nature."

Koby let out a breath. "I miss you, Jake. I wish you were flying down sooner so we could be together."

"I miss you, too Honey. But, like I said, I am not coming down to sit around all day, by my onesies while you're in all-day meetings."

"Jake, the conference is over. The post summit meetings are only two and a half hours in the mornings. I really miss you, sweetheart, can't you please come down earlier?"

Jake heard the loneliness in his wife's voice. After a brief pause, he said, "Okay, let me see if I can book off earlier. It's not a lot of fun sitting up here all by myself anyway."

Koby closed her eyes and breathed a little sigh of relief. "Thanks Hon. I don't know if Lou and Kate will be up for another boat ride when they get back, but I have a line on a sunset cruise that could be promising."

"All right, let me check with the powers-to-be at work and I'll be back in touch."

All the while Koby was on the phone, she was walking toward the taxi stand. After a short ride to her hotel, the taxi dropped her off and at the front desk, she left a note for Kate: *pls text me whatever time you get in. Hugs, Koby*

15

On the walk back, Lou debated how much he should share with Kate about what he had seen. The squiggly markings he had seen on tree trunks had mystified him. But Kate was as much a part of this as he was, and her insight always made a difference.

When he returned, he shared everything he had observed and imagined with Kate. The fact that someone had visited the island in the past gave them hope. They decided that once a day one of them would take a walk around the island, just on the off chance a boat might have come ashore. The other person would remain near the lagoon on the chance a plane might appear.

THE FOLLOWING MORNING, after a meager breakfast consisting of papaya and water, Kate stood up and put on her protective shawl. "Lou, you circled the island yesterday, so I'll do it today. Besides, I could use a good stretch of the legs."

With that, she went down to the water's edge and began

walking in the direction of the stream that flowed over the mudflats into the lagoon.

WHEN KATE WAS ABOUT HALFWAY around the island, the wooden poles Lou had seen embedded in the sand came into view. He had said they looked weather-beaten and narrower at the base, likely eroded from the constant wave action. When she reached the poles, she noticed one had a short length of rope tied to it. When she touched the remnant, it disintegrated in her hand.

Well, it's anybody's guess how long that's been there.

As she looked up and stared at the tree line, she thought, *Lou said the ceremonial site was on a plateau just above where the poles are.*

Then her eyes followed a single set of footsteps that came toward her from the tree line. *Well, it's unlike Lou to leave a clear trail, but I guess he did. Those tracks must lead to the path he said goes up to the plateau. I think I'll take a look around for myself.*

Once Kate reached the plateau and walked around, her mind began connecting the dots. *Lou's right, there is a ceremonial connection to this place. What that is, and whether anybody still comes here is the big question.*

As she stood at the base of a tall palm tree, she thought, *Some of these carvings are newer than others. But they're all similar, so undoubtedly, there's some significance to the sun.* She ran her fingers along the squiggly parallel lines and dismissed them as representations of lightning. After one final glance around the site, she turned and headed down the path toward the beach.

What she never saw was the dried-out skin, recently shed by its owner.

WHILE KATE CIRCLED THE ISLAND, Lou gathered firewood and created a fire pit in the sand directly in front of their camp. It wasn't long before the skilled woodsman had used the flint he'd found to light a fire and have a thick bed of hot coals ready to cook over. He waited until he saw Kate returning before he skewered the fish he'd caught in the lagoon and had it roasting over the fire. As Kate approached, Lou raised his arm and waved, but Kate didn't quicken her step until she smelled the smoke and the aroma of fish.

She no sooner reached the fire, then Lou motioned to the large coconut shells they'd been using to carry water. "Kate, drink some water."

When she finished refreshing herself, Lou was using his knife to scrape the cooked flesh off bones and onto a large leaf.

"The fish will be hot, Kate but help yourself." Neither spoke as they devoured their first cooked meal in days.

As Kate finished the last morsel of fish, she turned to her husband. "How long do you think we'll be here, Lou?"

"Hard to say, Kate. My guess is they've dumped us off in the middle of nowhere, but we might get lucky. If I know Jake, he'll be looking for us as soon as we don't return."

Kate let out a sigh. After a moment she said, "At least now we can make a fire, that's an improvement."

Lou nodded. "I collected enough wood from the underbrush for us to light a signal fire. There's nothing like smoke to attract attention."

Kate reached over and rubbed her hand along her husband's shoulder. "I'm so glad you paid attention in Survival class."

"You can thank Grey Elk for that one. He made sure Jake, and I were trained in the ways of the Abenaki. My people have used smoke to signal others for generations."

"Well, let's follow Grey Elk's advice and build this fire up so someone besides us can see it."

Lou shook his head. "Nah, we'd just be wasting firewood. Like I said, we're in the middle of nowhere. Unless someone was in the vicinity, this whole damn island could go up in smoke and not attract any attention. We'll let this fire go out, then I'll show you how to start one, using a piece of flint.

LATE INTO THAT EVENING, the two castaways sat on the beach lost in their own thoughts, staring at the dying embers from the fire Kate had made. The only sound was the lapping of waves upon the shoreline. When Lou finally lifted his head and looked out across the dark water, he breathed in heavily.

"That cool offshore breeze sure feels good, doesn't it?"

Kate merely nodded. She'd noticed the change in temperature, but her mind had been elsewhere. Her motherly instincts were kicking in and thoughts of her young twins were coming on strong. Whether she would ever see them again consumed her thoughts. Lou's mind was more pragmatic. His focus was on their immediate survival and returning to the world they knew. As he leaned back, he gazed upward as an array of stars began to appear.

"Kate, I think it would be wise for us to continue taking turns going around the island, we might get lucky. If a plane or a boat appears, one of us will always be here to light the signal fire."

Kate was leaning forward, gazing into the coals, her knees pulled up against her chest, her arms on top of her knees, her head resting on her arms. Slowly she turned toward the man who made her life complete and nodded half-heartedly.

By no means was Kate apathetic, her energy was just down. The sun and heat of the day had taken a lot out of them.

THE DAYS WERE BEGINNING to roll one into the next. Monotony had become another challenge to deal with. The only measure of time was the passing of the sun. Out of necessity, they had settled into a routine. A couple of times during the day, one of them would walk over to the stream, quench their own thirst, fill the coconut shells they had carried over with water and return to camp. Every day Lou would spear a fish or two in the lagoon. One of them would search for edible fruit or eggs, while the other remained at camp. Gathering food, staying hydrated, avoiding the sun and listening for the sound of a plane, while scanning the horizon for a ship pretty much defined their daily island life.

ON THE DAY after their most important discovery, Kate had volunteered to walk around the island again out of sheer boredom. Waves lapped against her feet as she walked along the shoreline as she had the day before. For some reason, she was paying far more attention to small shorebirds darting along in front of her than her own surroundings.

Then, just after traveling nearly halfway around the island, she came up short. Directly ahead, in the wet sand, was a footprint!

That's not Lou's print, he passed this spot two days ago. The tide would have washed his footprints away by now, she reasoned.

Looking toward the tree line, she saw more footprints traveling all the way up the sand, and covered her mouth.

Mother of Jesus, we're not alone!

Then, further down the beach, she spotted an outrigger canoe pulled up onto shore.

Do I go back for Lou? Or do I follow the footprints myself?

In the end, her curiosity overpowered her caution, and she followed the footprints on the beach.

WHEN KATE finally realized the footprints were leading to the trail she had taken the day before, she stopped. Curious, but now cautious, she continued more slowly. Well before the plateau, she stepped off the trail and worked her way up through the underbrush.

Years earlier, Lou had schooled her in the ways of the forest, including the basics of an Abenaki game known as "Butterfly Hide and Seek." The game developed the ability to blend into one's surroundings, remain quiet, and be invisible to others.

Now, moving with the stealth of a warrior, she circled around the clearing to a high point opposite the trail overlooking the plateau. Once she had a good line of sight, she concealed herself in the lush flora that covered the hillside. After quietly waiting for over half an hour, and not seeing anyone, Kate decided to retreat.

By now, her endurance was low due to their meager diet over the past few days, but she jogged back around the island as fast as she dared. Once she crossed over the mudflat, she saw Lou in the distance and began waving an arm over her head, yelling to her husband.

Lou saw Kate running toward him, waving, well before he heard her. There was no doubt something was up, and he began running toward her.

"Kate! What is it? Are you okay?"

By the time they came together, she was out of breath. "Lou . . . I saw . . . we . . . we have visitors!"

"Where?"

Kate pointed toward the center of the island before bending at the waist and propping herself up with hands on her knees. After inhaling deeply, she said, "On the far side. There's a canoe . . . I saw a canoe . . . and a set of footprints."

"Did you see anyone?" Lou looked down the length of beach. *Was Kate being followed?*

Still out of breath, she said between breaths, "No . . . I didn't. I even went up to the plateau."

"Kate, let's get you into the shade." Lou could tell Kate was dangerously close to suffering heat stroke. "I want you to stay here and wait for me. I need to go back and get you some water. When you're refreshed, we'll go look."

As Lou jogged back to camp, Kate stayed near the tree line and sat down in a small patch of shade, slowly regaining her breath.

The water Lou brought back was warm, but still refreshing and provided fluids Kate's body needed. He had also brought back the spear gun, and they stayed in the shade until Kate nodded she was ready to go again. When they moved out, they stayed close to the tree line.

When they reached the far side of the island, the canoe with an outrigger was little more than a distant sail on the horizon, heading away from the island. Lou raised his hand to shield his eyes from the sun. "Well, whoever it was, they're gone."

Kate sat down on the sand. "Damn it. I should have stayed."

"No, there's no telling what could have happened, if you had. I'm glad you didn't."

Lou studied the footsteps leading from the forest to where the boat had been. "Let's go up top and see if they left any clues that might tell us why they were here."

At first glance, nothing on the plateau appeared to be any different. Then, Lou noticed what had been placed in the center of the stone edifice. It would change everything.

16

Immediately after Jake spoke with Koby, he sent a text message to the night supervisor at Canada Post Corporation, letting him know he wished to "book off" earlier than originally planned. Within a couple of hours, word came back that he could leave two days earlier. After sending a text message to his long-time travel agent at *Travel by Tatten*, he called Koby back.

"Koby, I'll be coming down the day after tomorrow. I'm not sure what time I'll get there, but I have a text into Linda Tatten. I'm guessing I'll get there sometime in the afternoon."

"Fine."

"Fine?" Jake said. "I thought I'd hear a little more enthusiasm in your voice than that."

"I'm sorry, sweetheart, I . . . I just spoke with the front desk people again. It's after ten and they still haven't checked in."

"Hon, they're probably having a great time and extended, that's all."

"I hope you're right."

"That's gotta be it. So, how was the conference?"

"It was good, but I'm so glad it is over. I had dinner with Dan Shively and his wife June last night. Everybody is talking about his latest discovery. Jake this is so huge, it's almost unbelievable."

"What's it about?"

"He's found the ruins of an entire city on the floor of the Caribbean somewhere down by Saint Vincent and the Grenadines."

"And?" When Koby hesitated, Jake repeated his question, "And?"

"He wants me to be part of the exploration team."

"When's that happening?"

"The dive won't happen until the fall, Jake, but this is really huge. It's a once in a lifetime thing. He said I can choose how long I participate."

Jake heard the excitement in his wife's voice. "Well, if that's what you wanna do, go for it. We'll figure out how to work it. Gigi and I will be fine."

"I haven't committed yet, but I know I want to. I'm going to fly down there with Dan tomorrow morning. He wants to take some aerial photos."

"Will you be back when I arrive?"

"Oh, absolutely! We're only flying down to take a few shots of the area."

"You're sure you won't end up staying over somewhere?"

"Positive, Dan needs to get back, plus, there's nothing down there but uninhabited islands. The only place we could even land is in the water."

LOU AND KATE had now been stranded on the island for over a week, yet the nightmare felt a lot longer. Each day blended into the next. The only way they had to measure passage of time were the daily marks Lou notched on the trunk of a palm tree. So far, neither had heard a plane nor seen a ship on the horizon. Their main task now was to survive.

Lou was the primary hunter, and Kate willingly took on the role of gatherer. With an ability to make fire, their diet consisted of fish cooked on a skewer, baked plantains, and fresh papaya thanks to plentiful fruit trees around them. Occasionally, they roasted a few land crabs and to Kate's surprise, they tasted like Maine lobster. But without drawn butter to accompany the dish, she wasn't very excited about it.

Kate had painstakingly rearranged coconuts on the beach to now read "SOS" However, upon waking one morning after another squall, she found half the coconuts floating in the lagoon. So she reconstructed the distress signal further away from the shoreline.

As isolated as they were, and unsure of what would happen, there were moments Kate began looking forward to. Since their camp was situated on the western side of the island, toward sunset, the two of them would sit side by side, on the beach, waiting for the sun to go down.

As she sat beside her husband, she leaned into him. "It's funny how simple life can become. The only thing we have to look forward to on this blasted island is making love at the waterfall and seeing a green flash the moment the sun touches the horizon."

Lou responded by putting his arm around Kate's shoulders and giving her a squeeze. Tilting her head to the side and squinting to avoid looking directly into the sun, she added,

"Another thing that's funny is how quickly the sun travels across the sky. You don't realize it until it's already low on the horizon."

"Yeah, blink and you'll miss the flash."

"Lou, did they tell you in survival class what causes the flash?"

"Do you really wanna know?"

"Yes," Kate nodded.

Lou took a deep breath before responding. "As the sun sets, it shines through a denser layer of the atmosphere. Cooler colors like blue, green, and violet refract more than warmer colors do. The atmosphere scatters the blue and violet waves, leaving the green wavelength. That's what causes the flash. Now you know."

Kate looked at her husband. "They actually covered that in survival class?"

"No, it never came up."

"Then how do you know all that?"

A smirk appeared on Lou's face. "Jake told me."

"No, I'm serious, where did you learn it?"

"From Jake."

Lou paused a moment, but before Kate could say anything, he continued. "Jake has been fixated with anything involving the sky and the atmosphere his whole life. When we were growing up, he went out on the lake every day just before sunset, just to watch the sun go down. I always knew he'd end up doing something connected with the sky. When he and I went to McGill University he majored in meteorological science."

Kate tilted her head. "I didn't think Jake had a serious bone in his body."

"Oh, there's definitely a serious side to him."

"That's funny, in all the years I've known him I've never seen it."

As Lou continued watching the sun move closer to the horizon, images of Jake's past escapades flashed through his mind. After a long pause, he decided to share a little more about his cousin.

"Jake can be self-disciplined when he wants to be. Years ago, when he and I signed on with the Joint Task Force Two Commando Unit, the first thing they put us through was martial arts training. Jake took to training like a duck to water. He was so damn good at it; they made him an instructor. I thought he'd stay in and make a career out of it, but he didn't. I was actually surprised when he mustered out."

"Oh, come on, you didn't see that happening? Jake wasn't cut out for military life."

"You're probably right. I think he stayed in just long enough to get his martial arts instructor certificate. He's into all that certification stuff. I think he's certified to fly just about every small plane there is." Lou paused for a moment. "But his sense of humor gets to me at times, as does this stupid obsession he has with Grey Poupon. We used to fight growing up. Everything was a joke to him. But if either one of us got in a jam, we had each other's back. Every kid in the village knew, if you took on one of us, you dealt with two of us."

Kate pulled her knees up closer to her chest and wrapped her arms around them. "Do you really think Jake will try to find us?"

Lou nodded. "There is not a doubt in my mind. But he's gotta find out we're missing first."

"What makes you so sure?"

Lou hesitated as he picked up a piece of coral the size of a walnut and tossed it into the lagoon. "Because he's every bit the tracker I am, Kate. Growing up, there were times I thought he might even be a little better at it than I was."

After a few seconds passed, Lou added, "It could take a while, but he'll show up. And once I have you back in civilization, Jake and I are going after the son-of-a-bitch who left us here."

Kate changed the subject. "I still cannot believe I shelled out all that money for this grand vacation and we ended up here! I vetted Nisbett and that stinking boat of his six ways from Sunday."

Lou waited before saying, "Nisbett wasn't on that boat, Kate."

Kate leaned back and placed her hands in the sand directly behind her. "I think I've come to that same conclusion. How did you get there?"

"It just didn't make sense, Kate. Chartering is how the man made his living. He couldn't start doing something as stupid as marooning people and expect to stay in the charter boat business."

"I've rerun everything in my mind, trying to figure out what I've missed," she said. "And I agree. Whoever that man was, he wasn't the man I exchanged emails with."

"Kate, quick, look! There it is, did you see it? Did you see the flash?"

"I did," she lied. Her thoughts had distracted her, and she'd looked away for just that instant.

As Lou stood up, he brushed the sand off his backside. "When we don't return to Barbados, Koby will do two things: First, she'll notify the authorities, then she'll call Jake. In the meantime, all we need to do is stay alert and keep a healthy attitude."

"Did they drill that into you in Survival 101."

"Yeah, with a jackhammer!"

Late that night, just at high tide, a fast-moving storm with high winds hit the island.

17

When the *Marlin Sea* left San Juan harbor, she was sailing northeast toward the Bahamas. Carlos twisted and stretched as he leaned forward in the helmsman's chair trying various positions, hoping to find a comfortable one. But he was just plain tired from being on the bridge for days as they deadheaded in the open water.

Sanchez was below deck, asleep, after making love to a bottle of tequila. Carlos calculated they were about fifty nautical miles east of Turks and Caicos and had another full day to go before reaching the Bahamas. He would have gone straight on to Bimini, but Sanchez wanted first to spend a couple of days on Devil's Cay, a small island in the Bahamas.

At this point, Carlos was the master of his own destiny. The only thing he needed was to provide the cartel with a description of the vessel he was bringing in before he approached Bimini.

Carlos had never met his handler. All he knew was that the man was known as The Chameleon, had significant influence inside the cartel, and lived in the islands. Carlos assumed the only reason his handler wanted advance information about the yachts he brought in was to keep unauthorized boats away.

By cartel standards, the two privateers had been wildly successful. They had already brought in five yachts. Everyone was happy because everyone was making money on the scheme.

Carlos had stayed true to the plan he initially shared with Sanchez. Yet neither pirate had the slightest clue of the unintended consequences their scheme had most recently created. What Carlos never anticipated, or planned around, was the wrath and resources of Number 10 Downing Street.

BACK IN SAN JUAN, Tom Mullin sat in an easy chair at home. His brain never stopped working, even when he was not at work, albeit his thoughts rarely deviated from anything beyond the challenges he faced at the dock. His wife had long ago given up on Tom's ability to remember anything related to family, or their personal life, and had become the self-appointed coordinator of all family and social obligations.

"Tom, when did you say Jim Nisbett would be coming for dinner?"

The sound of Kathie's voice broke her husband's concentration. "What did you say?"

"I asked you when Jim was coming for dinner. I need a little time to make those conch fritters!"

Damn, Tom thought, *I forgot all about him. He should have been back by now.*

As usual, when Tom failed to immediately reply, his wife used a different tone, one that always worked. "*Tom*...are you going to answer me?"

"I'm thinking, Kathie. He was supposed to be back days ago."

"Well, give him a call. You've got a marine radio sitting in the den. Go in there and find out where he is, and when he's coming."

Tom got up and went into his home office. He didn't need to hear one more time how he had used the money on that radio his wife had been saving to use on a new dishwasher.

After Mullin spent a considerable amount of time on the radio, he still couldn't reach anyone with even the slightest information on the whereabouts of Jim Nisbett, or the *Marlin Sea*.

As he emerged from his den, he said, "There's not a soul out there who's seen hide nor hair of Jim. Now that just doesn't seem right."

"No, it doesn't."

Mullin nodded. "I think I'll go over to the Coast Guard station in San Juan harbor. They may know something."

THE U.S. COAST GUARD had no specific information on the whereabouts of the *Marlin Sea*. But among the communications they did have, was one issued by Saint Kitts regarding two missing British subjects who had been on the *Marlin Sea*. The station in Puerto Rico had picked up several "distress calls" over the past few months but had taken no action as the calls were well beyond U.S. waters and they had received no request for mutual aid.

What they also didn't know was that those Mayday calls were all bogus calls initiated by Carlos.

But now, Mullin pressed the point that the *Marlin Sea* had been in U.S. territorial waters, was overdue, and not responding to radio contact with the officer on duty. Failure to communicate or be overdue at a destination are both considered legitimate reasons for the U.S. Coast Guard to initiate a Search and Rescue operation in all waters they patrol.

Mullin knew Jim Nisbett hadn't been planning to remain in U.S. territorial waters when he left, but he kept that knowledge to himself. Eventually, the duty officer logged an incident into the Search and Rescue system. Although it was listed in the "Awareness" stage, notification did go out across the Caribbean:

"If a distress call came from the *Marlin Sea* over channel 16, or there was an eyewitness report of an emergency, the classification would immediately move from "Awareness" to "Alert," or even to "Distress."

LOU STARED out at the lagoon next to their campsite. The storm left it cloudy and clogged with floating debris. As the noon hour approached, he decided to venture beyond the reef to do a little spearfishing.

He made his way down the beach toward the break in the reef, where fresh water from the stream emptied into the sea. A wide delta of sand extended a dozen yards beyond where the reef would have been but then the bottom dropped off sharply into the depths. He knew from experience that fish would be lurking there, just as they waited beyond the rocky shelves in his lake back in New Brunswick.

Wading through floating seaweed, Lou paid little mind to the swirls on the water's surface until the tranquility of the moment was shattered. A seven-foot blacktip reef shark erupted from the water with startling speed, followed closely by four more dorsal fins. The predators were in hot pursuit of a school of fish heading straight toward Lou.

He was in shallow water, but still, his heart beat a little faster as he took in the scene. It was a vivid reminder of the ocean's untamed nature.

"Looks like it's feeding time at the trough."

A wry smile formed on his lips as he turned around. *I think two or three papaya will hold us over until the lagoon settles down.*

Reef sharks were skittish and would not have bothered Lou. But the mature bull shark who had entered the area was a different story. He was a man eater.

As Lou walked back along the beach, he had no idea how close he had brushed up against certain death again. His mind wandered back to his childhood in New Brunswick.

Everything I know about fishing I owe to my grandfather. Grey Elk taught me how to find the best spots, the right techniques, and most importantly, the value of patience.

It's difficult to say whether a bull shark has patience, but they do have memories. Studies have shown that sharks can recall things from the past and will recognize shapes for up to six months. Whether the bull shark recognized Lou's silhouette as the intruder it had met just a week earlier when he came from the boat, mattered little. Outside the lagoon, the bull was the undisputed apex hunter. And patience or no patience, the bull shark would be waiting.

18

When Koby's cell phone went off the following morning, she awoke with a start. After fumbling in the dark, she found her phone, pressed the button, and took the call. "Hello?"

"Koby, it's Dan, Dan Shively."

Turning on the light next to the bed, only slightly more awake, Koby looked at the display on her phone . . . 5:20 a.m.

"Dan . . . what's up?"

"I just got a call from my pilot. He says the weather down around Saint Vincent and the Grenadines is going to turn nasty by late morning. A storm went through during the night, but it's clear now. He says there's a window for us to get down and back, but we need to leave a helluva lot earlier than we planned." Shively paused a moment before continuing.

"I realize it's early, but I didn't want to take off without at least giving you a call to see if you still wanted in. I promised my dive team I'd come back with more arial photos of the area. I leave the Caribbean tonight, this morning is my only chance. Can you be at the airport in an hour?"

Koby ran her fingers through her hair, still half asleep. *My chance to see this lost city, even from the air, is too good to pass up.*

"Yes. Yes, I can make it," she lied. She had just about an hour to get ready and be at the airport.

"Are you sure?"

"Positive!"

"Good . . . make it earlier, if you can, I'll meet you inside the charter terminal. Oh, and don't worry about breakfast, I'll have a thermos of coffee and sweet rolls."

As soon as the call ended, Koby shuffled off to the bathroom, still not fully awake, but determined to be at the airport by six-thirty.

TWENTY MILES off the coast of Saint Vincent, the morning sun had barely risen when a sleep deprived Lou Gault emerged from their makeshift shelter. He had awakened several times during the night and walked down to the beach.

From the distant sounds of thunder and sporadic illumination on the horizon, he could tell the approaching storm would be more than a tropical squall. Each time he had returned to the shelter, he brought a little more firewood back in with him before lowering the awning that hung out over the opening to their shelter. The awning Lou designed served two purposes, it provided a shady retreat during the day and could be lowered during a storm to keep them dry.

Late in the night, a driving rain accompanied by fierce winds had pelted the island for just under an hour before moving on. The lean-to Lou had built made it through the storm unscathed, but the beach was a different story.

Between high winds and a nearly full moon, the incoming tide easily breached the reef and had come up higher than usual. Kate's SOS message had completely washed away. The bonfire Lou had made ready now lay in ruins, its wood scattered helter-skelter along the beach. Clumps of shredded sea grass and other debris, including a long wooden plank, gave testimony to how far up the beach the tide had come.

As Lou appraised the damage, he had one thought. *Well, at least we didn't suffer anything we can't rectify after breakfast. While Kate fixes her SOS sign, I'll make a bench with that plank. It'll be nice to be able to keep our butts off the sand for a change.*

Kate was also an early riser. When Lou returned to their shelter, she was just returning from passing her morning water.

"Have you gone down to the beach?"

"Yeah," Lou nodded.

Kate heard the frustration in his voice. "Is it a mess?"

"Yeah, but it's no big deal. We'll put it back together after breakfast. I put some wood inside the shelter last night to keep it dry."

"I noticed you had."

As Lou reached into the shelter for the spear gun, he said, "I'll be right back. . . going down to the lagoon."

When Lou heard Kate sigh, he turned to her. "But, before I go to our *'grocery store,'* is there a particular fish you'd like to dine on this morning?"

A smile appeared on Kate's face. "No, just pick up whatever's on sale!" Neither of them had completely lost their sense of humor and they'd joked about the lagoon becoming their private supermarket a few times.

With that, Kate walked over to the man she loved. As she lifted up on her toes, Lou let the spear gun fall to the ground and wrapped his arms around her. When their lips finally parted, Kate nestled her head against Lou's chest and wrapped her arms around the man who meant everything to her.

"Kate, we *will* get through this."

"I know, I . . . I just want it to be over. During the night, I kept waking up thinking about the twins." Kate paused slightly. "Lou, I just don't want them going through life wondering what happened to their parents."

Lou tilted his head back and closed his eyes. Kate's words had catapulted a memory into his consciousness, one that Lou rarely allowed to enter his thoughts:

He was sitting cross-legged in a sweat lodge; his cousin, Jake, beside him, their eyes cast downward. Grey Elk, their grandfather, was summoning the spirits of their ancestors to the Abenaki death ritual. Their faces were smudged with ashes. Lou was only four at the time, but the memory of the ceremony he sat through after his parents' passing was as vivid today as it was then.

Years later, the two orphans had learned how their parents had perished. They were returning from a heritage pow-wow in Vermont. Their plane was struck by lightning as it passed over a remote mountainous area. It took two days before the rescue parties could reach the mangled fuselage and the remains of those who had been onboard. No one had survived.

After a moment, Lou opened his eyes, inhaled, and let out a deep breath. He kissed Kate on the forehead.

"I love you," he said.

With his thoughts cleared, he walked over to a nearby palm tree, took out his knife and made another notch in the trunk, marking yet another day. Then, in a whisper, he repeated himself.

"We *will* get through this."

Picking up the spear gun, Lou headed down to the lagoon.

As Kate watched Lou wade into the water, she gave thanks. "Lord, we are grateful to be alive and have the means to light a fire."

IMMEDIATELY AFTER BREAKFAST, Lou and Kate went out onto the beach and began reconstructing what the storm had destroyed during the night. It took less than an hour, and while neither of them were ever any more than thirty or forty yards from camp, neither saw the visitor who was checking out their campsite.

ABOUT THE SAME time Kate was stepping back to admire her repaired SOS sign, the wheels of a Gulfstream G550 touched down on the island of Barbados. The sleek metallic black plane taxied past the main terminal and headed directly to the commercial freight hangars where it came to a stop.

Within seconds of its arrival, a black limousine drove forward and parked beside the plane. The limo driver no sooner opened the rear passenger door than the door of the Gulfstream opened and an unusually tall male, wearing a white linen suit, exited.

The man known within the cartel as The Chameleon had arrived. He stepped off the plane and entered the back seat of the car.

As the limousine approached the gate, it did not slow down. The official on duty saluted and waved the vehicle through. Cartel money opened many doors in the islands.

19

T hree thousand miles to the north, skis attached to a Smyth Air de Haviland Otter set down on a frozen windswept lake and taxied over to a dock in central New Brunswick.

Earlier, Jake had trekked over to the lodge where Chef Angelo had insisted on making breakfast for his friend before he left for Barbados.

When Jake heard the plane coming up the valley, he finished off his last swig of coffee. "Angelo, that's my ride, buddy, gotta get going."

"Travel safe, my friend, eh? And don't forget - bring back some Cuban cigars."

Jake hadn't shared Koby's concerns with Angelo about Lou and Kate's delayed return. For all Lou's chef knew, Lou was still basking somewhere in the warm Caribbean sun without a care in the world. Jake had, however, given his cousin, Laughing Gull, a heads up. Since he was going down earlier than expected, he had hinted there was a slight chance she might have the kids longer than originally planned. She hadn't minded.

BACK IN BARBADOS, Koby Callahan stood half-awake before the closet in her hotel room trying to decide what she was going to wear. Between concerns about Lou and Kate's whereabouts, flying down to Saint Vincent with Dan Shively, and Jake coming down earlier than planned, Koby hadn't slept very well. As she pushed the shower curtain aside and reached to test the water temperature, her mind was elsewhere.

How could such a massive underwater structure, like the one Shively just discovered, have remained undetected all these years?

What she didn't know was that Dan Shively didn't just happen upon the site by chance. He had received a few anonymous letters months earlier, all postmarked from Barbados, encouraging him to visit the location.

Shively was a world class explorer, but the Caribbean had never interested Dan since he wasn't a treasure hunter. Like many of his contemporaries, he thought the Caribbean was barren, aside from some eighteenth-century shipwrecks, and offered less opportunity for discovery than the Mediterranean. But details in the letters had intrigued him enough that he had set sail for the Caribbean islands known as the Lesser Antilles. As for the hidden city, well, luck always seemed to play a role in the world of archeology.

For several weeks Dan's ship, *Magnavox II*, had followed a grid pattern off the coast of Saint Vincent. Dan had been about ready to give up on his rare venture in the Caribbean when the scopes scanning the bottom came across a unique structure. At first, Dan and his team weren't sure what was below. But once they sent a robot down, it was obvious they had come across a spectacular discovery, one that had literally and figuratively fallen into the abyss.

KOBY MADE it to the airport on time, and soon afterward the plane was taxiing down the runway.

"Sorry about the paper cups," Dan said, pouring out coffee. "Hope the pastry will make up for it."

The flight down to Saint Vincent took a little over an hour. Other than small talk, the two occupants sitting behind the pilot kept their thoughts to themselves as they drank their brew and stared out the windows.

At one point the pilot pressed a button on the intercom. "We're approaching the general area you wanted to see, Mr. Shively. Those small specs up ahead are the extreme outer islands of Saint Vincent and the Grenadines." Both Dan and Koby leaned forward to get a better look out the forward window.

After a few minutes, the pilot pushed the button on the intercom again. "We'll veer off to the right just ahead. I'm not seeing much turbulence near the surface, so we'll take a chance and drop down a little. If it gets bumpy, I'll take her back up and we'll circle around a bit." Dan held his right arm up in agreement.

Before takeoff, Shively had attached a high-resolution remote camera to the underside of the right wing. As he waited for the monitor to power up, he looked down at the water.

The site we found is down deep, but it looks calm. Hopefully, I'll get some decent photos, he thought.

The beautiful blue Caribbean waters were exceptionally calm and clear this morning, and the tide was slack. Dan and Koby were both glued to the monitor positioned on Dan's knees as the plane circled the area. They passed over several shapes, including the watery graves of sunken ships. They were still a distance from the primary target site and in shallow water when a structure resembling a road unexpectedly showed up on the monitor's screen.

Dan pressed the intercom button he had in his hand. "I just saw something of interest. Can we circle back over the area we just passed?" The pilot gave a thumbs up and pulled back on the joystick.

On the next pass, Dan was ready with the cameras. As they flew back and forth over the underwater structure, Dan's fingers clicked away, capturing picture after picture like an excited child playing with a new toy.

"Koby, I can't believe what we're seeing! We're going to completely rewrite history!"

LOU AND KATE had just finished putting things back together on the beach when they heard a plane off in the distance. Kate was the first to spot it. Lou was working as fast as possible to start a fire and didn't look up.

Even though the plane was a good distance away, Kate went down to the water's edge and began waving both arms.

"Lou, I think it's circling back. Do you think they've seen us?"

The plane continued making a wide arc as Kate cupped her hands around her mouth and began shouting. "Hello! This way!"

She turned to her husband. "Lou, I think they're coming straight at us now!"

Lou still didn't look up. He was on his knees desperately trying to light the signal fire. It took a couple of tries before a small flame lit underneath the dry tinder he had brought into the shelter during the night. Everything else in the pile was wet. But once he had the flame going, a thin trail of white smoke began to rise into the air.

As Lou continued feeding the fire, he glanced over at his bikini clad wife. Kate was animated, jumping up and down, waving her arms and yelling. He knew no one on the plane could hear her, but secretly he hoped they could.

The plane was still flying low off in the distance. Kate glanced over at Lou. The fire was smokey but still small. When the sound of the plane's engine altered, Kate turned back and looked up. To her horror, the plane's wings had tipped, banking right.

"NO!! WAIT, don't turn! Keep coming straight! Lou they're turning!"

Kate ran a few paces along the water's edge toward the plane, waving her arms. Lou placed more dry tinder on the fire and carefully blew on the flame, hoping to ignite the semi-dry debris and send up more smoke.

The plane circled around several more times in the distance, but never close enough to see Kate's SOS sign, or Lou's thin trail of smoke. They hadn't attracted the plane. In the end, their efforts had no impact.

As he sat back in the sand next to the fire watching as the plane headed further away from them, Lou chastised himself.

"It's my own damn fault! We didn't have enough dry material to send up a smoke signal."

Kate came over and knelt in the sand beside him. "No, it's not your fault, it's nobody's fault. Who knows if they would have even seen the smoke or come to investigate?"

"Kate, I know it's my turn to circle the island today, but let's switch. I need to make a second shelter just to store dry wood."

AS THE PLANE turned and headed out to the original discovery site, Koby looked out the side window and saw a small sail heading toward the island with a peak in the middle of it. As she continued looking at the island, she raised a hand to her forehead and shielded her eyes from the sun's glare.

Hmmm, that looks like a little bit of white smoke rising up from that island. Imagine that. We're in the middle of nowhere, but I guess people can survive anywhere, even way out here.

20

L ate that afternoon, Koby stood in the airport, waving her arm as Jake exited customs. The expression on her face was grim. Jake hadn't seen that look since the time their young daughter, Gigi, was bitten by an aggressive water snake while playing down by their dock. Even though she had a scar from that encounter, her enthusiasm for the out-of-doors was still intact.

Jake gave his wife a squeeze after receiving a peck on the lips and something less than an enthusiastic embrace. "I kinda thought you'd be a little happier to see me."

Koby sighed and squeezed him back. "I'm sorry, honey. I just can't get it out of my head that they're not back yet. This is so unlike either of them."

He pushed his fatigue from the long flight aside and nodded. "Have you talked with the port authority?"

"Only over the phone."

Jake thought for a moment and changed subjects. "How's the weather been?"

At first, Koby paused, trying to see the relevance of Jake's question. Then she made the connection and responded. "We've had a couple of storms, but nothing the boat they went out on couldn't have handled." As they made their way through the terminal Koby pointed to the left.

"The taxi stand is over here."

"How close are we to the docks?"

"We'll go right past the wharfs on the way to the hotel."

"Let's check them out before we head over to the hotel. Who knows, they may have come in while you were at the airport, if not, we'll ask around."

Koby put her arm around Jake's waist and leaned into him as they waited in line for a taxi. "I'm sorry, Jake. You know I'm happy to see you. I've missed you a lot. It's just that I have this terrible feeling about Kate and Lou."

Jake kissed his wife on the forehead. "We'll figure it out, hon. Lou isn't going to put himself, or Kate, at risk unnecessarily. Besides, for all they know, I'm not coming down for a few more days, and you're still tied up in meetings."

Koby let out a breath. "You're right, I may be overthinking this. Oops, let's go, this is our taxi."

WHEN THE TAXI arrived at the wharfs, Jake made a mental note of the driver's name and medallion number. "Can you deliver my luggage to the hotel?" he asked, handing the driver his credit card.

"Sure, mon, no problem."

"Good. We're staying at the Hilton. Leave it with the desk in the lobby and add an extra five dollars to the fare."

Turning to Koby, he said, "Do you know which wharf they're coming in at?"

"Two."

Once Jake had his credit card back, he turned them toward the water. "Okay, lead the way."

WHARF TWO WAS A LONG STRETCH; halfway down they passed the homeless man Koby had spoken with earlier. Again, he was stretched out on the same bench. As they passed, Jake whispered, "I guess Barbados isn't immune to the homeless here, either."

"They call him Johnny Coconut. I think that bench is his happy place. Every time I've come down, he's been there."

When they reached the end of the wharf, Jake placed his hand on a piling and looked out towards the mouth of the harbor. "Do you remember which slip they left from?"

"Fifteen."

"Let's go back, maybe someone in one of the nearby boats can tell us something."

THERE WAS ONLY one boat tied up near slip fifteen. It was an elegant well-kept lady named *Adele* that sailed out of the Isle of Saint Paul. Jake walked halfway down the slip, cupped his hands around his mouth and shouted, "Ahoy, the Adele, is anyone aboard?"

A man poked his head up from the engine compartment and wiped his brow with his forearm. "I'm here, what can I do for ya?"

"I'm wondering if you know when the *Marlin Sea* might be returning?"

"Not a clue, just got in myself."

Just then a woman came out on deck and the man asked her, "Adele, do you know when Nisbett is due back?"

The woman stopped and looked down to the left for a moment before shaking her head. "Nope, no idea."

Jake tried a different tactic. "By any chance did you hear the owner over the radio while you were out on the water?"

The man looked at his wife before answering. "Nope, we didn't hear Jim. Are you chartering with him?"

"No, friends of ours went out with him. We're just trying to figure out when they're coming back in."

The man pointed toward the beginning of the wharf. "There's a kiosk up there. The sign says, 'Boat Charters.' They handle all bookings. They oughta be able to tell ya when Jim's due back."

"Thanks."

As Jake walked over to where Koby was waiting, he noticed the homeless man now sitting up.

AS THEY APPROACHED THE KIOSK, Koby recognized the woman behind the counter as the same one she had spoken with earlier. "I stopped here the other day, Jake. All she could tell me was everything depends on the tides."

"Well, there's no harm in asking. She may have heard something since yesterday."

As they approached the kiosk, the woman stood up. "You want to book a char-tah? Got good deals for you!"

Jake smiled. "Nope, I just have a question. Do you know when the *Marlin Sea* is due back in port?"

"You wanna book dat boat? I make it happen for you."

"No, no, I just have a question. Do you happen to know when the boat is due back? I'm only interested in when it's coming in. Have you heard from the captain? The captain's name is Jim Nisbett."

Before the woman said anything, she gave Jake the once over and again checked Koby out. "Noooo . . . no word from him. He come back when he come back."

Jake smiled and gave the woman a nod. "Thanks." As they walked away, Jake smirked. "Well, that was helpful. Was it the port authority, or the harbor master's office you said you spoke with?"

"Both, actually. When I went over to the port authority office, they tried to reach him on the radio, but couldn't. I spoke with someone at the harbor master's by phone. They didn't have any information, either."

"Well, the harbor master is only going to be able to tell us if a boat is in port. Let's go over to the port authority, maybe they've heard something."

THE PORT AUTHORITY building was one street over from the water. As soon as they entered the building, they encountered a long counter separating the public area from the work area. The same middle-aged islander Koby spoke with earlier stood behind the counter, his fingers dancing across a keyboard as if time was running out. The name tag over his shirt pocket simply read, "Charles."

"Give me a moment folks, I'll be right with you."

Jake nodded and leaned up against the counter. "No problem."

Koby looked around the office. The obligatory ceiling fans were in motion, the furnishings were typical government issue, functional but far from stylish. There was a bulletin board on the wall behind them, cluttered with official looking documents, some so yellowed they might have been older than the building.

As the man behind the counter hit the "send" key, he looked up. "Now, what can I do to help you?"

Jake spoke up. "We're trying to track down the whereabouts of a boat named the *Marlin Sea*. It's a few days overdue returning to port. We're wondering if you might have any information on its whereabouts?"

"*Marlin Sea* . . . that's Jim Nisbett's boat." The man pursed his lips and breathed in heavily. "Nope, I haven't heard anything about Jim. When was he due back?"

Koby spoke up, "He was due back three days ago."

"If I recall, you were in here the other day asking about him. We tried to reach him on the radio," the man said, looking at Koby.

"I was."

"It's not like Jim to be late; he runs a tight ship. When were you supposed to go out with him?"

"We're not," Jake said. "Friends of ours went out with him. They were supposed to be back three days ago."

Koby spoke up, "Would you happen to know if he ever extends a cruise after he leaves port?"

"Oh, I wouldn't know anything about that, ma'am. I guess, if the opportunity came up and he could, he would. Hell, that's what he does for a living."

"Charles, do you think you could try to reach him by radio one more time?"

The man behind the counter winced as he shook his head. "Sorry, ma'am, I've been told to stay off the radio, unless there's an emergency warning that needs to go out."

Jake took out his wallet and displayed his Auxiliary Royal

Canadian Mountie badge. "Is there any chance you could just inquire if anyone's heard from the *Marlin Sea* lately?"

Once Charles realized he was talking with a fellow public servant, he smiled. "Yeah, sure, no problem, I can do that." Charles glanced at the wall clock, walked over to where the radio was, sat down and picked up the mic.

"This is Port Barbados calling Jim Nisbett on the *Marlin Sea*. Come in *Marlin Sea*."

After a brief pause, Charles repeated the message. "It looks like he's either not within range, or his radio is out. He would have answered by now. Let's see if anyone's seen him."

Jake nodded.

"This is Port Barbados calling. Has anyone out there heard from the *Marlin Sea* recently? She sailed out of Barbados over a week ago."

Within seconds, a crackling voice came back. "Are you talking about Jim Nisbett?"

"Yes, Jim Nisbett's boat, the *Marlin Sea*."

Again, there was a crackling sound. "Nope, I ain't seen, nor heard from Jim in over a week."

Another captain came on the air, "He was in Saint Kitts a couple weeks ago; maybe he went north."

Three other boats answered as well, not one reported seeing the *Marlin Sea*, or hearing Jim on the radio.

As Charles prepared to stand up, an unusually tall man, dressed in an obviously expensive, well-tailored white linen suit emerged from an inner office and cleared his throat. "Did I just hear you asking about the *Marlin Sea*?"

Charles swiveled around in his chair and pointed toward the counter. "Yes, sir. These folks are concerned that the boat is late returning to port."

Without saying a word, the tall man walked over to the counter and extended his hand to Jake. "My name is Montez, Inigo Montez. I am the chief of staff here. Please tell me, precisely what is going on?"

Jake reiterated the same narrative he had shared with the man who had been standing at the counter when they arrived.

Koby watched Montez's expressions as he listened to Jake. The man's face seemed to shift from curiosity to surprise and finally to interest. After Jake finished talking, Montez paused, fingered the pencil thin mustache above his upper lip and appeared to ponder the situation. "I do not know of this captain you speak of. But it is unfortunate that he has caused you to worry. From what I have overheard, he has a reliable reputation."

Jake nodded. "That's our understanding, as well. But, if no one can reach him on the radio, and he's three days overdue, that alone is reason for us to be concerned. It sounds like we need to go to the police."

Montez had been staring at the bulletin board behind Jake, only half listening, but when he heard the word "police," a sudden change came over his face. "This is not a police matter. There is no evidence that a crime has been committed. Why do you wish to speak to the police?"

Jake momentarily looked at Koby before responding. "Because our friends are missing. We need to file a missing person report and get a search party going."

Montez quickly cleared his throat and waved his right hand, signaling stop. "Actually, by talking to *me*, you are doing everything you need to do. Yes, a boat returning late *is* a concern, but that is not a crime, nor is it a matter for the police."

"You don't believe the police need to be involved?"

"Of course not. There is no need to involve them just because a boat is overdue. Now, if your boat was *stolen*, then, yes, that would be a police matter. However, in Barbados, I, not the police, have jurisdiction over anything to do with the sea." Montez lied.

Noticing the frown on Jake's forehead, Montez continued gaslighting. "Involving the local police is the last thing you want to do. The police will only complicate matters with unnecessary red tape. However, if you wish to have everything delayed, then, I invite you to go to the police. Is that what you wish . . . to delay things?"

Jake seemed confused by what he was hearing but shook his head. "No, of course not; that's the last thing we want to have happen."

Montez paused, then puffed himself up like a peacock. "The police have jurisdiction over the land, they are not trained to deal with what happens on the water." Montez lied a second time.

"So, you're saying don't go to the police?"

Montez responded quickly. "Exactly, you are off-islanders. I ask that you just follow my lead. Trust me."

"We're specifically asking that you begin a search and rescue operation," Jake said, anxious to get things moving.

Montez nodded. "If you will excuse me, I will be back in a moment."

Jake could hear Montez typing on a keyboard. When Montez returned, he placed a single sheet on the counter. "Once you fill out this official document of inquiry, I will be authorized to launch an investigation on your behalf."

Koby nodded. "Good, that's exactly what we want to do."

"Once you've finished filling out the paperwork, call for me. I'll get things started for you."

The form was straightforward. Once Koby finished filling it out, she took a picture of it with her iPhone and called out.

"Mr. Montez, we're finished, what's next?"

21

When Jake and Koby left the port authority office in Barbados, Jake was far from satisfied that they had done everything possible to locate his cousin. For the moment, whatever search and rescue operations Barbados would initiate was in the hands of a man named Inigo Montez, someone neither Jake nor Koby had strong vibes about.

As they stepped into a taxi, Koby turned to her husband. "What's your take on Montez?"

"He's one of the more interesting officious, bureaucrats I've met. Given the way he was dressed, odds are a little cash was involved in his appointment. I don't think he'll go far. How about you?"

Koby shook her head; she was used to Jake's sense of humor. "I agree. Wasn't it interesting, though, how adamant he was that we not go to the police?"

"You'd think they'd be joined at the hip on a small island like this."

The words "small island" caused Koby to flashback to an image she had seen earlier in the day. *Well, I suppose Barbados is a small island,* she thought. *But it's nowhere near as small as the islands Dan and I flew over this morning. It's hard to believe people choose to live that far off the grid. But they must. There was smoke coming up from that one with the mountain.*

Not thinking it important, she didn't mention it to Jake.

AFTER JAKE REGISTERED at the front desk and they were alone in the elevator, Koby wrapped her arms around her husband and gave him a squeeze. "I cannot even begin to tell you how glad I am you're here! I'm already feeling better."

"Good, I'm glad." The next thing Jake said wasn't anything Koby expected to hear. "Once I unpack, I'm going back over to the wharf and have another look around."

"Oh, hon, I can't go, I'm too exhausted. I've been on the go since I arrived here, and Dan had me up early this morning. I just want to go down to the pool and relax."

"Stay here, I won't be long. I'll meet you at the pool. I just want to check it out one more time."

"Promise?"

Before Jake could answer, the elevator reached their floor, and the doors began to open. Jake pressed the emergency hold button and embraced Koby. "I promise, sweets. And as soon as I'm back, I'll change into my suit and join you at the pool."

LIKE LOU HAD DONE EARLIER, Jake walked to the wharf area, just to get a feel for the island's culture. A subtle whiff of marijuana emanated from a few of the storefronts as he passed, but for the most part the air was filled with the aroma of spices and smoke from street vendors barbecuing tropical dishes.

Arriving at the wharf area, Jake noticed a different woman behind the kiosk counter selling charters. Unlike the one he had spoken to earlier; this woman was much older and seemed totally disinterested in anything other than the paperback she was reading.

When Jake came to a crosspoint and had to choose which wharf he wanted, he turned right and followed the signs to Wharf Two.

As he walked along, he wondered, *Lou, where the hell are ya, cuz? Why the hell hasn't Kate contacted Koby?*

When he reached the fifteenth slip, he stopped and stared at the empty berth. His right hand went up to the top of his head, then down and across the back of his neck. As he let out a sigh, he said to no one in particular. "*Marlin Sea*, where are you?"

"She no back."

Jake swirled around, to see who had spoken. The only person nearby was the disheveled homeless-looking man he had seen earlier.

"Did you just say something?"

"She no back."

"I can see that. Tell me, what do you know about the *Marlin Sea*?"

When the man didn't respond, Jake came close to walking away, but there was something about the man that held his attention.

Without saying a word, the homeless man reached into his left pocket and took out what appeared to be a business card. Next, he reached into a different pocket and pulled out a pen. Jake watched with amusement as the man scribbled something on the back of the card. Then with far more dexterity and swiftness one could expect from a street person, the man stood up and walked over to Jake.

"You want to know 'bout *Marlin Sea* . . . do this." With that, he handed him the card, turned, and walked away.

Jake stood there, head tilted slightly left, watching the man leave. Finally, he looked down at the card and read it. The name on the card read "Peninsula Club," one of the more upscale restaurants on the island. After staring at the front, he turned it over expecting to see gibberish. Instead there was a crisp message:

Meet Mr. Lee – 7:30 a.m. - tomorrow.

RETURNING TO THE HILTON, Jake changed into his bathing suit and headed down to the pool area. Koby had laid claim to two lounge chairs and was lying in the sun.

"Madame, may I get you a drink?" He said quite formally.

At the sound of her husband's voice, a smile appeared on Koby's face. "I love how you read my thoughts."

"Would Madame, care for a glass of Chardonnay?"

"No, I'll have a skinny bitch."

Jake cocked his head. "Say what?."

"A skinny bitch. I'll have a skinny bitch."

Like her husband, Koby had a sense of humor and enjoyed playing harmless practical jokes. But Jake wasn't quite sure if he was being set up. After a slight pause, he asked, "So, is the bartender going to know what I'm talking about, when I tell him I'd like a . . . *skinny bitch?*"

Koby looked over to see who was behind the bar. "Yes, he should. Everyone has been ordering it. If he doesn't, tell him to fill a tall glass with ice, add an ounce of vodka, a splash of cranberry juice, a slice of lime, and top it off with plain soda water."

"No . . . little umbrella?"

"Nope."

"Okay, I'll be right back." But as Jake walked across the pool area, his thoughts were not on the drink order.

Do I tell Koby what just happened over at the wharf, or wait? She has one last day of meetings. If I tell her now, she'll likely ditch her meeting. This may be a whole lot about nothing. I'll fill her in, if anything comes of it.

THE FOLLOWING morning Jake arrived at the posh Peninsula Club at twenty-five minutes past seven. Except for the maître d' who was also acting as the host, the lobby was empty.

"Good morning, sir, is it one for breakfast?"

"No, I'm meeting someone here, I'm early."

The maître d' nodded. "And who might that party be?"

"A Mr. Lee."

Jake looked around to see if anyone was coming. "I was told to meet him here this morning."

"And your name, sir?"

Jake studied the maître d' for a moment before he replied. "Name's Gault, Jake Gault."

The maître d' nodded and slipped a small card out of his coat pocket. After scanning whatever was on it, he looked up. "If you'll follow me, sir, I'll show you to your table."

Jake followed the maître d' across the room. When they reached a table on the far side, the maître d' stopped and placed his hand on the back of a chair. "Your host will be with you shortly, Mr. Gault. May I start you off with coffee?"

"Coffee will be fine, thanks . . . hazelnut, if you have it."

"I believe we do." With that, he turned and headed toward the kitchen area.

Jake's eyes scanned the large dining room. It was beyond upscale. The ornate tray ceiling was adorned with two rows of crystal chandeliers. The alabaster ceiling was at least twenty feet high. Marble pillars blended into the walls, framing alcoves. The tables were covered in white linen, napkins folded into decorative fans graced the center of each setting. Small vases, filled with tropical flowers added a touch of color to the room. A few other people were also dining in the room. Most of the tables were deuces, although there was a party of four at the far end.

Here a lone man sat against the wall directly across from him. Jake had barely seated himself when a pleasant looking young islander arrived with a carafe of coffee.

"May I bring you anything else, sir?"

"No, I think I'm set for now, thanks."

At forty minutes past the hour, the maître d' returned. "Sir, if you would, please follow me." The voice intonation was clear, it was a directive not a request. When Jake reached for his coffee, intending to take one last sip, the maître d' held up his hand. "That won't be necessary, sir. I'll have a fresh carafe sent your way."

Jake wasn't entirely sure what was going on, first the mysterious invite, now he apparently was changing tables. His senses were fully alert as he placed his napkin on the table and pushed his chair back. Standing, he casually glanced around the room. The table across from him, where the single diner had been, was empty.

That's odd, I didn't see him leave.

The server led him to an alcove where a man and a woman

were already seated. Their backs against the wall, their line of sight facing the entryway. Jake recognized the man immediately as the one who had been sitting across from him moments earlier.

"Good morning, Mr. Gault. Please . . . if you would, have a seat."

His accent was undeniably upper crust British. Waving his arm in a dismissive motion, he continued. "My apologies for all this, we needed to be sure you weren't being followed."

The man's attire screamed affluence. Other than stubble on his face, his grooming was impeccable. There was an air of sophistication about him. The woman beside him was attractive and dressed equally impressive. As Jake gently pulled out a chair, his mind was racing in several directions.

I've met these two before. It's their eyes; I recognize their eyes.

The man with the British accent was about to say something when the young server reappeared with another carafe of coffee. As soon as a fresh cup had been poured for Jake, the man said, "Thank you Nigel, that will be all for now."

Once they were alone, Jake's host raised his own cup. "To our good health."

The woman at the table smiled, raised her cup, and made a motion with it toward Jake as she nodded. Jake followed suit and raised his own cup. As he took a sip, he took in the features of the man across from him.

"I'm sure you're curious as to what this is all about."

Jake gave a slight nod as he lowered his cup. "That did cross my mind."

The man reached across the table. "Name's Lee, Frank Lee."

Jake smiled as he shook hands. *Yeah, I'll bet your name's Frank Lee.*

Jake lifted his cup, as if to take a second sip of coffee. "Tell me, how is it that a guy like you and Johnny Coconut ended up being pals?"

"We're a team."

"Really?"

Frank Lee glanced over Jake's shoulder before lowering his voice. "We da same one, mon."

Staring down, Jake returned his cup to the saucer and smiled as he touched his fingertips together. "Very good, I hadn't quite made the connection."

"I'll take that as a compliment. Both of my parents were Shakspearian actors. Unfortunately, when I failed to follow in their footsteps, their only child became their biggest disappointment in life."

"Until you handed me a card, you had me believing you were a wharf rat. My wife said she had seen you there during the week. What took you so long to make contact?"

"We needed to check you out first."

"Really?"

"There is a lot of . . . shall we say *rubbish* that goes along with our work. One cannot be too careful."

Jake turned to the woman. She had been attentive but had remained silent so far. "Have we met?"

Without saying a word, the woman looked at Frank Lee and waited. Once he nodded, she turned toward Jake. In just above a stage whisper, she said, "You wanna book a char-tah?"

Jake smiled but suddenly grew impatient and cut to the chase. "Okay, you both go to the head of the class. If you've checked me out, then you know why I'm here and what I'm trying to do. So, who are you, and how can you help?"

Frank Lee tilted his head, but the expression on his face remained the same. "I didn't realize *Canuck's* were as blunt and to the point, as the Yanks."

Jake bristled upon hearing the word "Canuck," but let it pass. He had been called worse.

The woman spoke next. "Mr. Gault . . . how shall I put this? Several British *tourists* have gone missing in the Caribbean, of late. We are uncertain how, or why, this is happening. We've learned of your wife's concerns regarding the *Marlin Sea* a few days ago, which set things off. Your interest involves your cousin, I believe, is that correct?"

Jake nodded, wondering just how much of an open book his life had become. "Mind telling me what your interest is in my cousin?"

The woman cleared her throat with a nervous cough. "There isn't one, really. Well, not precisely, anyway. Our interest is the *Marlin Sea*. The boat has a connection with the disappearance of a chap who had a rather notable record with the crown. After setting out on the yacht, he and his wife went missing.

Now, we're questioning whether the true captain was onboard at the time. We know for certain he was *not* when your cousin boarded. Our people have been tracking the vessel's whereabouts for the past few weeks now. When she left Barbados, she was supposed to head for Saint Lucia. Instead, she traveled southwest to Saint Vincent. Since then, the yacht has maintained a northerly course."

At that point, Frank Lee cleared his throat, and the woman paused. After looking at her companion, she nodded, and he took over.

"We know everything about that boat, Mr. Gault, just like we know everything about you. We know why your wife is here, what the both of you do for a living, where your child is currently, and the same goes for your cousin and his wife."

Jake sat back in this chair, elbows resting on the arms, tips of his fingers forming a tent as they came together. Then he lowered his head until the tips of his index fingers touched his lips, and he stared at the tablecloth for a moment. Finally, he looked up.

"Mind telling me who the hell you two are?"

"Well, like I said, my name is Lee . . . Frank Lee."

"And my name is White, Lily White. MI6 at your service."

22

J ake leaned forward in his chair. "All right, let's dispense
with the charades. You seem to know a whole helluva lot
about me. Who *exactly* do you work for?"

Just as Frank was about to respond, Lily touched his
arm. After clearing her throat, she looked directly at Jake. "We're
with British Intelligence. As I've said, MI6, to be exact. Frank is a
level two operations officer. Several of us have been temporarily
assigned to a special investigation here in the Caribbean."

"So, what brings MI6 to the Caribbean?"

Lily looked at Frank and gave him the go-ahead signal.

"We used the word 'tourists' before. That was a euphemism.
Two of the people who have mysteriously disappeared were
high ranking, respected members of MI6," Frank said. "They
were here on holiday with their families. Their disappearance
sent shockwaves throughout the agency and Number 10
Downing Street."

Lily interrupted. "Their being here was strictly on the hush-
hush. Only a handful of people in the agency knew about it. It's

still unknown if they were deliberately targeted. If that is the case, there's an internal leak. Everything's on the table at this point. We were about to write off the *Marlin Sea* as unrelated, until your wife kept showing up inquiring about it. By the way, I hadn't intended to disclose this, but we checked you out rather thoroughly, and know you are some sort of Mountie."

When she paused, Frank jumped back in. "Both of the yachts our people were on sent out mayday messages. Search and Rescue responded quickly but haven't found even the slightest bit of debris floating in the water. Both yachts seem to have disappeared without a trace."

After processing everything he'd heard, Jake said, "Tell me again how the *Marlin Sea* plays into all of this?"

Lily smiled. "A missing MI6 retiree and his wife went out on the *Marlin Sea* a few weeks ago. It was a two-day trip. They had a son who followed in his father's footsteps and joined MI6. When his parents failed to respond to his repeated calls, and didn't return to their hotel room, he made it known to the higher ups. Naturally the concern was the agency was repeatedly being targeted by someone in the Caribbean."

Lily looked at Frank for confirmation before continuing. "The retirees' remains floated ashore in Montserrat. We were able to identify him through dental records. His wife is still missing. Our people have been tracking the *Marlin Sea's* movements ever since."

Jake took a breath and exhaled slowly. "So, the *Marlin Sea* is still out there?"

Frank nodded. "It is. We have her under surveillance."

"Where is she now?"

Lily pulled out her cell phone and her thumbs raced across the keypad. "She's due east of Turks and Caicos, heading northwest."

Jake tried to envision the location on a map. *Shit, I should have brought Koby, she'd know exactly where it's supposed to be. Well, she can tell me later.* After a pause, he said, "Where's she heading?"

"Miami, maybe Ft Lauderdale . . . even the Bahamas is still a possibility; she's still out in deep water."

"If you know where she is, why haven't you picked her up?"

"The evidence implicating her is only circumstantial, no charges have been lodged. At this point, she is considered a subject of interest, nothing more. For the time being our people will continue to monitor her whereabouts."

Jake had been leaning forward, listening intently. But when he heard MI6's plan was just to monitor the *Marlin Sea's* location, he sat back in his chair. "Let me get this straight. All you plan to do is monitor her whereabouts. I thought you said the captain was missing. Isn't mutiny a crime? Doesn't an act of piracy give you cause to board her?"

Frank Lee raised his right hand, signaling a pause. "We have no proof she's been hijacked; she could have been sold. If we attempt to board her on the high seas, without just cause, we violate any number of international maritime laws. The sentiment is to let her be, for now, anyway. The States have a Search and Rescue alert out on her. Once she enters US territorial waters, they'll board her."

"The States are involved in this?"

Frank looked at Lily, as if he needed approval to respond. Once she nodded, he continued. "Inquiries about the *Marlin Sea* have come out of Puerto Rico. We're not sure what triggered that. So, now two countries are apparently interested in her whereabouts."

Jake's coffee was cold by now, but he took a sip anyway. "Actually, make it three countries. Barbados has joined the arena."

When Lily heard Jake mention Barbados, she perked up. "Say more about that."

"My wife and I filled out a 'request for inquiry' with the port authority yesterday."

Lily's eyes glanced at Frank for a split second, then she returned her gaze to Jake. "You said 'port authority?'"

"Yes."

Lily seemed to sit up straighter. "Have you gone to the police as well?"

"No, we were advised that would only delay things."

Lily shifted in her seat. "I see."

Jake noticed her reaction but decided to take the conversation in a different direction. "You said you have been tracking the *Marlin Sea*. Can you tell me where's she been?"

"Yes, we've reconstructed her whereabouts based on harbor master records."

Lily picked up a tablet that had been sitting on an empty chair beside her. When the screen came up, she continued. "I can go back further, but on the day the second missing yacht sent out a mayday message, she was in Nassau. When she left Nassau, she traveled to Turks and Caicos, then made a stop in San Juan. She was next seen in Saint Kitts where she picked up our MI6 retiree and wife. She was supposed to return to Saint Kitts, but there is no evidence she ever did. Next, she showed up in Barbados, which is where your cousin and his wife boarded. From there the boat traveled down to Saint Vincent. The harbor master in San Juan reported her entering and leaving that harbor. Since then, she has been on the move."

"You said, 'you question if the true captain is aboard.' Why is that?"

"The pattern doesn't jibe. The real captain has a reputation for being precise and on time, plus there's no evidence he ever returned to Saint Kitts. If he did, he didn't enter the main harbor. Now, he's overdue returning to Barbados where a party of four is patiently waiting to board his boat. The behavior is inconsistent with Nisbett's operating style. The man is punctual to a fault."

"I've heard that about him before. So, what's MI6's plan?"

"Well, to be clear, it has truly little, if anything, to do with your own mission. We're here to investigate the loss of two highly respected MI6 officials and the disappearance of two rather expensive yachts belonging to the royal family."

"So, you're not interested in the *Marlin Sea*?"

Frank and Lily again exchanged looks, before he responded. "The *Marlin Sea* is only of interest to us if it sheds light on our primary mission; if not, you are correct, it's of no interest to us."

"So, I'm pretty much on my own?"

"In a manner of speaking, yes. However, we'll continue to feed you any information that comes our way regarding the yacht."

Jake glanced at his watch; it was approaching 9 a.m. "Well, I'm certainly grateful for all you've shared."

"Frank and I are only here for a few more days," Lily said. "We trust you'll honor the importance of confidentiality which surrounds our masquerade."

"You have my word on that."

23

The sole purpose of the second shelter Lou constructed, was to house firewood. It was identical to those the Abenaki had built for generations. As he began collecting wood, Kate set out on the daily trek around the island. After days of walking along the water's edge, the task had become routine, and Kate found herself working to stay alert. More than anything else, the antics of shorebirds scurrying ahead was the only thing that held her interest.

This day had started out no differently than the previous day. Except for thin wispy threads of clouds in higher elevations, the sky was clear. Later in the day, puffy moisture ladened cumulus clouds would appear, and rain would offer a brief respite from the heat.

Until then, the bright sun would cause her to squint. She longed for her sunglasses, but they were aboard the *Marlin Sea*, along with everything else she'd carefully packed.

Although desolate and lonely, the surrounding beauty of the

island was undeniably breathtaking. The only sound that came to her ears were waves pounding up against the reef and an occasional squawk from a gull gliding overhead.

Kate had traveled almost halfway around the island, mostly with her head down and lost in private thoughts, when she reached a bend in the shoreline and sounds of excited shorebirds caught her attention. She looked up and stopped dead in her tracks.

At first, Kate thought her eyes were playing tricks on her. The entire beach ahead was erupting and appeared to be moving toward the water. Shorebirds were circling overhead; others were on the beach, wings flapping wildly. More were flocking towards the phenomenon that was playing out on the beach. It was sheer bedlam.

It took a moment, but as soon as Kate shielded her eyes from the sun, she realized what was happening: Hundreds of miniature newborn turtles were scurrying frantically toward the safety of the water. Their flippers flailed madly, like tiny wind-up toys. The only thing missing was the whirring of a mechanical sound.

When the shorebirds began dive bombing and snatching the helpless hatchlings, Kate's first instinct was to run forward and scatter the birds, but she soon realized enough turtles would survive.

In a matter of minutes, the mad dash to the sea was over. A few weak stragglers still struggled in the sand and would fall prey to the gulls. But most had made it to the water.

As she continued walking across the disrupted beach, Kate's eyes wandered across the remains of what she had witnessed.

And so goes life in this paradox between paradise and survival of the fittest. Thoughts of life's challenges raced across her mind.

Then visions of her young twins filled her consciousness. *Will they survive? What will become of them if we never return?*

It wasn't until she reached the halfway point around the island that she glanced up, and for a second time, froze in her tracks.

MEANWHILE, on the island of Barbados, Jake sat across the lunch table from Koby. He had just briefed her on the breakfast meeting he'd had with the two MI6 operatives and Koby was not pleased.

"Jake, you know how worried I am. I cannot believe you didn't tell me you were meeting these people at the Peninsular Club."

"I wasn't sure if it was going to amount to anything Koby, and this morning was your last post conference meeting."

Koby pursed her lips, eyes glancing upward as she took in a breath. "I just wish you had told me, Jake. The meeting was basically over yesterday. We accomplished everything we needed to do. The only reason we met today was to say goodbye." Koby paused. "All right, let's not make an issue of it, just tell me again what they said."

"They're here trying to figure out how a couple of MI6 colleagues, and their families, disappeared without a trace in the Caribbean."

"And how does the *Marlin Sea* play into this?"

"One of their retirees went out on that yacht with his wife. When the man's body washed ashore and the wife disappeared, MI6 began tracking the whereabouts of the boat, that's all there is to it. As of this morning, the boat is east of Turks and Caicos heading north."

"Jake, there is no way Kate and Lou would just take off and extend their cruise for this length of time without saying anything to us. That is just not like them."

"You and I both know that."

"You said they know where the yacht's been?"

"Yeah, the day Lou and Kate boarded, it sailed to Saint Vincent and the Grenadines, from there it's been heading north."

Koby sat back in her chair. Her hands pressed together, as if in prayer, touching her lips as she reflected on what she'd heard. After half a minute, she looked up and shook her head.

"No, Jake that can't be right. That is *not* the itinerary Kate showed me. They weren't going to Saint Vincent. They were going north to Saint Lucia. After a couple days at Saint Lucia, they were going up to Martinque, after that they were returning to Barbados."

"I'm only telling you what the spooks told me."

"Well, they're wrong, Saint Vincent wasn't on their itinerary. Kate purposely chose that boat because she wanted to snorkel the waters around Saint Lucia."

Jake shrugged his shoulders. "Koby, the harbor master in Saint Vincent reported the *Marlin Sea* coming into port and docking the same day it left Barbados."

"That can't be right! When they left Barbados; they went to Saint Lucia."

"Koby, honey, there's no record of the *Marlin Sea* pulling into port on Saint Lucia."

"And there wouldn't be. Boats like that stay clear of the main harbors once their passengers are on board. The beauty of yachting is that you drop anchor wherever you choose."

"Well, if that's true, doesn't it also mean they could have changed course and gone to Saint Vincent?"

Koby paused to let Jake's words sink in. "Did they overnight in Saint Vincent?"

"No, the harbor master's records showed the *Marlin Sea* coming in and pulling out within an hour."

"Jake, even if they did decide to change their itinerary, and go to Saint Vincent, they'd still be back by now."

He nodded in agreement. "I wonder if they were even onboard when the *Marlin Sea* pulled into that harbor in Saint Vincent."

Koby's thoughts flashed back to her recent flight with Dan Shively. They sat in silence, each with their own thoughts, until Koby spoke up.

"You know, the other day, when I flew down to look at Shively's archeological find, we flew over the small islands off Saint Vincent. Just as we were leaving the area, I saw a small column of white smoke coming up from one of the islands. At the time, I didn't think too much about it. But now I wonder if it might have been a signal fire."

Jake paused. "If it was Lou, it would have been one helluva smokey fire, there's nothing subtle about him." Still, in his head, Jake wondered if the trail he needed to pick up was somewhere near Saint Vincent and the Grenadines.

"Is MI6 working with the port authority?"

"I doubt anyone on the island knows they're here."

"We need to share the information you learned this morning with Inigo Montez."

WHEN THEY ARRIVED at the port authority building, Inigo Montez was in his office, on his phone. As soon as Montez learned that Jake and Kate were waiting to see him, he hung up and walked over to the counter.

"How splendid of you to come in, I was about to call you."

Koby's eyes widened in expectation. "Have you found them?"

Holding up both hands, Montez put on a show of concern. "No, no, not yet, but we will. The search is underway."

Jake dismissed Montez's theatrical antics. "What was it you wanted to share with us, Mr. Montez?"

"Why, that the investigation is now officially underway. But you must understand, it is still very early. I have instructed my team on the urgency of this matter. I can assure you any unnecessary protocols which might delay things have been suspended. Now, that being said . . . "

Anxious to pass along the information that Jake had learned, Koby decided she wasn't going to wait for Inigo Montez to finish.

"Mr. Montez, we just learned that when the *Marlin Sea* left here, she traveled down to Saint Vincent."

Montez's pleasant demeanor changed, and his eyes flashed. His next words came out as a challenge. "How do you know that?" Then, with a much softer tone, he said, "Excuse me, what I . . . what I meant to say was, what makes you think so?"

Jake nudged Koby, cautioning her to not divulge anything about the true source of their information. Koby took a breath before responding. "The harbor master's log in Saint Vincent has a record of the *Marlin Sea* entering and leaving their harbor the same day she pulled out of Barbados."

Montez's eyebrows narrowed. "That can't be true, there must be a mistake." Again, Montez's demeanor seemed adversarial, his words coming across more as a declaration than curiosity.

Jake cleared his throat. "It's true."

Montez paused and when he spoke next, his tone was neutral. "It is important that any information you gather comes directly to me so it is verified. How is it that you came across this?"

"We've been calling around," Jake lied.

Montez straightened up. "Please, you must not interfere. Allow me to do my job. I assure you, I will inform you as soon as I have *anything* to report."

Jake read Montez's body language and saw where the conversation was likely to go. "Fine. We appreciate your willingness to keep us in the loop."

Montez glanced at his wristwatch; the meeting was over. "Most assuredly. My team will brief me later today. I am confident they are fully aware of this bit about Saint Vincent. But if, for any reason they are not, I will pass your information along."

Jake extended his hand, to shake with Montez. "Well, we certainly can't ask for anything more than that. Koby, let's not take up any more of this man's time."

As soon as they were both outside the building, Jake whispered, "That dog won't hunt."

"What? What does that mean?"

"Koby, either Montez is an officious buffoon, which I doubt, or something else is going on."

After a pause, Jake continued, "Come on, let's go see if what he said about this not being a police matter is really true."

THE BARBADOS POLICE had an entirely different story about how things worked on the island.

Koby was dumbfounded. "So, let me get this straight: Mr. Montez does not have a search and rescue team currently working this?"

"No ma'am, not unless he's paying for it out of his own

pocket. The only role the port authority has in any search and rescue operation is relaying information and providing dock space. Search and rescue operations fall under the jurisdiction of the Coast Guard."

As Koby was about to say something further, Jake put a hand on her shoulder. "Let it go, hon. We need to go talk to the right people."

The police sergeant reached for the phone on his desk. "I'll let the Coast Guard know you're coming, then I'll have a talk with Mr. Montez. He is new on this island, but it's inexcusable he did not immediately refer you to the Coast Guard."

WHEN JAKE and Koby walked into the U. S. Coast Guard office, they were met by a young lieutenant. After filling out a missing person report and sharing what little they knew about the disappearance of Lou and Kate, they headed back to their hotel.

Not more than a quarter block away from the coast guard office, Koby turned to her husband. "Jake, what are we going to do about Inigo Montez?"

"Nothing."

"Jake, he lied to us. We wasted valuable time because of him."

"Let it go. The police will have a conversation with him. Other than that, he's not even in my rearview mirror."

THE APPROACHING darkness forced the coast guard to hold off launching an air and sea search until the following morning. When dawn arrived the following day, and the subsequent four days, spotter planes and patrol boats canvased the area of the Caribbean known as the Lesser Antilles. But over a hundred miles lay between Barbados and a small, unnamed island in the ocean . . . with a peak on it.

Each day, the coast guard's report was the same: "No sign of the *Marlin Sea*."

On the sixth day, a paragraph was added: "Active search and rescue operation will cease after the seventh day."

24

L ou counted the notches he'd made on a tree. The next day would be their twenty-first on the island. Three times in the past week, they heard small planes in the vicinity. Each time Lou lit the signal fire, but the planes never came to investigate. Two days earlier, the outline of a freighter had appeared on the horizon. Again, Lou lit the signal fire, and a great deal of smoke went up, but it was questionable whether anyone aboard even noticed.

The only clothing the castaways had were the bathing suits they'd worn the day they snorkeled in the lagoon. Kate's bikini was expensive, but far from the most durable piece of clothing she'd packed. Early on, she had put her bikini aside to save it and had covered herself from the waist down with a makeshift loincloth crafted from large leaves. For the most part, Lou did the same, except when he was spearfishing in the lagoon. Both had become cautious about being in the sun and throughout the day applied aloe to soothe their peeling and blistering skin.

More than ever now, the days just blended one into the next

while they settled into a routine. Life had become boringly simplistic: gather food, wait for the day to pass, watch the sun go down, and sleep. To offset the monotony, Lou had crafted a checkerboard. At night, they'd tell each other stories of their upbringing, other than that, survival chores filled their day.

Each time Kate circled the island, she alternated the direction she took, just for a change. This day, she was traveling counterclockwise. As she walked along the beach, her thoughts were, as usual, on her twins and their own survival. It was only by chance she looked up and saw not one, but two large ocean-going canoes pulled up on the white sandy beach sitting next to each other. Her first reaction was to drop down and lessen her profile.

Kate remained motionless. The beating of her heart blocked out all other sounds. After sensing the canoes were unattended, her curiosity edged her forward, and she began crab-walking along the water's edge. As she worked her way toward the canoes, the incoming tide erased the footprints she left in the soft watery sand.

The dugout canoes were each about twenty feet long. A single mast, with a loosely furled sail, rose up from the center of each and the outriggers extended from their right side. Footprints in the sand alongside the dugouts went directly toward the path leading to the plateau on the hillside above. Kate counted them.

There's at least four or five of them. Without any backup I'm not particularly fond of those odds, she thought.

Turning, she crab-walked back to where she'd first seen the canoes, knowing the tide would erase her tracks, leaving no evidence of her presence. As soon as she felt far enough away, she stood up and paced herself as she jogged back to the lagoon.

LOU WAS GATHERING MORE debris to store inside the second lean-to when Kate came running back to camp.

"Lou, we have company!"

"Where?"

"On the far side, just below the plateau. Two canoes, I counted at least four, maybe five sets of footprints."

Lou nodded, his hand instinctively checking his knife at his side. He reached down and handed Kate the wooden spear he used to fish from shore.

"Let's go."

They headed inland. The overland route would cut their travel time in half, but more importantly, it would provide cover.

They traveled uphill, past the small pond beneath the waterfall and around the far side of the dormant volcano to a vantage point overlooking the plateau.

Five males were directly below in the clearing. Two were using palm fronds to sweep the ground, while another watched. Two others stood next to the stone edifice, talking. It was a hot day, yet all five of them were clothed in some sort of dress that extended from the waist to just above their ankles.

Four of the men were dressed in plain garments, the other had a more elaborate garment with vibrant colorful images on it.

"What's your take on it?" Kate whispered.

Lou's eyes were scanning the plateau below. Finally, he whispered, "I'm not sure. It looks like they're preparing for something. The pile of wood on the stone altar has been built up. The two sweeping the ground and the one watching appear to be younger than the other two."

"You can tell that from this distance?"

Lou nodded. "Watch how they move, that's what gives them

away." Lou no sooner said that, when the two who had been sweeping tossed their makeshift brooms aside and joined the others. The two who had been talking shook hands. Then four of the men removed the simple garments they had around their waist, folded them, and placed them on the stone edifice. Clothed only in breechcloths, they turned and walked in single file toward the path leading to the beach.

Lou cupped his hand over Kate's ear. "Stay here, I wanna see where they're going."

When Lou reached a vantage point near the path that offered a clear view of the canoes, he waited. Shortly, the four who had left the plateau appeared on the beach and pushed both canoes into the water. After maneuvering the canoes around to face open water, they climbed aboard and began paddling away. Once the canoes were clear of the surf, the man sitting in the forward position of each boat took hold of the halyard and raised the single sail.

Now that is interesting, Lou mused, *they're leaving the one above behind. Why?* Lou remained where he was, his mind racing, eyes locked on the canoes as they sailed away. When he realized he had left Kate alone longer than he intended, he worked his way back up toward the clearing.

Lou moved with such stealth; he was virtually invisible. When he reached the edge of the clearing on the plateau, the islander who had remained was still standing near the stone altar. But Kate wasn't where he left her.

Surprised she had moved; Lou took what he felt was a concealed position among the underbrush. Then, soon after Lou knelt down, the man at the altar turned around. . . and looked directly at him.

Lou was close enough to clearly make out the man's features.

He was much older than Lou had first thought. Like the others, he was short and stocky. His shoulders and upper arms were muscular, likely from paddling ocean-going canoes. Earlier, the man's back had faced Lou and a large tattoo in the shape of a cut leaf covering one entire side of his face hadn't been visible. A circular tattoo, resembling the sun, covered the center of his chest. Other than a machete hanging from his waist, and the ornate garment, nothing else was notable.

The man's eyes continued looking straight at Lou. To Lou's surprise, he finally spoke. "I wondered how long it would take before you reappeared."

The man's voice was guttural, but his tone wasn't threatening. While surprised the man spoke English, Lou was more dumfounded that he was visible. He had used every bit of stealth he knew while coming up the hillside and thought he had remained completely hidden.

Now motioning with his hand for Lou to come forward, the man continued, "Why have you come to the island of our ancestors?"

Stepping from his concealment, Lou saw the wooden spear Kate had been carrying now leaning up against the stone edifice. Even from a distance, the man noticed Lou's eyes lock onto the spear and Lou's hand reach for the hilt of his knife.

"She is not harmed."

"Where is she?" Lou's voice divulged none of the rage he was feeling. As if on cue, Kate stepped into the clearing, wearing a brightly adorned full-length tunic. The old man's eyes never left Lou. When he saw Lou's body relax slightly, he continued.

"The rituals are near. Move carefully. The spirits punish those who dishonor them."

Lou's eyes scanned Kate. He could tell from her demeanor no harm had come to her, but now he had even more questions.

In one fluid motion, the old man reached into a handwoven basket and pulled out a garment identical to his own. As he held the cloth out for Lou, he said. "Wrap this around your waist, it is unwise to offend the spirits of the ancient ones."

When Lou didn't immediately make a move to accept the offering, the old man gestured with his hand, indicating it was not a choice.

As Lou wrapped the cloth around his waist, the old man continued. "You are too tall to be a Carib, yet your raised cheek bones tell me you are not like the ones who come from across the great water."

Lou nodded, his hand subconsciously reached for the talisman which usually hung around his neck, but quickly remembered it wasn't there. "My people are known as the Abenaki. Our lands are far to the north."

After a pause, the man responded. "What brings the Abenaki to this most sacred of all islands?"

Lou hesitated before answering. He had expected to be using sign language with the man, or at least some form of broken Spanish.

"It was not our intent." As Lou nodded toward Kate, he continued. "We were left here against our will. We seek to return to our own lands, in peace."

"How did you come here?"

"By boat . . . the boat marooned us here." Lou wasn't sure if the man would understand the word *marooned*, but he used it anyway. "We have no way of leaving."

"How long ago?"

Lou wasn't sure if they shared the same numbering scheme, so he held up his hands. After flashing all ten fingers twice, he added one more finger.

"Three weeks?"

"Yes, you speak English well. How is that?"

Smiling, the man responded, "The missionaries. They come to our village to educate us and try to make my people like them. But they only care about their own ways. My people are not like the Caribs, we will not let them change us."

"Who are your people?"

The old man seemed to stand taller as he spoke. "We are descendants of the ancient ones. My people were here long before the *Igneri* arrived and long before those who came later."

The name Igneri registered with Lou, he majored in *The Origins of Western Culture* at McGill University in Montreal years ago. Yet, he wasn't familiar with any people known as *the ancient ones*. Finally, he said, "What name did the others call your people?"

The old man smiled. His teeth were brilliant white and perfectly aligned. "My people were here long before the Igneri, before the Arawak, before the Taino even before the Myan, the Inca, and the Aztec. But they did not know of us."

"How is it that the others did not know of you?"

The old man made a sweeping gesture with his arm. "Long before the others came, the sea swallowed the land of my people. We are few now. We come here to honor the spirits of the ancient ones."

"You keep saying, 'the ancient ones.' Who are the ancient ones? What name did they call themselves?"

"They had no name; there were no others. We were the only people then. Our people were scientists and artists. They built a great city. The sky gods came and helped them create our culture. They worshiped the sun and the sky gods who came from the stars and who lived in the great cosmos.

Lou looked at Kate who had moved beside Lou by this time. The story was a little too far-fetched for him to believe at face value. "So, what happened to your people? Where are they now?"

"The god of the sea was jealous of his brother, the sun, and decided to punish him. He waited until the sky was dark and his brother was asleep. Then he came and swallowed the city of the ancient ones. When the sky gods came and saw what had happened, they were angry and came no more."

"Yet, some of your people survived?"

"Not many, . . . but some. Those who lived in the great cities on land where the sun sleeps, had all come to our central city to celebrate the gods, but the sea swallowed them, too. There are only a few of us now. When the Caribs came, we fought them, but they were too strong and too many, so my people fled to these smaller islands. Then the Spanish came and conquered the others, but they did not know of my people because we hid from them."

Lou had always been a student of history, and his curiosity was peaked. "Did the city that sank into the sea resemble the temples the Myan built?

"The Myan were not builders. They were squatters. They came after and took the empty cities the ancient ones had built on the lands beyond and made them their own. When the Myan died off, the Aztec and the Inca came. The cities the ancient ones built were not in ruins, so the Aztec and Inca lived in them. When the Spaniards came, they did not know of the ancient ones, they killed the Aztecs and the Inca who had knowledge."

Lou's mind raced as he tried to absorb all he was hearing. "Are your people known as the Toltec?"

"No, but that is the word the Aztec used to describe our lost culture. Like the Myan before them, the Aztec and the Inca tried to embrace our knowledge of astronomy, our system of government, and the farming ways of the ancient ones."

"They did more than try," Lou said.

"No, they only used what they found. They did not advance the knowledge the ancient ones left behind. The belief systems that defined the cultures that followed were flawed. Everything was built around ritualistic pageantry. They glorified themselves they angered the sun god. When the Spanish came, the sun god did not come to help them, and they vanished."

Kate had heard enough. "Can you help us get off this island?"

Her question jolted Lou back to reality. "We need your help. When will the canoes return?"

"My people will come once the sun crosses the sky four times."

Kate was anxious. "Is there any way you can tell them to come sooner?"

The old man shook his head. "They will not come again until the stone calendar tells them it is time. Only then will my voice travel to *Xibalba*, the realm of the dead, and be heard by the spirits of the ancient ones."

Lou realized all the time they had spoken, neither had told the other their name. "My name is Lou, Lou Gault. This is my wife, Kate. Will you help us leave this island safely?"

"I am Bion."

Kate asked again, "Will you help us leave this island?"

"When the canoes return you will go, I will help you, but you must wait."

Four days, Lou thought letting out a sigh. Then he expressed his gratitude. "Thank you, Bion. What can we do in return?"

"We will talk about that tonight. I will come to the far side where you camp."

"You know about our camp?"

Bion acknowledged Lou's question with a single nod. "I

have traveled there three times. Once when you first arrived, once when you slept, and once after the storm when you were both on the beach. I will come and we will eat together."

As Lou extended his right arm to shake hands, he thought, *I wonder what else I will learn from this one?*

25

Later that evening, after they had dined on a spit-roasted chicken, plantains, and greens that Bion brought, they let the cook fire die down, as they traded stories.

Lou had studied the cultures that had once populated Central and South America as well as the islands in the Caribbean. However, he'd never come across people known as "the ancient ones."

"Bion, tell me about your ancestors. How advanced were they?"

"They learned much from the sky gods, who traveled among the stars. That is who helped them build great cities and taught them to use the sun and moon to create calendars and count the days. But after the sea god swallowed the land, the sky gods came no more.

"When the sun god awoke and saw what his brother had done, he was not happy. To punish his brother, the sun god created waves so the sea would never rest. After that, the churning of water and sound of waves kept the sea god awake and he could not sleep. This upset his stomach.

"Finally, the sea god spit out pieces of land it had swallowed, and the islands were created. But when the sea god still could not sleep, he cleared his throat and spit out stories of the ancient ones that had been caught in his throat. When the sun god saw that his brother had created the islands, and given the stories back, he made the tides so his brother could rest twice a day."

Lou nodded. "The Abenaki use stories to help our young ones learn the history of our people, too."

Bion nodded. "The history of the ancient ones is not lost; it is the technology that is lost. The ancient ones walked across the water in great canoes that did not need paddles. The sky gods showed them how to move among the clouds."

As the night went on, Bion shared many stories about the city states of the ancient ones, including how they were connected by trade, diplomacy, and marriages. The social structure and dynamic political landscape was fascinating.

When Bion told of the sacrifices the ancient ones made to the gods to ensure agricultural fertility and cosmic order, he tread carefully.

Then there came a point when Bion decided enough stories had been shared and he rose up. "I will return tomorrow . . . for dinner. We will talk more."

In the nights that followed, Lou would learn there were only two cornerstones that framed the strong alliance existing among the ancient ones: a common religion and common cultural beliefs. What Bion would also touch upon was how the sky gods had leveraged the harmonious arrangement and balance within the universe to travel among the stars.

EACH DAY, Jake and Koby walked down to the wharf area while the Barbados coast guard sent out teams in search of the *Marlin Sea*. Jake would take a seat on the far end of the bench Johnny Coconut sat on, while Koby chatted with Lily at the charter boat reservation kiosk. But the MI6 operatives had nothing new to share.

ON THE NIGHT the *Marlin Sea* left the harbor in Puerto Rico, it had traveled to a small, secluded island in the Bahamas. There was a time when the locals referred to the island as *Hermosa Rosa*, but the beauty that once was no longer existed. More recently, the small port that defined the island was approaching a level of wickedness equal to the infamous Port Royal, the Caribbean hellhole of the seventeenth century that had also sunk into the sea.

The cartels now controlled the island and corruption was rampant. Brothels and bars lined the streets where once rose bushes draped over picket fences. Each morning, the bodies of unfortunate souls who had foolishly tested fate were gathered up along with the rest of the garbage. There were no limits, everything and everyone could be bought, if not in a shop, then on the streets, or the dark sordid alleyways. The faceless people who ran the shops had no scruples, and would traffic in anything, human flesh included.

Carlos had never been fond of the island now known as Devil's Cay, but Sanchez was a big fan. Having misgivings about spending time among thieves and other bottom feeders, Carlos only tolerated it because it appealed to Sanchez. They had frequented the island before, and the locals knew the two men had money to spend.

Whenever he was in port, there was a sweet young thing who hung on Carlos' arm and willingly shared her bed with him. As for Sanchez, he enjoyed the nightlife and excitement that came from every time his blade ended the life of some fool who tried to cheat him. For two whole weeks, the *Marlin Sea* sat in port, completely off the grid. Or so they thought.

WORD SPREAD QUICKLY among the higher echelon in the cartels that Carlos and Sanchez were on Devil's Cay and the *Marlin Sea* was sitting on a swing anchor. People like Inigo Montez kept track of the comings and goings of everything that happened on the island. He knew the Caribbean like the back of his hand.

Montez, himself, had come from humble beginnings. Like Francisco Pizarro (the cruel Spanish conquistador who rose in stature from a humble swineherd to leading an army and conquering the Inca), Montez had great expectations. He rose quickly within the ranks of the cartels and now was living the good life.

His network was like a spider's web, nothing happened that his network wasn't aware of. The eyes and ears who worked for him monitored all communication in the Caribbean, including encrypted messages of MI6. More than once, Montez's network saved his life, earning him the nickname The Chameleon. Without question, the minions he controlled willingly did his bidding. Even the upper echelon of the cartels considered Montez as lord and master of the Caribbean. And given the money he poured into the cartel's coffers; he had a free hand.

But Montez's network wasn't the only clandestine operation collecting information in the Caribbean. When word of the *Marlin Sea*'s whereabouts reached Johnny Coconut, he was anxious to share it with Jake before leaving the island of Barbados for good.

To Johnny Coconut's surprise, Jake didn't come to the wharf the last day he was there. So, before Johnny bid his final farewell to the bench he'd occupied for weeks on end, he took out another Peninsular Club business card, wrote a note on the back, and jammed it into a crack in the wooden bench, hoping Jake would find it sometime soon.

IT WAS JUST after 3 p.m. when the coast guard released their final search and rescue report before suspending the operation. After reading the impersonal document, Koby looked up at her husband.

"Jake, I don't care what their policy is, they can't just stop looking for Lou and Kate!"

"Unfortunately, they can, and they have," Jake said. "So, it's up to us now. They're out there somewhere, and you and I are going to find them."

Koby took a deep breath and let it out slowly. "I just feel like we've wasted so much time. First with Montez, now with the coast guard. Do you think they're still alive?"

Jake was only half listening. He already had a plan and was scrolling through a weather app on his iPhone. "Forecast for tomorrow is clear. We'll get an early start and head down to Saint Vincent. The trail may be cold, but if Lou and Kate are alive, I know he'll help us find him."

Koby hadn't allowed herself to accept the possibility that any real harm had come to the couple, so she accepted Jake's plan. "I agree, given the time of day the *Marlin Sea* went into Saint Vincent, there's zero chance it went anywhere near Saint Lucia that first day."

THE FOLLOWING MORNING, Jake and Koby were waiting inside the hangar when Bruce Russell, owner of a small flight school, entered the building. "Morning folks, you're early if you're here looking for lessons."

"We're not." Jake said and pulled out his pilot's license and FAA CPL certificate, handing them over to Bruce. "We'd like to take one of your birds for the better part of the morning, maybe longer."

Bruce scanned the documents Jake presented. "Are you certified on a Cessna Grand Caravan?"

"I am. You can look it up if you've a mind to; I'm certified on that, and a host of others as well. My usual bird is a de Haviland Otter."

Bruce was a cautious man, and knew he would check Jake's credentials, like he did with any pilot, before they would even touch the tie down straps.

"I think I'll need one that's fitted with pontoons, just in case I need to set her down in the water," Jake said.

"Setting down in the water's a lot different than on a landing strip. Have you done many water landings?"

"I fly a mail plane up in New Brunswick. I set down in water more than a few times every day."

"I'll bet you do," Russell said, looking at him directly. "Just the two of you going up?" But Russell didn't wait for an answer. "Here, fill out this flight plan while I see what I have available that we can fit a pair of floats on."

Bruce Russell was gone a little longer than Koby expected. She hadn't slept well in weeks and was tired. Even the wait for Jake to fill out the paperwork seemed like one more unnecessary delay. She whispered to her husband, "What's taking so long? We're only renting the thing."

"It won't be long now. I told him to top off the tank. After that, he's gotta do a ground check, then I'll do a preflight. When you're depending on pontoons, ya' really wanna be sure those babies aren't gonna fall off. You lose one, and you're in for a lot more than a bumpy landing, like tipping into the drink, or worse!"

Moments later, Bruce came through the door and gave Jake a thumbs-up sign. "You're all set Mr. Gault. Just have her back before we close, otherwise, you're paying for another day."

Jake looked at the sign on the wall: Closing time 5 p.m.

KOBY WASTED no time boarding the plane and settling into the co-pilot seat before Jake finished his pre-flight inspection. Once Jake strapped himself into the pilot seat and both engines were purring, he pushed the thrust lever forward and taxied the Cessna up behind a Beechcraft also waiting to take off.

As soon as the Cessna lifted off, Jake pressed the intercom button. "We should have good visuals today, Koby. When we get down around Saint Vincent, I think the first thing we do is fly over the outer islands. I have a hunch they may be holed up on one of those smaller ones. Keep your eyes peeled for anything in the water like a wreck."

"Jake, if they ran into a problem with the boat, someone would have gotten on the radio and called for help by now. Besides, you said MI6 is tracking the boat."

"Let's not rule anything out. Maybe the radio wasn't working."

"There's usually a spare radio on board, but you're right." Despite offering those encouraging words, she kept the rest of her thoughts to herself.

And there were flares on board. If they were on one of the islands, they should have been able to send up a signal flare when a plane or a boat came near.

SMALLER ISLANDS off the coast of Saint Vincent number well into the hundreds. Some are no bigger than spits of sand surrounded by a reef. Others are lush and densely populated with an array of green tropical flora.

Around mid-morning, Jake looked down at the fuel gauge, he'd already used up two-thirds of the gas he had on board. "I thought these Cessnas were better on fuel. Must be the floats causing drag. Koby, we'll make a couple of passes around the islands directly in front of us, then we better head over to Saint Vincent and take on some more fuel."

"Read me the coordinates so we can get back to where we left off."

Jake looked down at his instrument panel. "Latitude, 3.2510° N, longitude, 61.1863° W." When Jake banked the plane right, he saw dark clouds to the south.

"Whoa, where the hell did that mess come from? The weather app didn't say anything about that."

"I saw it off in the distance a while ago, Jake."

As the Cessna headed for the island of Saint Vincent, Jake shook his head. "That looks like it could be a nasty system. We might need to think about refueling and getting the heck outta here before things get a little too bumpy for this little 'ole Cessna."

"Either that, or we spend the night on Saint Vincent. That would save us from having to go back and forth from Barbados."

Jake inhaled as he thought about it. After letting his breath out slowly, he turned to Koby and smiled. "This looks like it's just a passing squall." But even as he said it, Jake wasn't convinced it wouldn't be a whole lot more.

26

When nothing panned out on the islands below, they headed to St. Vincent for fuel. Just as Jake finished topping off the tank, gusty winds and ugly dark storm clouds reached them on the island.

"Koby, this one doesn't have the look or feel of a fast-moving tropical squall. We might be on the ground here for a while. Stay in the plane; as soon as I pay for the avgas, we'll taxi over to an area where I can tie this bird down."

AN HOUR LATER, Jake sat across a table from Koby looking at a lunch menu in a hotel not more than a mile from the airport.

"Jake, I think we did the right thing staying over. I just looked at the radar image on the weather app and this is a huge storm." Jake shrugged his shoulders, as he perused the menu. Koby didn't need any acknowledgment and continued talking.

"We did pass over a few sunken wrecks this morning when we covered the islands north of Saint Vincent before this storm grounded us. I bet Lou and Kate are on the islands to the south. We should probably start off by going south tomorrow. Do you agree we go south?" When Jake didn't respond, Koby said, "Are you listening? What do you think?"

Jake looked up with a start. "What do I think? I'm not sure about the Dover Sole, I think I'm going with the baked grouper, it sounds good, and it comes with a nice Grey Poupon reduction sauce."

"Jake, for god sakes, will you be *serious* for once in your whole life!"

"I *am* serious. I'm not going to take a chance on the Dover Sole." Koby closed her eyes and shook her head.

"Koby, hon, relax. I heard every word you said. We saw several sunken wrecks and I agree we go south next. If Lou was anywhere near where we were today, he would have sent up a signal."

"Aren't you worried?"

"Somewhat, but if they're alive, and he's not injured, Lou's got things under control. They may be roughing it, but they're doing fine."

"Jake they've been missing for weeks! How can you even think that way?"

"Because I know Lou. He's a survivor. A couple of weeks camping out may not be the reason he came down here, but he's in his element. He can fish, he can hunt, he can forage, he can make a fire. If he doesn't have a flare, he can send up a smoke signal. Anything we didn't learn from Grey Elk about survival, they taught us in commando school."

"You're that comfortable?"

"I am, even though I'm as anxious to find them as you are, I'm just keeping my cool about it and not letting my emotions take over."

Koby placed her napkin over her lap. "Then tomorrow let's go find the island where I saw a thin sliver of smoke rising up.

THE STORM LINGERED over Saint Vincent throughout most of that afternoon. When the anemometer at Argyle International Airport recorded winds exceeding thirty-nine mph, the World Meteorological Organization gave the tropical storm the moniker, Gretchen.

The planes that managed to shelter inside hangars at the airport fared well, but that wasn't the case for those tied down in the open. The Cessna Jake had rented appeared to sustain some surface damage to its paint from flying debris. Before he would take it up again, he would give it a thorough ground inspection.

AN HOUR before the storm reached Saint Vincent, it hit the small island where Lou and Kate were sheltering. Once again, the wind and storm surge wiped out the beach. But otherwise, the castaways suffered no damage. By the time Bion, their nightly dinner guest arrived, the storm had passed beyond the island.

"Canoes will come tomorrow," Bion said in greeting. "One will take you to the island we come from. From there, you will travel to the bigger island."

"What time?" Lou asked.

Bion closed his eyes and paused before answering. After careful thought, he said, "Before the sun is directly above."

THE FOLLOWING MORNING, after the storm passed, Jake made sure the Cessna was safe to take up. Once he completed a routine preflight check, he and Koby took off and headed south, toward more islands. They'd been in the air about forty minutes when Jake pointed downward.

"Whaddya make of all that over on the left?"

Koby propped herself up higher in the seat and looked over the nose of the Cessna. "Hmmm, looks like a whole armada of sails down there. I wonder what's going on."

As Jake pushed the joystick forward, he looked to the left. "Let's drop down and get a closer look see."

They made a wide circle around the flotilla twice.

"I count twenty-three, Jake. They're all about the same size and every one of them has an outrigger. Those are island boats. There must be some kind of reenactment going on."

During their second pass, the coxswains all raised arms and waved. Everyone else continued digging paddles into the water, propelling the canoes forward.

"Well, whoever they are, and wherever they're going, they're all doing it together."

Koby twisted in her seat and as she turned around. "Where do you think they came from Jake?"

"No idea; somewhere close by, I'd say. Those boats may be sea-worthy, but they're small. I doubt they've traveled far, but ya' never know. It looks like they're going to that island with the peak in the middle."

"Do you think there's a village on that one?"

"Nah, these islands are too small to sustain a population of any size for any length of time. And there are no amenities to speak of this far out."

As they passed close to the island, Jake looked down. "There's a nice lagoon on one side of that one. But the beach is strewn with debris. I doubt that place is home to anybody."

"Well, the mess on the beach could be a result of the storm."

"Yeah . . . maybe. We'll take a closer look on the way back. I wanna check out the islands further down first."

KNOWING they were going to leave the island on this day, neither Lou nor Kate felt a need to reconstruct the SOS sign on the beach or rebuild the signal fire. Even if they had, when Jake's Cessna passed overhead, Lou and Kate were already in the middle of the island, on their way to the to the plateau.

When Lou heard the plane, he stopped and looked up, but couldn't see anything through the dense tropical canopy.

"Lou, do you think they're looking for us?"

"Hard to tell; it could be. But in any event, we're getting off this island today."

"Do you think it's Jake?"

"It's either Jake out looking for us, or someone doing a little sightseeing. Any organized search and rescue would have ended by now."

Just our luck, Kate thought, *the one time there's no sign on the beach.*

BION STOOD beside the stone altar, a brightly colored headdress now adorned his head. When he saw Lou and Kate emerging from the undergrowth, he waved them over.

"You must leave before I summon the spirits of our ancestors." Then, as if choreographed, he handed Lou a short version of the wrap he had lent him earlier. "Put this on so the spirits of the ancient ones are pleased."

Kate had never taken off the full-length shift Bion had given her when they first met. Now, as Lou wrapped the fabric around his waist, Bion looked up at the canopy of leaves overhead.

"Come, the boats that bring my people approach. I must meet them as they come ashore." With that, Bion picked up an elaborate staff and proceeded toward the path leading down to the beach.

They no sooner arrived by the water than one-by-one, canoes began coming ashore. Bion made the rounds as each canoe beached, welcoming its occupants and chanting as he touched the bow with the tip of his staff. As he moved down the line, a group of men followed him. When the last boat landed, Bion's followers gathered around him.

Lou couldn't discern what was being said, but he noticed Bion pointing at him several times, then pointing out to sea. Finally, he saw heads nodding and in unison, the group began walking toward him and Kate. In the distance, two men had pushed the last canoe to arrive back into the water and were turning it around, so it faced out to sea.

"Two of my people will take you now. I bid you well as you journey to your lands."

Kate looked at Lou in almost disbelief. *Is this really happening? Are we really getting off this island?*

Lou reached out and locked arms with Bion. "Thank you, my friend." Turning to Kate, he said, "Come on, Kate, let's not keep anyone waiting."

ONCE JAKE'S Cessna passed beyond the island Lou and Kate were on, it traveled a distance to the southernmost islands in the chain.

After circling those islands for close to an hour, Jake leaned over to Koby. "I don't think there is an island down here we haven't flown over at least several times. Let's head back and look around the island with the peak."

Koby nodded. *I wonder if that's the one that had the thin trail of smoke I saw.*

"There's nothing but open water until we get to that island Koby, but let's keep our eyes open for anything that could be floating on the surface."

IT TOOK ABOUT twenty minutes for the Cessna to fly up from the southernmost islands to the one with a peak in the middle. A few times, Koby thought she saw something with a geometrical shape on the seabed, but she was more interested in looking for flotsam on the surface. As the island with the peak came into view, Koby's eyes searched for columns of smoke. Jake was first to break the silence.

"I thought we might get another glimpse of the sails we saw earlier, Koby, but I guess we won't."

Koby ignored Jake's comment, but her thoughts shifted to the people in the boats they had seen earlier.

It's funny, I thought where we live is remote, but the people in those boats are really off the grid.

"It looks like there's a good stretch of beach up ahead," Jake said. "I'll make a couple of passes over the lagoon and up the shoreline. If they're there, we'll flush them out of those palm trees."

After making a couple of low passes, Jake asked, "See anything?" Koby shook her head.

"Nothing but a lot of debris."

"Well, if they were camped on this side of the island, at least one of them would be out on the beach by now, waving their arms."

Koby let out a sigh. "I'm not giving up hope, Jake, but it's not looking good."

"Let's circle around this island and take a look at the other side."

No sooner had the Cessna come around on the opposite side of the island than the line of boats pulled up on the sand came into view.

"Well," said Jake, "I can tell you right now, Lou's not on this island. If he was, he'd have every one of those natives standing on the beach waving at us. Either that, or he'd have taken off with one of their boats by now."

Jake paused as he circled overhead. "We'll make a couple of passes along the beach anyway . . . just to be sure."

Three low flying passes later, and Jake tipped his wings before heading out to sea. "Well, it was a roll of the dice, and it came up snake eyes. We're back to square one, Koby."

Jake was far from giving up, still, he was discouraged. "Let's talk about *plan B* on the way back to Barbados."

Koby heard her husband's comment, but was busy scanning the horizon and didn't acknowledge him. "Jake, there's a single sail way off in the distance, all by its lonesome. Let's go check it out."

"Koby, it's just an anomaly. Let's head back."

"Maybe so, but sometimes anomalies happen for a reason."

"Yeah, and sometimes people going on a picnic go back for something they forgot."

"Like what?"

"I don't know . . . napkins, salt, pepper, whatever."

"Jake, what if it *is* them?"

"And what if it isn't? I don't want to end up ditching this thing in the water because we ran out of fuel."

Koby looked over at the fuel gauge. The needle was below a quarter full. "Have you switched over to the reserve tank yet?"

"No."

"Then can we *please* just check it out?"

Jake heard the frustration in Koby's voice. "All right, I see it, we'll swing over." As he altered course, he glanced once more at the fuel gauge. The needle was low, but with the auxiliary tank, he had more than enough gas to reach Saint Vincent and refuel.

THE SINGLE SAIL had traveled about six miles from the island as the Cessna approached. Jake dropped down, but not as low as he had done when they were checking out the beaches.

"Looks like there's a few people in this one, Koby."

"Yeah, it's funny, too, they're all waving."

As they flew overhead, Jake asked, "Did you get a good look?"

"I tried, but not really. Circle back and go down a little lower."

Jake was about to go into a turn when he heard the telltale sound of the engine missing. Moving quickly, he switched over to the auxiliary fuel tank. Pontoons or no pontoons, the last thing he needed was to lose the engines and be forced to make a water landing in the middle of nowhere.

After the engine sputtered a few times, it settled down and Jake went into a turn and circled back. "Okay, when we come up on them, this time, take a good look . . . they'll be on your side."

Koby propped herself up in the seat to give herself the best possible view as the plane flew by.

"Did you get a good look?"

"No, I couldn't, the sail was in the way. We need to go back!"

27

As the single engine plane banked left and came back around, Kate rested her paddle on the gunwales. "Lou, do you think that's Jake?"

"We'll know soon enough, Kate. Whoever is flying that plane is coming back."

This time as Jake approached, the pontoons were no more than thirty feet above the surface of the water.

Lou raised his paddle overhead and held it there with both hands as the plane roared past. "That's Jake," Lou said, "he's the only one crazy enough to fly that damn close to the water."

AS JAKE ROARED passed the outrigger, he knew from a single glance who the two people sitting in the middle of the canoe were.

Got 'em! he thought. *I knew you'd be out here somewhere, cuz.*

Koby was straining to see out the side window. "It's them!" she cried excitedly. "Oh, my God, we found them!"

Below in the canoe, the native in the stern leaned forward and touched Lou on the shoulder. "Is this the one you said would come for you? Is this your friend?"

"Yeah, no one else is that crazy."

"Oh, Lou!" Kate cried, "Oh, Lou!" No other words would come, only tears.

JAKE MADE another quick bank to the left and came back around. This time as the plane approached, he did a wing rock.

Lou lowered his paddle and smiled. The nightmare was finally coming to an end. They were going home.

The man seated behind Lou repeated his question. "This is your friend, yes?"

"Yes, yes, this is my friend! He's totally crazy, but he is my dear friend."

The man in the stern turned to look at the plane. "Will he follow us now until we reach land?"

"No, he won't have enough fuel for that, but he can land on the water. Let's furl this sail and see what happens."

The man in the forward position came back and within seconds, the sail was down. "Now your friend will know we wait for him."

Kate was seated close to the mast. She had stowed her paddle and was holding on to both gunwales with her hands. The surface of the water wasn't placid, but neither was it exceptionally choppy.

Now Jake had turned again and was coming in low, into the wind. As soon as he graced the water surface with the pontoons, he taxied over to where the canoe was drifting and feathered the prop.

Once Jake was broadside to the canoe, he slid the pilot's

window open and quoted a line from an old commercial: "Pardon me, would you have any Grey Poupon?"

Lou smiled and gave his cousin the finger.

With that, Koby cupped her hands around her mouth and yelled. "Kate! Are you all right?"

When Kate waved her hand and nodded, Koby moved to the passenger section, opened the door, and stepped out onto the pontoon.

"Looks like we're going for a ride, Kate," Lou said. He turned around and shrugged to the man behind him. "Thanks for the lift, but this is where we get off."

As Kate shifted into a kneeling position, Lou reached forward and placed his hand on her shoulder. "Hold on Kate, something big just passed beneath us."

"What? Like what?"

"I'm not sure, I only saw it for a split second. Let's get the canoe right up against the pontoons." The dark shadow passing beneath the canoe was as long as the plane's pontoons and about as wide.

All four people aboard the canoe used their paddles to draw the canoe closer to the plane floating on top of the water. Koby was standing on the right pontoon, one hand on a wing strut, the other reaching out.

When the shadow passed under them a second time, Kate saw it and froze. "Lou what is it?"

Before Lou could say a word, Koby held her hand up. "Everybody just stay where you are. I need to figure out what's circling below."

Koby waited, hoping to see the shape again. Finally, she said, "I saw more than one. Whatever they are, only two large species travel together in these waters: Black tip sharks or dolphins. If they're sharks, there's more than two and believe me when I say, we don't want to do anything to provoke them."

Minutes passed. When whatever was below did not reappear, Koby motioned the canoe closer. "All right, they've moved on. Let's get you guys aboard."

Kate was first. As she stepped out of the canoe, Koby took firm hold of her right arm. At that moment, two bottlenose dolphins surfaced just outside the framework of the outrigger. The noise was enough for Kate to quicken her step, and she propelled herself into the cabin.

Lou was next, but before he stepped onto the pontoon, he removed his hunting knife from the sheath on his belt. Holding the knife by its blade, he handed it to the coxswain. "Here, a little something to remember us by." The man took it and smiled.

As the canoe drifted away from the plane, the islander in the forward position hoisted the sail. The man in the stern waved with his free hand, working his paddle like a rudder with his other.

THE CESSNA HAD BARELY LIFTED off the water when Jake's voice came over the intercom. "You are now free to move about the aircraft."

Jake's attempt at humor fell on deaf ears. Koby and Kate were still hugging each other and rapidly talking together. Lou was looking out the window watching the canoe reverse course back to the island.

There was more than enough gas in the reserve tank to reach Saint Vincent. The foursome could have flown back to Barbados after refueling, and save a day's rental fee, but didn't do it. Instead, they decided to stay overnight at one of the small hotels on the island of Saint Vincent. All four were in great need of relaxation and being in the company of loved ones who would go to the ends of the earth for each other.

ASIDE FROM A FEW scrapes and bruises, and deep tans, the two former castaways were in decent shape and elected to wait until they reached Barbados before being checked out by a physician. However, after over four weeks on the island, their appearance left a lot to be desired.

Once Jake was in line to refuel, Koby went over to the shop inside the charter terminal and picked up a couple of XL tee shirts, flip flops, sunglasses, and baseball caps. Kate's disheveled hair and Lou's beard would have to wait, but at least they'd look somewhat like respectable beach bums when they walked into the hotel.

After Lou and Kate checked in, the two couples parted. Lou and Kate went up to their room to shower like civilized people, and their rescuers set out to purchase sets of clothing and other necessities for their returned family.

They had all agreed to hold off going to the police until they'd had time to talk amongst themselves at dinner.

THE FIRST THING Kate did when she arrived in her room was to place a call to Lou's cousin, Laughing Gull, in New Brunswick, Canada. After hearing the exuberant voices of their young twins, her mind was greatly eased.

The next thing she did was disrobe, step into the huge roman shower where Lou was already, and make love to him, just as they had several times under the waterfall on the island.

More mentally exhausted than physically tired from their

ordeal on the island, Lou said, "I told you it would all turn out well, didn't I?"

AS KATE TOWELED OFF, she said, "I'm not sure how much of this adventure we should share with the kids."

"It'll all come out in the wash at some point, Kate. Right now, I'm thinking about all the survival skills I need to teach those two."

As Kate examined the array of toiletry articles the hotel provided for their guests, she said. "Lou, there's time for that. Let's just let them to be children a while longer. They're not even eight, yet."

While Lou admired the curves on his naked wife's tanned body, he smiled. "You're right." But what he didn't share was just the opposite.

Jake is their mentor. He'll step up their training now, just like Grey Elk did after our parents died.

"Lou, was that the door I just heard?" Without waiting for an answer, Kate wrapped a towel around herself. "I gave Koby a key to the room. She said she'd leave a set of clothes for us on the bed. If that was her, we need to move along, they'll be waiting for us in the restaurant."

Lou wasn't listening to Kate's words. His thoughts had already shifted. Soon, he and Jake would pick up the trail and go after the man who deliberately left them on a deserted island in the middle of nowhere.

But mostly, he was thinking about the talisman he had left onboard the *Marlin Sea*.

28

After weeks on end of dining on nothing but fish, eggs, and land crab, Lou, and Kate both opted for an entrée of red meat at dinner. Throughout the meal, the two cousins purposely kept the conversation upbeat and light. Once the table was cleared, Koby and Kate set out to shop for clothing and a few travel essentials. When the sommelier reappeared with an assortment of fine cigars, Lou, and Jake each selected a hand rolled Cuban and headed outside.

IT WAS early evening when the two cousins took ownership of a bench set back from the sidewalk outside the hotel. The sun was low in the sky, but this time of year sunset was still a couple of hours away. Once Jake had his cigar lit, he passed the lighter to his cousin.

"Any ideas on how you think you want to start out, Lou?"

Lou turned over the perfectly wrapped cigar in his hand a

few times before responding. "I'm still working on the front end, but I'm damn clear on how it's all gonna end."

As Jake leaned back, he lifted his chin up and blew a couple of smoke rings in the air. "I ran into some spooks in Barbados."

Lou let that sink in before speaking a word. "What'd they have to say?"

"They've been tracking the *Marlin Sea* for over a month."

"Did they say why?"

"There's some connection to the disappearance of a former MI6 operative."

Lou took a deep pull on his cigar. "Well, let's hope they don't get too upset when they figure out we're in the hunt."

"I don't think they'll care. The two I met were close to pulling out."

"Did they tell you anything we could use?"

"Just that the boat was last seen leaving San Juan. They figured it was going to either Miami or Fort Lauderdale and that the Yanks will board it when it re-enters U.S. territorial waters. That's about all they had, Lou."

"Did they say why the States are involved?"

"Puerto Rico issued a search and rescue advisory."

"Sounds like there's a whole bunch of folks interested in this one little boat, Jake, and not a one of 'em is any good at it."

"When we get back, we'll take a walk down to the wharf. There's a spook posing as a homeless guy hanging around there. He might have something new to share."

"I saw that guy. His eyes betrayed him. So, he's MI6, huh?"

"Yeah, so is the gal in the kiosk."

"What else?"

"The head guy at the port authority isn't worth spit. He sure in hell didn't want the police involved."

"Then he's got skin in the game."

Jake nodded, "That did come to mind."

The two men sat in silence a few minutes, each consumed by their own thoughts. Finally, Jake cleared his throat. "Ya know, we could just put this one in the bag and go home." Lou didn't wait a second before responding.

"Can't."

Jake took a slow draw on his cigar and let it out. "I believe I know why but tell me anyway."

"The talisman that belongs to our people is on that boat."

"I thought you looked a little naked around the collar, cuz."

"That, and I intend to square things with the son-of-a-bitch who left us on that island."

"MI6 doesn't believe the real captain was on that boat when you went out."

"I figured that. Man would have had to be a damn fool if he was."

Lou paused and knocked ash off the tip of his cigar. "The first thing I learned early on about Kate is that woman doesn't take to fools kindly. She had that captain checked out. She never would have signed on with him if he hadn't passed her sniff test."

Jake breathed in heavily, holding his cigar at arm's length. "It's likely we'll be on the trail awhile. I'd feel better if the gals were back home."

"They're itching to get back to the kids anyway."

Jake let out a puff of smoke. "I believe that very sentiment may have come up once or twice during dinner."

Anyone, passing the two men sitting on the bench could easily have mistaken them for brothers. But physical looks aside, they were far from a matched set. Their personalities were almost the opposite of each other: Jake defused his life challenges with humor, serendipity guided his life choices; Lou was more stoic, and a disciplined planner. That said, they'd always been a team, and people learned early on that you didn't want them on your trail, unless you needed their help.

THE FOLLOWING MORNING, all four travelers left Saint Vincent's airport an hour after dawn. Air traffic going in and out of Barbados wasn't heavy, but for some unknown reason, Jake was placed in a holding pattern awaiting clearance to land which chewed up time.

Once on the ground, the reception they received wasn't anything they anticipated. As soon as the Cessna taxied over to the terminal designated for private aircraft and stopped, two black limousines sped out onto the tarmac. In less than a minute, the occupants in both vehicles had exited and circled the plane. They were dressed in casual island attire, but one held up a badge and began signaling those inside the plane to come out. Jake and Lou had taken the front seats. Without turning his head, Jake said, "I count six, but they may have backup. Whaddya thing, cuz?"

Lou eyed the men on the ground. It was obvious from their posture they were disciplined professionals, which meant only one thing, they were carrying.

"I'm not sure."

"Shit, I hope I'm not in a handicapped spot. Travel and Leisure magazine just did a full-page article on how airports are cracking down on that."

"Be quiet."

Jake smiled and waved at the man holding the badge as he shut down the engines. "At least they're not dressed in black. Did you ever see the flick 'Men in Black?' I don't fancy my memory being erased."

Turning around, Jake said, "Ladies, they're probably going to tell us we have to move, so for the time being, stay where you are."

But Kate's police instincts had already kicked in. As she looked out the window and assessed what was unfolding, she said, "Let's not overreact. This is obviously a case of mistaken identity. Let's all stay calm and just let whatever's going on, play out."

Koby was all too familiar with life in the tropics. Her thoughts had taken a different path. "I agree, but what we don't know yet is whether that badge is legitimate."

Lou and Jake both exited the passenger side door on the Cessna and stood with their hands out to the sides.

The man holding the badge stepped forward. "Who's in the plane?"

Lou motioned with his head, "Just our wives. Do you need them out here?"

"Not at the moment, and you can both relax, this is not an arrest." As the man secured his badge, he said, "The name is Edwards, Donald Edwards, MI6. Sorry about all this, but we weren't exactly sure if you were traveling alone."

Lou inhaled deeply and let out a frustrated sigh. "Mind telling us what this is all about?"

"Which one of you is Jake Gault?"

Jake raised his hand. "That would be me."

"We need to speak with you regarding an investigation."

Jake's mind immediately went back to the breakfast meeting at The Peninsular Club. "Are you talking about Lee and White?"

"Not their real names, but yes."

"All I can tell you is that we had breakfast together. We spoke a few times after that, but there's not a helluva lot more to it than that."

"We need to determine if your actions compromised their presence on the island."

"If I did, it wasn't deliberate, nor is it anything I'm aware of. I kept the whole thing to myself. I never told anybody about the meeting," he lied. "Besides, they said their time was almost up there."

"You'll need to come with us."

"Hey, hold on, I thought you said this wasn't an arrest."

As Edwards motioned for one of his men to come forward, he said, "It isn't, just consider it an informal inquiry."

Lou saw where this was going and wasn't about to be separated from his cousin. "That's not exactly true; he filled me in on everything."

"And you are the other Gault, the one who was aboard the *Marlin Sea?*"

"Correct."

"Then you'll need to come along, as well. What about your wives? Do they have any knowledge of Frank Lee and Lily White?"

Jake took out his wallet, presented his RCMP Auxiliary badge and told a slight untruth. "I can assure you, they do not."

Edwards studied Jake's face for a moment before responding. "Okay, for now your wives get a pass. But tell them to stay put."

"So, how long do you anticipate detaining us?" Lou asked.

"How shall I put this? It's rather difficult to explain at this point."

"Are we talking *hours?*"

"Actually, I'm afraid things have become rather sticky, of late. For the time being, I suggest you place your travel plans on hold."

Jake exchanged looks with Lou. Both knew what the other

was thinking and nodded. Jake was the first to speak, "Give us a moment. We've been on the road for a while. Our wives are tired, and anxious to return home and be reunited with the kids. We need to let them know what's going on and that they're not free to travel."

Edwards nodded, turned, and walked over to the limousine he'd arrived in, sure there would be no surprises.

WHEN LOU and Jake reentered the plane, both wives were sitting on the edge of their seats with questioning expressions. Kate was the first to speak.

"Lou, what in heaven's name is going on?"

"It appears Jake and I are going to be detained."

"Why? What for?" Koby asked. "We haven't done anything wrong."

Jake responded, "Relax, hon, no one's being charged with anything. There's an investigation going on and they want to speak with us about the *Marlin Sea*. That's all there is to it."

Kate let out a sigh. "Lou, I just want to get home. How long is this going to take?"

"They're not sure, they told Jake and I to put any travel plans we had on hold for a few days."

Both women simultaneously blurted out, "A few *days*?"

Jake responded saying, "Yeh, a few days. Look, you're not involved in this. You two should be free to travel shortly to pick up the kids. We'll follow as soon as we're given the okay."

"Jake, I don't like the sound of this."

"Neither do I," said Kate. "I don't believe we're hearing even the half of it."

Lou held up his hand. "Kate, slow down, we're telling you everything these folks just told us."

"Who are 'they?' They don't look like any pictures of a Barbados cop I've ever seen."

"They're not, they're MI6."

Kate's eyes widened. "MI6? MI6 has no jurisdiction here! This is not the United Kingdom. Let me out, I need to talk to whoever is in charge."

Lou placed a hand on his wife's shoulder. "Kate, connect the dots. They're asking for our help. Right now, you and I have no ID, and even if you did, you don't even come close to looking like the photo on your ID. Let it go. Jake and I will follow as soon as we can."

The back-and-forth conversation, pseudo arguments for and against, took a while. Finally, all four of them emerged from the Cessna and walked over to the limousine parked in front of the plane. When Edwards stepped out, Lou cleared his throat.

"We have one slight problem."

"What's that?"

"Our wives would like to travel home now."

Before Lou could say more, Kate spoke up. "The problem is, my husband and I left our passports aboard the *Marlin Sea*."

"This is not a concern of mine."

Kate looked Edwards straight in the eye. "Oh, I believe it is. Here's the reason: you have absolutely zero jurisdiction here and thus, no lawful right to detain, interrogate or even question any one of us. However, my husband and I do need passports to get home. I know you are aware that one phone call to my superiors and your cover is blown. So, here's the deal: in exchange for two temporary passports, which I'm sure you're capable of providing, I'll stand down and allow you to question my husband and his cousin. Do we have a deal?"

Edwards hesitated. "This doesn't need to become an embarrassing international incident," she added.

Edwards turned and snapped his fingers. Another MI6 operative emerged from the limousine.

"What's up?"

Edwards motioned with his head. "Get a hold of the consular in Bridgetown. I need passports for Lou Gault and Kathryn O'Grady-Gault."

After a simple salute, the man took out his cell phone.

"Problem solved. Anything else?"

Kate stared at Edwards for a moment. "Just like that?"

Edwards nodded, "Yes, ma'am, just like that. Or should I address you as *Lieutenant* O'Grady-Gault?"

When Kate didn't respond, Lou and Jake looked at each other and shrugged their shoulders.

"Nope, I guess that's it," Lou said.

"Good, you're staying at the Hilton. We'll have passports delivered to the front desk within the hour. Oh, and one last thing: don't check out. We have your room under surveillance."

"Is that it?" Lou asked.

"For now, yes. We'll be in touch later in the day to get your statements."

AS SOON AS both limousines drove away, the foursome went off in three separate directions. Jake walked into the hangar and just about maxed out his credit card settling the cost of the Cessna rental with Bruce Russell. Lou went over to the main terminal and booked two one-way tickets to Canada for the wives. Koby and Kate taxied back to the hotel, so Koby could pack up her belongings.

They had agreed to regroup at The Conch Grille inside the main terminal. Jake was the first to arrive and grabbed a table next to the window overlooking the runway. Lou was the next to arrive. He noticed Jake's credit card sitting on the table next to a glass of water. "Did you order already?"

"Lou, I don't think there's enough left on that damn piece of plastic to buy a damn grilled cheese sandwich."

"I called American Express last night from Saint Vincent's. They'll have a replacement card waiting for me at the hotel."

Jake changed the subject. "How soon are they flying back?"

"I was able to get them on a direct to Halifax at noon."

"Are they sitting together?"

Lou nodded. "Yeah, but to do it, I had to go First Class, otherwise they were each in a middle seat."

Jake glanced over his cousin's shoulder. "Well, here they come." He waved his arm at the women. "I'm sure they'll be happy about the upgrade."

THE DEPARTURE GATE for the flight to Halifax was at the far end of the terminal. After a light brunch and more stories exchanged, Koby whipped out her credit card, paid the bill, and the foursome headed to the gate area.

As they walked through the terminal, Kate turned to her husband. "Lou, no delays please, and no shenanigans. I want you back home, safe and sound. No exceptions, agreed?"

"Kate, I've got plenty of reasons to be back home."

Kate merely smiled. She'd been married long enough to ask, "Does that mean you'll be home as soon as you can?"

"That means I'll be on a plane flying home as soon we're done with this." Lou was deliberately being evasive, and Kate knew it, but chose to let it go.

When they arrived at the gate area, the first-class passengers were already beginning to board.

Both wives knew exactly what their husbands intended to

do. Koby hugged Jake. "Play it safe, sweetheart, this isn't a game."

"Koby, I'm going to echo what Lou said to Kate, I have plenty of reasons to get back home."

Kate stood on her tiptoes and tousled her husband's hair. "I'll be waiting."

Lou smiled and gave her one last hug.

"Lou, come home safe and sound."

"I will. We both will."

As soon as their wives entered the jetway, Jake turned to his cousin. "Let's head over to the wharf. There's someone over there we need to talk to."

As he turned to leave, Lou noticed one of the MI6 types watching them from a distance and hesitated. "Jake, I think we need sit down with MI6 first, we don't need them watching our every move."

MI6 HAD a limousine waiting outside the airport. It wasn't long before Lou and Jake were whisked over to what had previously been the island's customs house. When they stepped across the threshold of Donald Edwards' makeshift office, he looked up.

"Good afternoon gentlemen, have a seat."

As Lou suspected, the meeting was an interrogation, albeit cordial. Both sides held their ground and neither side held anything back. Lou's goal was simple: he wanted to eliminate any interference from MI6. The only goal the Brit's had was to understand how the Canadians played into the picture. Once it was apparent both sides had achieved their objective, Edwards leaned back in his chair and breathed in heavily.

"It's interesting how we both ended up in the same boat, fugitively speaking, of course. The fact of the matter is, neither of us has any jurisdiction here. As sticky as it is, I say we should agree to partner up on this, like chaps, and pass along any new information to the other. Are you in agreement?"

Lou and Jake exchanged glances, nodded to each other, and stood up. Lou extended his arm to shake hands as one of Edward's aides entered the room. "Sorry to barge in on you, sir, but I need to brief you on a development."

Edwards nodded. As he stood up to shake hands with Lou, he said, "Can we give you a lift anywhere?"

"No, we're good, but thanks."

AS SOON AS they stepped outside, Jake said, "So, what's your take on that?"

"It sounds like we're in the same hunt for different reasons. I'm not sure how much help they'll be, but they'll leave us alone."

As Jake waved down a taxi, he said, "I never knew my life was such an open book. *'Are my eyes really brown?'*"

When Lou didn't pick up on his Bogart quote from the movie *Casablanca*, Jake dropped it.

"Let's go pay my friend, the oracle, a visit."

29

Sharing a taxi, the two cousins headed over to the wharf while piecing their plan together. "The spooks have been keeping tabs on the *Marlin Sea*," Jake said. "As soon as we get an update on the last sighting, we'll take off."

When Lou didn't respond, Jake shot him a glance. "I've seen that look before Lou, what's on your mind?"

"I still don't get it. If someone had stolen the boat, why the charade? There's a piece to this we're just not seeing."

"There's a couple of pieces we're missing Lou. Hopefully, the spook you're going to meet will have something to share." As the taxi pulled over to the curb, Jake reached for his wallet. "This is where we get out."

Lou was surprised when he saw Jake hand the driver his credit card. "I thought you said you ran that thing dry."

Jake smirked. "What, you think I only have friends in low places?" When he saw the quizzical look on Lou's face, he shrugged. "They increased my limit. I'm a big spender, now."

AFTER JAKE PAID THE FARE, they entered the wharf area and headed toward the brightly colored kiosk all the charter boats used to book reservations.

"Jake, before we go anywhere, I need to pick up a knife and some more clothes."

About to crack a joke, Jake stopped abruptly. Lou instantly went on alert, his eyes scanning left and right.

"What's up?"

"I'm not sure. One of the spooks was working that kiosk, but she's gone."

Lou kept scanning the area. "You sure that's not her?"

"Yeah, there's no way in hell that's Lily White."

"Who?"

"Nothing. She said her name was 'Lily White,' that's all. Forget it, let's go down to the bench and pay my friend, Johnny Coconut, a visit."

"You think he'll be there?"

"He's been there every time I've come down here. He's my oracle. Last time we spoke, he said his trackers had placed the *Marlin Sea* in San Juan. Unless he tells us something different, I say we grab a Gulfstream and boogie on up to Puerto Rico and start from there."

"Gulfstreams are pricy."

"Gulfstreams are three times faster than that Cessna I had. Besides, the guys we're going after have a bit of a head start."

"I hope the bastard hasn't tossed my stuff overboard."

"Stuff, you can replace, Lou. The only thing we're after is the talisman Grey Elk gave you. That's different, maybe Johnny Coconut can save us some time."

They'd walked only a few steps down the wharf, when Jake stopped short, again. "Shit! He's not here, either. Where the hell is he?"

"Looks like your oracle took the day off, Jake."

Standing in front of the empty bench, Jake just stared at it, hands on hips. "Shit, if that doesn't beat all! Well, let's go . . . you said you needed a knife."

"Hold on. Let's not dismiss what Grey Elk taught us. Let's look around. Maybe this friend of yours left us a sign." As Lou's eyes studied the bench, his thoughts shifted back to his conversation with Donald Edwards.

It's interesting, MI6 is keeping track of this boat, yet they won't board it, even in International waters. That tells me whatever we're going up against is bigger than a single boat gone rogue.

"All right, let's go, we're wasting time here Lou." Just as Jake turned to leave, Lou nudged him with an elbow. "What?"

Without saying a word, Lou walked over to the bench and pulled something out of a crack in one of the back slats of the bench. It was a small card. One side read "Peninsular Club," but there was writing on the back.

"This mean anything to you?" Lou handed it to Jake.

"Well, I recognize the front."

When he flipped it over, he read the cryptic message on the reverse aloud: "M.S. at Devil's Cay. Well, it looks like the spook left me a gift."

"So, let's figure out where the hell Devil's Cay is and get a move on."

JOHNNY COCONUT HADN'T SAT on the bench for the past thirty-six hours. He had received instructions to pack up, pick up Lily White, and travel on toward Montserrat. Even though he thought it odd that the message had used the previous day's encryption scheme, he dismissed it. Protocols changed daily and people were moving about.

When Lee arrived at the small bungalow Lily was using, he used the coded sequence they'd agreed upon as he knocked on the door. Usually, Lily wasted no time coming to the door. But when she didn't respond after a second knock, he tried the handle. The door was unlocked.

She's probably still in the shower; he thought as if he let himself in. He also knew her disguise required a lot of makeup. His rationale was more hopeful than true, but, again, he dismissed caution.

The living room was dark, window shades down, which wasn't anything unusual. Still, something was amiss. It took only a moment for his eyes to adjust to the low light.

The man with the double aliases, "Frank Lee" and "Johnny Coconut," had been in the room enough times to know how the room was set up. Everything appeared to be in place, but something was different. The light near the overstuffed chair by the hallway wasn't on as usual. Lily had never been fond of the dark and always kept that lamp on.

He stopped, hoping to hear water running through the pipes, indicating someone was taking a shower. But when he couldn't detect even the slightest sound, Frank removed the pistol from his ankle holster. Rising off his heels, he moved slowly toward the hallway, listening for anything, even the tiniest sound.

The bedroom Lily had chosen to use was the first door to the left once entering the hall. It was there he found her lifeless body on the floor. Her legs were angled in a grotesque manner. Obviously, she had struggled. The thin cord that ended her life was still wrapped around her neck.

Now, the MI6 operative was on full alert. His heart pounding, as well as breaking; he had hoped their relationship might evolve into something more than professional.

He reached down to check for a pulse with his left hand, but there was none. He could tell her death had been recent since the body was still relatively warm. Then, about to stand up, he heard a bullet chambering and froze.

The man in the white linen suit stood nearby. He had known about the two MI6 operatives for over a week. Everything that happened in the Caribbean eventually was known to the one they called "The Chameleon," a man as ruthless as they came.

Wasting little time dispatching yet another human being unfortunate enough to get in his way, a single shot to the back of the head ended the life of another promising and talented MI6 operative, Frank "Johnny Coconut" Lee.

As the killer wrapped a linen handkerchief around the barrel of the silencer, he began unscrewing it. Briefly, he tried to recall the number of notches he could have had on his handle by now, if he had been into that. The sound of a horn on the street brought him back to reality. But, he knew he was safe, they all feared him. After all, he was The Chameleon.

The Chameleon ruled the Caribbean. Nothing happened without his approval. He was also the handler for Carlos. It had been no one other than he who had to approved Carlos' plan to steal yachts in the Caribbean. Carlos saw it as a favor. He was also the one who made sure Carlos' partner would be Antonio Sanchez, a man as ruthless as himself.

The Chameleon had made a lot of money off Carlos' scheme. And if everything stayed below the radar, he stood to make a lot more money and higher stature within the cartels.

Now, with Lily White and Johnny Coconut gone, MI6 was effectively out of the cartel's way. But there was one more threat. He had tried to throw the Canadian tourists off the scent, but they had persisted. Now The Chameleon was laying the groundwork to address that, too. There was no doubt in his mind, those representing the biggest danger to his scheme would take the bait he'd left on the bench. Soon, he intended to eliminate them, as well.

WHEN THE TWO cousins left the wharf area, they went in separate directions. Jake needed to retrieve his luggage before heading over to the airport, and Lou headed into town to do a little shopping. He found a suitable knife in a dive shop to replace the one he had given the native islander. He picked up a small carryall bag along with the clothing items he needed in an adjacent store. Still operating without a cell phone, Lou thought of his own phone left on the *Marlin Sea*. For now, they'd make do with Jake's aging iPhone 7.

Jake had to make a decision a little more complicated than Lou's. Devil's Cay had an airport and a good runway, but it was short. The challenge wasn't landing a Gulfstream there; no, the runway wasn't long enough for the jet to take off. In the end, he went with a Beechcraft King Air 350. The prop plane was slower and would add an extra ninety minutes to the flight, but at least he wouldn't run out of runway when he tried to take off.

When the attendant at the counter ran Jake's credit card, he made an offhanded comment. "This is funny, you're the second plane we have going to Devil's Cay today. That doesn't happen too often."

BY THE TIME Lou arrived at the airport, Jake was finishing up his pre-flight inspection. "Throw your stuff in the back, cuz, I only have one more thing to do." With that, Jake headed back into the terminal.

Minutes later, he returned with a brown paper bag. As he strapped himself in, he asked Lou, "Did you eat?"

"Nah."

Pointing to the paper bag, he said, "Help yourself, I ordered us a couple of ham and Swiss on rye. There should be enough Grey Poupon on them, but if you need more, I had them throw in a couple extra packets."

Lou rolled his eyes. *Of course you did.*

The sound of the props kicking in, blotted out further communication until the men had their headgear in place. Once cleared for takeoff, Jake turned to his cousin. "Buckle up cowboy, we're gonna take this bird for a ride."

Lou wasn't listening, his thoughts had already shifted to the *Marlin Sea* and how he planned to settle the score with the man who'd left him stranded on an island. The only concern he had was how long it would take to pick up the trail. But neither Lou, nor his cousin, knew anything about the island aptly dubbed "Devil's Cay."

Unbeknownst to the cousins, the other person traveling to Devil's Cay from Barbados that day had left in a prop plane a few hours earlier, and he knew everything there was to know about Devil's Cay. He also knew what was about to unfold on the island.

JAKE HAD a good tail wind and the flight from Barbados went smoothly. Lou believed the element of surprise was in their favor. Unfortunately, he was wrong. The element of surprise belonged to two others on Devil's Cay, neither of whom had the same agenda.

The sun had already set when Jake touched down on the runway. Clouds in the western sky were a brilliant orange-y-red, but that wouldn't last. Soon they would turn deep purple, darkness would come, and the evil that lurked on the island would emerge.

The Customs Department was an almost non-existent entity on Devil's Cay. The island was part of the Bahamas, but there was no question this small island, well off the beaten path of cruise ships, belonged to the cartels.

Customs officials made more from the cartels than they took home every week in their government paycheck. They didn't care who came or who went, nor what was inside anyone's luggage. After Lou and Jake breezed through Customs, they passed through a set of sliding doors and were literally accosted by a swarming group of young girls eagerly peddling colorful, but cheap necklaces to everyone who emerged through the doorways.

Lou was in the lead, and somehow, he managed to plow his way through the gaggle of screaming young girls pushing necklaces into his face. Jake wasn't as fortunate. The youngsters swarmed around him as if he were a queen bee attempting to leave the hive.

"Jake, meet me at the Avis sign. I'll get a set of wheels."

Jake nodded, his right hand instinctively reaching down to check that his wallet was still where it belonged.

With all the chaos surrounding them, neither cousin noticed the tall man in the white linen suit, leaning up against a pilar. The fedora atop his head slightly obscured his face, but his eyes saw what he had come to see.

WHEN LOU DROVE off the Avis lot, he handed the rental agreement to his cousin. "Put this thing in the glovebox."

Jake pressed the button to open the compartment. "Did you know Packard Motors was the very first company to ever put a glove box in a car? They called it a 'boot.' It wasn't until about twelve years later that a British woman, coined the phrase 'glovebox.'"

Lou wasn't listening to his cousin. He was preoccupied with programming his mind to stay on the left side of the road. Between concentrating on shifting with his opposite hand and dismissing the drivel Jake was spewing, he never glanced in the rearview mirror. If he had, he might have noticed the Avis gate attendant wave another car through the checkpoint without looking at any rental agreement paperwork.

"Yeah, she was a real race car driver, who knew, right? Dorothy-something-or-other. It wasn't Levi . . . what was it? Was it Levitt? Yeah, Levitt, Dorothy Levitt, a true pioneer in race car driving."

Lou finally turned and looked at his cousin. "Why do you keep all this worthless shit in your head?"

"We play a little trivia in the mornings while we're waiting for them to load the mail on the planes. I usually win."

"Well, this isn't a game, so, stay focused."

Jake glanced at the side view mirror a couple of times. "You been checking the rearview mirror?"

Lou looked up at the reflecting glass. "Yeah, I see him. I'm not sure if he's a tail or just heading the same way we are."

30

For the next half mile, Lou's eyes alternated between the windshield and the rearview mirror. Finally, his curiosity got the better of him. "Let's check and see if he's hanging on our backside."

When Lou broke from the flow of traffic and took a sharp right onto a side road, he kept his eyes on the rear-view mirror. When the car that was behind went straight, he let out a sigh. "Looks like they were just heading in the same direction."

What he didn't see was the dirt bike traveling behind the car that pulled over and stopped. Even if he had seen the bike stop, he never would have seen the man press the talk button on his helmet.

THE SIDE ROAD quickly changed from a paved surface to dirt as the landscape shifted from tropical forest to open fields. The section of the island they had entered represented the only respectable endeavor on the entire island - agriculture.

"Lou, GPS says we're now heading away from the wharf area."

"There's a line of telephone poles crisscrossing up ahead; must be an intersection. I'll make a couple of left turns and get back on the main road." Lou glanced in his rearview mirror but dust from the dirt road was so thick, it obscured the bike that was following.

Jake smirked. "Be careful when you make this next turn, you sure as hell don't wanna flip this muscle car over."

"Shut up. They only had Corolla's . . . okay?"

"I'm just saying."

Lou ignored his cousin's comment. "Take out your cell phone, smart ass, and see how far we are from the port."

As Jake fired up his phone, the man on the dirt bike adjusted his helmet microphone closer to his mouth. "Chico, I need you, man. Meet me at the entrance to the harbor."

"Where? Where the boats come in?"

"No, you fool! There's no road that goes there. Meet me at the beginning of the road that goes to the harbor. I need your help. I have a little job to do. Do you have your pistol?"

"*Si*, I will meet you there, *pronto*."

The *Marlin Sea* was anchored in a harbor only a few miles away from where Lou had turned off the main road. It wasn't an exceptionally large harbor, but that didn't matter to those who were in control of the island. The action on Devil's Cay occurred on land, not on water.

CARLOS SAT in a chair on the aft deck of the *Marlin Sea*. He was tired, which wasn't unusual. He hadn't really had a decent night's sleep since the day his older brother was murdered. For years, he had awakened from a reoccurring dream, always distraught over having missed a chance to avenge his brother's death. The dreams would haunt his consciousness for days after.

In one persistent dream, he would freeze and watch helplessly as the faceless murderer who killed his brother vanished into a shadowy mist. In another dream, he stood weaponless, as the killer emerged from the mist, only to sneer and mock him before fading back into the mist. Up until a year ago, the reoccurring theme had never changed, the shadowy, faceless killer always escaped into the mist. However, once he learned the name of his brother's killer, the shadowy image began to take on features. In his mind, he began visualizing the terror that would appear in the killer's eyes as he faced his own imminent death.

Like Carlos, his brother's killer was connected to the cartels. Carlos was relieved when The Chameleon sanctioned the kill that would right the wrong done to his family. The burden of not having avenged his brother had hung around his neck like an anchor for over a decade. Why The Chameleon had chosen Devil's Cay as the place for Carlos' revenge to take place was a mystery, but he cared less. He only knew that the man he wanted to kill would be there. Now the only thing Carlos had to decide was how and when it would happen. He knew his instrument of justice would be something other than a blade. Unlike Sanchez, he wasn't skilled with a knife, but that didn't matter, he would find a way.

THE TWO PRIVATEERS spent so much time together on the boat, they often needed a break from each other. Typically, they went separate ways as night approached.

Carlos frequented the same local eatery every night. His favorite dessert was the amorous island girl who waited on him.

She wore her hair in long dark ringlets that flowed below her shoulders. She willingly spread her legs in exchange for a more generous tip. But as much as she tried to entice Carlos to sleep over, he never did. Once their nightly tryst was over, he returned to the *Marlin Sea*.

Sanchez's approach to life was completely different. He wasn't fussy about who he bedded down with, and woke up most mornings hung over from tequila, lying next to a whore he'd never seen before, in some small sleazy room. At some point each following day, Sanchez would show up at the *Marlin Sea*, take a nap, shower, change his clothes and do it all over again.

THE SUN WAS low on the horizon when Sanchez jumped into the only shower aboard the *Marlin Sea*. Carlos had showered earlier. He had learned the hard way to shower before Sanchez took his shower if he wanted hot water.

Most days, by the time Sanchez finished his shower, pushed back the wet curtain, and reached for a towel, Carlos had already gone ashore. But this day was different. When Antonio Sanchez pushed the wet curtain aside, Carlos stood in the open doorway to the shower room, his right hand behind his back.

Sanchez did a double take. "What? What are you looking at? Are you so tired of looking at naked women, you need to see a naked man? Is that it?"

Sanchez reached for a towel. "Well, go ahead . . . take a good look."

Carlos didn't say anything, he just stared at Sanchez.

"Why do you stand there? Close the door, it's cold in here."

"You killed my brother."

Sanchez tilted his head, not fully grasping what Carlos had just said.

"What?"

Without saying another word, Carlos' right arm swung around in front of him. He raised a flare gun to belt level and pulled the trigger. The flare hadn't traveled four feet before it entered Sanchez's body. At such close range, the blunt tip of the flare ripped through Sanchez's skin with ease. The projectile would have come out the back side if it hadn't been for Sanchez's spine. The pyrotechnic composition ignited upon impact, and the inside of Sanchez's abdomen illuminated like a red glow stick.

At first, Sanchez simply stood there, looking down at his belly, amazed and confused. Then, as if on reflex, he stuck his hand inside his abdomen, in an apparent attempt to pull the burning flare out of his body. Finally, Sanchez looked up in disbelief and mouthed one word: *Why?*

Seconds after firing the first flare, Carlos loaded another into the chamber. When the second shot entered Sanchez's body the enigma known as *El Carnicero* slumped down in the shower. The two flares consumed his body from the inside like the fires of hell. Carlos stood in the doorway, watching as the dying man's hands grasped the fiery cauldron that had once been his belly.

It was over.

Carlos let out a deep sigh. He had finally avenged his brother. Now his thoughts shifted to the last message he'd received from The Chameleon: *Take the Marlin Sea to Bimini and wait there. I will have someone to replace Sanchez.*

If Carlos had any concerns about his future, his handler quickly put those to rest. Carlos was assured what the yachting community had begun referring to as "The Curse of the

Caribbean" was going to continue: the game of stolen yachts and missing people was not over.

THE STENCH from burning flesh quickly permeated throughout the yacht. Now Carlos was afraid the repulsive odor would attract unnecessary attention. After grabbing Sanchez's head by the hair, he dragged the killer's lifeless body to the aft deck. As he rolled the carcass onto the swim platform, there was a swirl in the water a few feet beyond the hull.

Sanchez's body didn't even make a splash when it rolled into the water. The body floated near the boat for minutes, but soon something beneath the surface came to nibble on it. At first, the nibbling was subtle, causing Sanchez's body to bob, like a cork in the water. But Carlos didn't stay to watch, nor was he there when the large jaws came up from the depths and tore a chunk of flesh from Sanchez's leg. No, Carlos had carried out his plan, Sanchez was dead.

Now he went up to the bridge, blew the bilge, started the engine, and reached for the line to disconnect the yacht from its mooring. He was eager to reach Bimini. In the past, he was always in a hurry to leave Bimini. But this time would be different. This time, he would wait there.

AT THE VERY moment Carlos was guiding the *Marlin Sea* out of the harbor, Lou was pulling into a parking space overlooking the harbor. Lou stared at the yacht, but didn't positively identify her until he saw the name on its stern.

"Shit!" he cried out in an exasperated expletive. "Shit!" and struck both palms on the steering wheel.

"Is that her?"

Lou took a deep breath and let it out slowly. "Now what?"

Jake spoke a little louder than usual to be heard over the loud, pulsating sounds of two dirt bikes just pulling into the parking spaces on either side of them. "Well, we could steal one of the boats over yonder with the big-ass kickers and board her on the high seas. They do that all the time off the coast of Somalia."

"Yeah, and get our heads blown off for trying. Let's think about this," Lou said. "Take out your damn phone, see who's renting boats, and where we can pick up some hardware."

Lou hadn't taken his eyes off the *Marlin Sea* and Jake was scrolling through apps when they heard simultaneous knocks on both side-door windows. In unison, the cousins turned a head to look out their own respective windows and directly into the business end of two 357 Magnums.

"*Señores*, it is time for you to get out of the car."

Lou smiled at the man on his side. Without moving his lips he said, "One of us could have done a little better job watching the back door."

When Lou didn't move, the man pointing the gun at him said, "Señor, I asked you nicely to step out of the car. You must do this, or I will shoot you, just like this." With that, the booming sound of a magnum broke the silence, and the left front tire went flat.

Jake turned his head and looked directly at the man on his side and pointed to his ear, as if he couldn't hear through the glass. The man merely smiled a toothy grin and motioned for him to come out of the car. As Jake pushed his seat back as far as possible, he nodded at the man holding the gun while saying to Lou: "Are you ready?"

"Yeah . . . on three."

Jake let out a snort. "No, not three, everybody does that . . . we'll go on two."

31

On Jake's count of two, the doors on the rented Corolla flew open and both magnums fired. The gunmen outside the vehicle were standing just close enough that the forward swing of the doors knocked the barrel of each magnum sidewise and the shots went into the engine compartment.

Up to that point, both assailants had felt confident they had the upper hand. The furthest thing from either of their simple minds had been a counterattack.

The man on Lou's side was still looking at his weapon, wondering what had happened, when Lou's left hand came down like a hammer, breaking the assailant's collarbone. With the man's gun arm now useless, Lou delivered an uppercut to the jaw, followed by a knee to the groin. As the would-be assailant slumped over in pain, Lou came down with a chop to the back of his neck, cracking his vertebra. That confrontation was definitely over.

The situation on Jake's side was totally different. The

gunman recovered quicker than his companion on Lou's side. As Jake exited the front seat, he saw the barrel swinging back toward him and went in low, hoping to stay beneath the bullet he knew was coming. When the magnum went off with a deafening sound, his head was inches away from the barrel. Nothing masked the pain as the bullet ripped a shallow path down the length of Jake's back.

Still, he hit his adversary mid-thigh, knocking him back a step, but the gunman remained upright. Jake had nanoseconds to act before the magnum fired again. Now he was in an awkward position with few options. His only chance was to keep his opponent off balance long enough to disarm him.

In a bold move, Jake wrapped his arms around the man's knees and pulled upward as he sprang from a squatting position. The move had zero technique; it was pure adrenaline, based on nothing but hope. But when Jake's opponent lost his center of gravity and became horizontal, he momentarily lost ability to control his aim. Three shots went off in rapid succession. One tore through Jake's shirt sleeve, ripping another hole in his flesh, the other two went wild. Jake's attacker somehow managed to contort his upper body into a semi-sitting position. Just as he was about to pull the trigger and take Jake out, a bullet entered his forehead and blew out the back side of his skull.

Jake let go of the dead man and turned around. Lou still had both elbows resting on the roof of the Corolla, a .357 Magnum in hand.

"I thought you might need a hand, cuz."

"I was hoping the Calvary would show up a little sooner."

"You've got a streak of blood going down your back, how bad is it?"

"I'm not sure, but it's beginning to hurt like hell."

"Well, let's take a look see at what we're dealing with."

Lou used his knife to cut open the back of Jake's shirt. The wound was ugly, but not deep, yet it was contaminated with fragments from the bullet and his shirt.

"Looks like the bullet didn't go deep enough do a lot of muscle damage, but it sure as hell plowed a path along the surface. I need to clean it out before the blood clots. Is there anything in your bag I can use?"

"There's a small wound kit in there. The one in the Beechcraft is a whole lot better."

"Well, let's see what I can do to get this thing cleaned up. Anything else I need to look at?

"Take a look at my left shoulder."

"I see it; that one's just a nick. I'd say we were damn lucky, cuz."

Jake winced as Lou poked around examining his back. "You'll have a scar, and you'll be sore for a while, but you'll heal."

"Thanks for the prognosis, but what I really wanna hear is, do you know what the hell you're doing?"

"Patching people up was pretty much an everyday affair when I was over in Afghanistan. The medics used to debate over which wound had the better chance of going septic. A bullet wound was bad, but a knife cut was worse. The bad guys used to dip their blades in sheep dung."

LOU DID his best to clean out the wounds. After applying antiseptic, followed by a thin coat of Vaseline, he covered the open wounds with sterile dressing. While Jake reached into his carryon, and pulled out a fresh shirt, Lou walked around to the driver's side of the Corolla and opened the door.

"Lou, you think we should tell the police about these two?"

"Take a look at the tats on their arms, they're identical. These guys are with the cartels." Lou glanced around the harbor before continuing. "In a small place like this? The police aren't going to do anything that crosses the cartels."

"You think the cartels are in on this?"

"Come on," he said wryly, "This was a hit. We were set up."

"And here I was thinking we were targeted because we were driving around in a muscle car."

Lou smirked and shook his head. "We just uncovered another piece of the puzzle. Let's see if we can figure out where the hell the *Marlin Sea* is headed."

"What about these two?"

"Leave 'em. Somebody will come along."

As Lou slid into the front seat of the Corolla, Jake said, "Cuz, I'm betting that thing isn't drivable. You got one tire out and a couple of bullets somewhere in the engine."

As he pocketed the keys, Lou grabbed the rental agreement. "We're not leaving any more of a trail than we need to. Grab your bag from the back seat." Then Lou used a handkerchief to wipe clean their fingerprints.

"You know Avis is going to hit you up for not bringing this chariot back to the airport," Jake said.

"Just grab your stuff and strap it onto one of those dirt bikes."

Then Jake saw the helmet resting on the seat of the dirt bike closest to him. "Wanna bet these dudes had radios in these fancy helmets?"

Lou reached for the helmet on the bike closest to him. "Let's see if there's any chatter." As soon as the helmet covered his ears, he heard a heavily-accented voice through the radio static.

"*Chico, where are you, man?*"

Lou smiled, placed a finger to his mouth and pressed the talk button. *"Aqui!"* he mumbled.

The voice on the other end came back immediately. *"Hey, where you been, man?"*

"Aqui."

"Here? I don't know where 'here' is, man. Where are you?"

Lou thought quick knowing he couldn't say much, but he needed to respond to keep the man on the other end engaged. Again, he put a finger in his mouth before speaking.

"Agua."

After a slight pause, another voice came through static. *"Did you kill the hombres?"*

"Si."

Now Lou waited. Seconds went by and the only sound was radio static. To keep the deception going, he decided on a ploy. Once again, he placed a finger in his mouth.

"Hola, Hola."

Almost immediately a voice came through the static. "I can hear you."

Lou intermittently pressed the talk button and spoke a combination of Spanish, English, and pure gibberish. *"Hola . . . boat . . . se han ido . . . hola!"* Lou could hear the other man clicking in, but he spoke over him. Finally, he stopped transmitting and listened.

"I can hear you, mon. The boat is gone."

Lou had one chance. Before saying anything, he pressed the talk button a few times to create static on the line. Then he said: "Donde?"

"What do you mean, 'where?' Where Carlos always takes them . . . Bimini."

Lou smiled, now they were armed and had two new pieces of the puzzle: a name and a destination.

Jake had donned the other helmet and was listening to the ruse. "I didn't know you were that well-versed in Spanish, *amigo.*"

Lou looked at his cousin for a moment, then quoted a line from an old Beatles song: "I get by with a little help from my friends."

"And all this time, I thought you were just a pretty face."

"Get your ass on that bike. We need to get over to the airport before something else happens."

WHEN LOU and Jake arrived at the airport, they went separate ways. Jake headed for the charter terminal, hoping the Beechcraft they came in on was still intact and Lou headed over to the Avis sign.

But as Lou walked toward the counter, his thoughts were elsewhere. *Nobody knew we were coming here, but the car behind us sure felt like a tail. Those bikers didn't just happen upon us by chance, they had headsets. I'd put money down the car that followed us was a tail. Neither of us paid any attention to our back door. We should have picked up on that from the time we left the Avis lot. Let's see if I can erase our trail a little, so we're not followed.*

When the attendant looked up from the counter, Lou slammed the keys down hard. The sound had the effect he intended on the young attendant.

"Sir, you . . . you're not supposed to bring the keys here, you leave them with the vehicle."

"Well, to tell you the truth, I didn't return it. I didn't return it because I couldn't return it. I couldn't return it because the damn thing wouldn't *start*! I had to find my own damn way back here. Here's the damn rental agreement. I want my money back, and don't even think about giving me a hassle."

The attendant scanned the rental agreement. "This has never happened before. I do apologize." After he read the agreement, his fingers raced across his keyboard. "Here's what I can do, a full size, with low mileage just came in. I'm going to upgrade you, at no charge, and you'll be on your way."

"Nope, not a chance in hell of that happening. I'm through with Avis. What you're going to do is give me a refund and erase this whole transaction."

"I'm sorry sir, I can't do that."

"You can't do *what*?"

"I'm not able to erase the transaction. Once an agreement is in the database, it's there. The only thing I can do is go in to correct an error."

Lou placed his newly acquired magnum on the counter. "Okay, so here's the way we're going to handle this: You're going to pull up the original transaction and give me a refund. You can do that, right?"

"Yes, I can do that."

"Good, I'm going to wait for you to do that."

It only took the attendant a few minutes to process the refund. "Okay, done. I've refunded your money."

"Good, now go back in and purge the card number."

The attendant shook his head. "I can't do that."

"You can't, or you won't?"

"I can't purge."

When Lou placed his hand over the magnum, he sent a clear signal. "But you said you can go in and make a correction, right?" Lou didn't wait for a response. "So, here's what we're going to do. Log into your transactional journal, find the agreement, change the last three numbers on the credit card to sixes and change the name to Al Smith. Then change the address fields to Number one Downing Street, London, England. How's that work for you?"

Lou noticed the attendant glance at the magnum. After a quick nod, he said, "I think we can do that."

As Lou walked away from the Avis counter, the only evidence of him ever having been there were the grainy images captured by the hidden security cameras in the airport.

WHEN LOU ARRIVED at the charter plane terminal, Jake was nowhere to be seen. Except for a man standing behind a counter with a cell phone to his ear, and a lone mechanic nearby, the place was empty.

As Lou approached the counter, he heard the man say, "Hold on, someone's coming." After placing his hand over the phone's mouthpiece, the man looked directly at Lou.

"Yes?"

"Did someone about my height just come in here and fill out a flight plan?"

Pointing to the tarmac in front of the terminal, he said, "Yeah, he's doing a preflight out there on a Beechcraft." With that, he turned around, placed the cell phone up against his ear and walked a few paces away from the counter. "Okay, I'm back, what's up?"

"Next time I give you a little job to do, I expect you to take care of it."

"I got a couple of guys on the Corolla."

"No, you *had* a couple of guys on it." The emphasis was on the past tense.

"What do you mean?"

"They just found your guys laying on the ground next to a shot-up Corolla."

The man behind the counter was silent. He waited for the man known as The Chameleon to continue.

"I'll text you a picture of who these two are. If they show up, I want you to take care of this. *Understood?*"

"Understood."

The man sounded relieved that was the only message. He had barely hung up when a text arrived. As soon as he saw the images, he hit the redial button and looked out toward the tarmac.

"Yes."

"They're just taking off."

"Who?"

After a slight pause, the man said, "The two in the picture. I didn't know it was them."

"Read me their flight plan."

The man took a deep breath. "They're going to Bimini."

"Are they in the air yet?"

"They're about to."

"Get a sea plane ready. You're flying me to Bimini."

32

Jake's back was throbbing. Sitting back against the pilot's seat with his bullet wound was going to be challenging, even though he knew he could endure the twenty-five-minute flight to Bimini. Confident Lou had cleaned the wound sufficiently, he still planned to visit a clinic once they were on the ground.

No sooner was he settled into the cockpit's seat finding some degree of comfort when Lou said, "Drop down, let's get a look at the yacht below."

Jake leaned over and looked out the side window. "You think that's her?"

"Hard to tell looking directly down. I need a side view. Go down and do a discreet flyby."

Jake had popped a couple of Advil earlier which took some of the edge off the pain in his back, but still he winced as he moved around, maneuvering the controls.

As the plane banked left, Lou said, "Tell me how you're gonna do this, first."

"I'll just do a few simple loop-dee-loops, to make it look like we're playing around. Then I'll come in close, so you can get a good look."

As Lou tightened his seatbelt, he saw the grin on his cousin's face. "Don't pull any of that crazy upside-down, barrel roll crap."

"Ah, cuz, where's your sense of adventure?"

"It'll be up your butt, if you pull any of that stuff."

"Okay, okay! We'll do *the kiddie ride* version." Jake had no intention of aggravating the wound on his back, but he couldn't help chiding his cousin. After he completed the equivalent of two touch-and-go-landings, Jake swung around and came in close to the *Marlin Sea.*

"That's the one we're going after, Jake," Lou said. *And I know exactly where I left the talisman,* he thought.

Jake pulled back on the joystick. "Okay, let's go see where the boats anchor in Bimini and where we're going to land this thing. There's a map in the side pocket between us. Pull it out and give me a lay of the land."

In seconds, Lou had the map spread out over his knees. "Looks like the airport is in what they call South Bimini. There's an anchorage nearby called Nixon's Harbor."

Jake glanced at the map. "There's not a whole lot of terra firma between north Bimini and south Bimini. Koby said it was small. She did a few dives down here and said the name Bimini meant 'two islands.'"

"Yeah, there's a few islands trailing off to the south."

"Have you figured out when you wanna board the *Marlin Sea*?"

"After dark."

"Well, she'll be a while coming in, so let's check out North Bimini first, see if there's a harbor up there she might be heading for." Jake paused as he looked at the landmass below. "Then we'll come back and see if the *Marlin Sea* dropped anchor in Nixon's Harbor."

"I thought you said you wanted to get your back checked out?"

"I will. Another ten minutes isn't going to kill me."

As they flew over South Bimini, Jake noticed a long single runway off to his right.

AFTER TRAVELING up the narrow west side of the island connecting north and south Bimini, Jake banked right at Paradise Point, crossed over to Round Rock, and headed south. As they approached Pigeon Cay, Lou said, "Doesn't look like there's much anchorage up here. Let's go back and draw a bead on the *Marlin Sea*."

"She's gotta be in Nixon's Harbor by now; she wasn't that far out when we flew over."

After circling the harbor twice, Jake asked, "Did you see her?"

"No."

"Me, neither."

Lou looked further out to sea. "She isn't in the channel; make another pass."

After their third pass, Lou said. "She went somewhere else."

"Well, she didn't go north. We would have seen her if she had."

Lou ran his index finger three quarters of the way down the map and stopped. "One of the dinky islands to the south has a cove."

"Well, let's give it a look, maybe that's where she's hiding."

AS THE BEECHCRAFT TRAVELED SOUTH, Lou kept his eyes on the water. "Jake, look down below the surface. Is it me, or is there a long straight line down there?"

Jake leaned his head against the side window and looked down. "Yeah, I see it; that must be The Bimini Road."

"What?"

"The Bimini Road?"

"What the hell is that?"

"It goes back to the sixties. Some guy spotted it from the air. It was a big deal for a while, everyone thought it was Atlantis. That was one of the reasons Koby came down here on a dive expedition. She said it was a popular location. I'm surprised we're not seeing a ton of dive boats."

"How'd you find out about it?"

"Koby told me. Some psychic got into the act, claimed he'd had a seance with someone who had lived in Atlantis and the ghost told him it was located near Bimini. The whole thing died down after they did carbon dating and analysis on the blocks. It's been debunked as something formed naturally through geological forces."

Lou was about to say something about the sunken city of the ancient ones near Saint Vincent when Jake said, "We're coming up on that cove; it'll be on your side."

The Beechcraft was halfway into a circle around the rim of the cove when both men heard the unmistakable pinging sound of bullets hitting the fuselage.

"Whoa, what the hell? Some crazy bastard is shooting at us!"

As Jake pulled back on the joystick and banked right, Lou's eyes scanned the area below. "I see her. She's tied up at a dock. Keep doing what you're doing, but be careful, there's a couple of guys with rifles down there."

"Bullshit! We're getting the hell outta here!"

Lou didn't immediately respond. Finally, after staring back at the *Marlin Sea*, he said. "There's a few more pieces to all this than a guy with a boat."

"I'm thinking the same thing, but say more."

"Look at all the people MI6 has over here. Someone went to the trouble of leaving a note on a friggin' park bench, hoping you'd take the bait. Those bikers on Devil's Cay didn't just happen upon us. Now a couple of guys are firing shots at us. Somebody wants the *Marlin Sea* to disappear, and we're getting in their way."

"All right, let's head back. Whatever your plan B was, I think it just became plan A."

AFTER SECURING the plane on the tarmac, Jake inspected the damage to the fuselage. A total of six bullets had hit the plane. The outer skin needed to be repaired and a window replaced. Once Jake was certain no serious damage had occurred, the two cousins headed to a local clinic.

WHEN THE PHYSICIAN who examined Jake was satisfied that his wounds were only superficial and free of contaminants, she cleaned and redressed the wounds. Then gave him a dose of pain medication.

Next, the two cousins headed to a dive shop. The proprietor was exactly the type of laid-back, salty beach-bum persona you'd expect to find in a place like Bimini. He was a little taller than average, athletic looking, tanned and his sun-bleached hair had that perpetual unkempt windblown look. His attire was simple: a faded tee shirt, a plain bathing suit and boat shoes. "Water's warm this time of year, guys. If you're only going snorkeling, you won't need wetsuits."

Lou dismissed the man's comment and kept shopping. After about twenty minutes, the two cousins walked up to the counter loaded down with jet black dive gear.

"Wow, you guys sure you wanna totally look like a couple of commandos?"

"I read where the Box Jellyfish are coming in," Lou lied. "I hate getting stung by those nasty buggers."

"Yeah, they're out there. You wanna stay clear of them, for sure. They sting like hell. Fella came in here last year . . . had welts all over his legs. Said it took a whole damn bottle of vinegar to put out the fire."

Just about every rack had a big sale sign on it. When Jake handed over his credit card he said, "Looks like you're running an end of season sale."

"I wish! It's a going out of business sale. Bimini's not the dive mecca it once was."

"What happened?"

"A rumor started going around that the water down here was toxic. It was all bullshit, of course, the water's fine. But once word got around, folks drank the Kool-Aid. Somebody started promoting the hell out of *Cabo San Lucas* and folks just stopped coming here."

"Is that where they go now?"

"Pretty much . . . that, and *Cabo Pulmo*. I've been to both. The dive shops over there can't keep up with business. They said they'll take everything I have left at the end of the month. It's funny, we all thought the Chamber of Commerce would step in and put an end to the rumors, but they never did. You'd think somebody paid them to look the other way while everything was falling apart. Now it's too damn late; the business is gone."

AS THEY WALKED DOWN to the marina, Lou turned to his cousin. "How far do you think it's to that cove?"

"Ten, maybe twelve miles . . . no more than that."

"Yeah, that's what I was thinking. We'll need something with a decent kicker to get over and back. Let's go look at the Zodiacs that first guy has for rent."

CARLOS NEVER HAD any intention of going to Nixon's Harbor. His destination was a small cove on North Cat Cay. He had radioed his pending arrival just a half an hour earlier. By the time he entered the cove, the dock had been cleared for him and the smaller boats were all ashore. The only thing sitting on a swing anchor was the sea plane that had just flown in from Devil's Cay.

When the men on the dock saw Carlos jump down from the bridge and secure the stern line himself, someone yelled over, "Hey, where's Sanchez, drunk again?"

Carlos shrugged his shoulders. "He no longer has the stomach for this."

With that, Carlos heard a familiar voice, one he had previously only heard over the phone. *Finally, I'll connect the voice with a face.*

"Carlos, I have someone I want you to meet." When he turned around, the man in the white linen suit stood no more than twenty feet away, flanked by four thugs. When Carlos didn't move, The Chameleon said, "Come, walk with me. I want you to meet someone."

Not sure what was about to happen, Carlos wondered if he had crossed a line when asking for permission to kill Sanchez. But when The Chameleon stepped forward and the four thugs remained at the dock, he relaxed somewhat.

The Chameleon sensed Carlos' uneasiness. "You have served me well, Carlos, you have made me much money. So, tell me, do you wish to continue doing this?"

Carlos was cautious. He had been a good soldier. He had never asked for anything other than permission to avenge his brother. Finally, he said, "I am only here to serve you, you know that." The Chameleon smiled. It was the answer he needed to hear.

"Good, then I will introduce you to Fernando. He is the one I have chosen to replace Sanchez."

Like Sanchez, Fernando Torres was a killer, younger, but just as ruthless. His weapon of choice was also the blade.

CARLOS HAD ALWAYS LEFT the island quickly, but this time, decided to stay in Bimini and spend one last night on the yacht. There was enough food onboard, and he and Torres could talk about how they would work together.

They sat in the salon well into the night, talking, and drinking tequila. In the morning, a small boat would take them to South Bimini and they would fly to a different island in the Caribbean to start their partnership.

ABOUT THE TIME Carlos and Torres had their fill of Tequila and retired for the night, a rubber inflatable with two passengers passed the tip of North Cat Cay. The man at the wheel pulled back on the throttle and shut the engine off as soon as the boat entered the cove. While the boat drifted, both occupants changed into their wetsuits.

Lou finished first and waited for his cousin to move to the bow. There was no need for words, they had been together so long, they knew each other's movements. Both men began paddling in silence toward the dock.

The moon was a waning gibbous, which offered enough light for the intruders to see without being seen by the guards they knew would be on the dock.

When Lou made the sound of the whip-poor-will, Jake took his paddle out of the water. The guards had congregated at the near end of the dock and the sound of their muffled whispers traveled over the water. But darkness shrouded their exact location. As the boat drifted closer, the location of the voices became more obvious. There was a scent of cigarette smoke in the air.

The men in the boat waited, listening, their paddles held at the ready. The guards were close, but the shadows on the dock made it difficult to discern exactly where they were. Suddenly, the voices stopped.

Lou's thoughts raced. *Have they seen us?*

Seconds passed. The only sound was from the water lapping up against the pilings, then someone on the dock cleared his throat. Lou's eyes no sooner turned to where he thought the sound came from then a man's face was briefly illuminated as he lit a cigarette. He could see them now. One guard turned and walked to the opposite end, the intermittent red glow of his cigarette continuing to expose his location.

The tide was out; spacing between the pilings underneath the dock was wide enough to maneuver the rubber boat under the dock and allow them to tie up next to a barnacle encrusted ladder.

Jake was first up the ladder. He moved with agility despite his injuries and stopped as soon as his eyes were even with the surface of the dock. The guard had his head down, the light from his cell phone illuminating his face. His AK-47 was leaning up against a pylon. Lou and Jake had no illusions, it had come down to a game of winner take all. Neither side would take prisoners.

The guard was too busy to notice Jake slowly slithering onto the dock. When Jake's foot left the last rung on the ladder, Lou moved up, stopping only when his eyes were even with the surface of the dock. Both men carried the magnums they'd taken from the fools who had tried to kill them out on Devil's Cay. But they would be held in reserve. The guards would be dispatched commando style, quietly, with stealth.

Lou watched Jake come up behind the first guard and take him out with only a muffled sound, then drag his body into the shadows. With one guard down, the two former commandos moved into the shadows and worked their way toward the second guard who had gone to the far end of the dock.

The whereabouts of the second guard wasn't clear until he flicked his cigarette butt toward the water. The red glow that arched from the dock into the air betrayed his location. That was all Lou and Jake needed.

33

The second guard was sitting against a container. Lou waved his hand to attract Jake's attention and pointed at himself. When Jake nodded, Lou moved forward like a cat stalking a mouse. Just as Lou was poised to strike, the man heard something and reached for his AK-47 while making a move to stand up. It was the last move he ever made. Lou grabbed the back of the man's hair with one hand, and with the knife in his other, ended the man's life with a single swipe. The only audible sound came from the rifle as it hit the wooden dock.

The two cousins were now no more than thirty feet from where the *Marlin Sea* was tied up. Just as they were about to board her, the door to the bunkhouse flew open where the cartel workers slept. Three men emerged, none of whom carried a weapon. One at the end waved his arms and called out into the dark: "Hey, amigos, if you are awake, don't shoot, okay? My mother will not be happy if you kill me while I pee." One of the others laughed.

Although the cartels had been using the small cove for months, outside of a dock, a cell tower, a storage shed, and a building that served as both kitchen and sleeping quarters, there was no further investment in the infrastructure. There was no plumbing, and whatever electricity they needed was provided by generators. The only sanitation facilities were a couple of chemical toilets located at the far end of the docks.

As the trio of men walked along the wooden planks, the one who had yelled out to the guards a moment earlier said, "Hey, amigos, hurry, I really need to go."

A much deeper voice responded. "If you need to go that bad, go pee in the water. The fish will not mind, they do it all the time." With that, the last man in line walked over to the edge of the dock and unzipped his pants. The second dead guard lay not even ten feet from where the man was relieving himself into the water. The guard's blood was still pooling around his neck. But there was just enough breeze that the other man didn't detect the metallic odor of blood.

Lou and Jake remained in the shadows, watching, and waiting long after the three workers returned to the bunkhouse and settled into bed before they approached the *Marlin Sea*. Other than the gentle sound of the water, the moonlit night was quiet.

JAKE HAD NEVER BEEN on the yacht before, and Lou had only been aboard for a few hours. But he had committed to memory everything he knew about the boat when he was back on the island. He remembered there were four staterooms aboard the ship, and he had left the talisman in the most forward one. As they moved down the hallway, Lou held up two fingers, indicating there would be two people aboard.

The door to the first stateroom was ajar. Once Jake cleared the room, he grabbed two pillows and handed one to Lou.

When they approached the door to the next stateroom, it was closed. Jake placed his ear against the door. After a moment he made a sign indicating he could hear heavy breathing. Lou nodded and pointed to his cousin, then back to the door. Jake nodded. He'd wait and enter when Lou determined which berth held the other man.

When Lou reached the third door, he placed his ear against it and listened. He couldn't detect any sound, but that didn't mean the room wasn't occupied. With knife in hand, Lou slowly opened the door. The light of the moon showed through the porthole and the bunk was empty. It could only mean the second person was in the forward stateroom, inches away from where he stood.

Lou moved to the last door and placed his ear next to it, hoping to hear heavy breathing, if not snoring. Seconds went by as he pressed his ear closer against the door, but the only sound he heard was his own breathing.

Slowly, he opened the door. Remembering he'd hung the talisman on a picture just next to a doorway, he reached in, feeling for it. But it wasn't there. Suddenly, the door opened wide, and the man who had marooned him, stood before him.

Then the sounds of a struggle came from the second stateroom. It wasn't loud, but it was obvious something was happening. The noise distracted Lou for only a fraction of a second, but just enough for Carlos to react. Lou's arm was still inside the cabin as Carlos tried closing the door, intending to pin Lou's arm between the door and the jamb. With his peripheral vision, Lou caught the movement and reacted, narrowly avoiding being trapped. Now Lou slammed into the door with his shoulder, knocking Carlos backwards. When Carlos tried to recover, Lou delivered a powerful blow to his opponent's temple, and Carlos' legs turned to rubber as he collapsed.

Moments later, when Jake saw his cousin had things under control, he signaled that he would circle around to make sure the rest of the yacht was clear. After that, he went back out onto the dock and retrieved the AK-47's the two dead guards no longer needed. Next, he went over to the bunkhouse and wedged a two-by-four up against the door. It wouldn't keep them in, but it would slow them down.

By the time Carlos came around, he was gagged and bound hand and foot. Lou pointed at his face. "Hi, remember me?"

Carlos shook his head slightly, indicating "no." When Lou removed the wetsuit cap covering most of his face, Carlos's eyes widened.

"Yeah, that's right, I'm the guy you left on that island. Surprised, huh?"

Lou had already lifted Carlos' wallet and now held it up. "Says here your name is Carlos Morales. Is that your real name?"

When Carlos made no response, Lou drew a line across Carlo's cheek with his blade, drawing blood. "We can do this a few ways. Just know that in the end I *will* find out why you marooned us. It'll be a helluva lot easier on you, if you decide to cooperate. Do you think you'd like to cooperate?"

When Carlos still didn't respond, Lou opened the front of Carlo's shirt with his knife. "We've taken care of your guards and the boys in the bunkhouse are too far away to hear the agony you're going to go through if you don't answer me. Even if they did, the AK-47 that will be pointed at them will keep 'em at bay. So, how about it, are you ready to tell me why you thought it would be fun to leave me and my wife on that island?"

When Carlos didn't respond, Lou said, "Maybe you'll find your tongue when I peel a layer of skin off your chest." The tip of Lou's knife made a small incision and Carlos grimaced, his head violently rocking back and forth. Finally, Lou heard a grunt.

"You ready to talk?"

Carlos nodded.

"You try anything stupid when I take the gag off, and this knife will end our conversation. Do you *understand* what I'm saying?"

When Carlos nodded, Lou reached forward, slid the blade under the gag and with the flick of his wrist, cut the gag in two. Carlos felt a sting on his lip since Lou had purposefully taken a small piece of skin with the tip of his blade. It was a shallow cut but served as a warning. As he held the blade of his knife across Carlos' neck he said, "Okay, tell me, why did you leave us to die?"

"So, you would live."

Lou tilted his head. Carlos' words didn't jibe with what he expected to hear. After a pause, Lou pushed down on Carlos' Adam's apple with the flat side of the blade and repeated his question. "Again, why did you leave us on that island?"

The pressure on Carlos's neck limited his ability to speak. "I . . . I left you there to . . . to give you a chance to live," he whispered.

"No, you left us there to die! Why?"

"No, I . . . I tell the truth. The one with me planned to kill you like he did all the others. I killed no one."

Lou pushed down harder with his blade on Carlos's throat.

"Others?' Don't lie to me. There was no one else onboard but my wife and me. What 'others?'"

Carlos closed his eyes for a moment. "I speak of the others. The ones on other boats. He killed them all."

Lou paused and reflected on what he was hearing. "What other boats?"

Carlos' voice was just a whisper now. "The other ones we took."

"What happened to Nisbett?"

Carlos frowned. "I do not know this man."

"The hell you don't! It was his boat you were on!"

Carlos inhaled. "He was killed. The other one killed him, too, just like he killed the others."

Lou began to frame the scenario Carlos was laying out. "So, you were in the business of hijacking boats and killing everybody on board."

Carlos was afraid to move, less the blade cut into his throat. He closed his eyes and breathed in. "*Si*, but I kill no one. I only killed the one I needed to kill."

Lou pushed down harder with the knife blade. "You just said you didn't kill anyone. Now you say you *did* kill someone. Which is it, Carlos? Which answer am I supposed to believe?"

"I only killed the one I wanted to kill. I did not kill the others."

Lou fired the next question. "Who did you want to kill?"

"I killed the one who took the life of my brother, the one who killed all the others, *El Carnicero*, the butcher. I was sick of him. He planned to kill you, too. But I liked your woman. She reminded me so much of a sister I loved but could not save. So I left you and her on the island. I did not want to see someone like my sister die again. He was not happy when I cheated him out of your deaths."

Lou still wasn't convinced he wasn't being lied to. His eyes wandered around the stateroom as he continued processing what he was hearing. Some of the pieces fit, but some of the puzzle was still missing.

Then he saw it.

The forward stateroom was originally designed to be the owner's suite. It was the only one with an adjoining head. When his eyes passed over the picture next to the doorway to the toilet area, he doubled back. He hadn't hung the talisman on the picture next to the exit door, he'd hung it next to the door going to the head. With Carlos still securely tied up, Lou got up, walked over to the picture frame, unhooked the talisman, and placed it around his neck.

Lou had become a good judge of character after years of running a remote hunting and fishing lodge. When his eyes returned to Carlos, he paused. "You don't strike me as a ringleader, Carlos. Who do you work for?"

When Carlos didn't respond, Lou poked him with the tip of his knife.

"I am a slave to the cartels, they control everything."

Just then Jake appeared at the door and spotted the talisman around Lou's neck. Then he listened as Lou relayed everything he'd been told.,

"Whaddya think?"

"There's no way of telling if what he's saying is the truth."

"We're not out of this yet," Jake said, "but maybe we've got some answers. You've got the talisman; we should leave now. Somebody else just came out of the bunkhouse. The longer we stay, the greater the risk the natives are gonna get restless."

"Only one came out?"

"Yeah, it looked like he was headed to the outhouse. If he wonders where the guards are and goes looking, we're gonna be in one hell of a firefight." Jake looked down at the wounds on the man lying on the bunk. "You've got the talisman, and he told you why he left you on the island. but I'd like to get out of here before somebody starts shooting at me, again."

Lou stared at the man on the bunk, and touched the talisman, thinking about this man who had left him and Kate on the beach to die.

Maybe his intentions were honorable. Do I need to kill him? I have the talisman. As his warrior spirit inside weighed whether he should take the man's life, memories of the carnage he had witnessed during the Afghan war entered his thoughts.

Finally, he said, "Open your mouth, this is not your day to die!" Lou stuffed a facecloth inside Carlos' mouth. "Don't yell out, or we'll say you played along."

After saluting Carlos, Lou and Jake hurried down the hall. Jake was in the lead. When he reached the gangway, he stopped short and hunkered down.

"Whassup?" Lou whispered.

"The guy who just went to the john is walking around the dock."

"Follow me. We'll go over the stern and swim to the boat. No sense attracting unnecessary attention." Those words were no sooner said than the man roaming the dock discovered the first dead guard and ran toward the bunkhouse.

"*Despierta rápido!* Quick, wake up!"

By the time a horde of men came streaming out of the bunkhouse, Lou and Jake had already reached the rubber boat and had traveled underneath the dock guiding it hand over hand until they emerged just beyond the stern of the *Marlin Sea*.

When floodlights lit up the cove, they used their paddles to stay within the shadow created by the outline of the yacht, as they battled the incoming tides, completely unseen.

Once Lou felt they had traveled far enough, he stowed his paddle, flipped open the cover plate to the ignition switch and turned the key. When the outboard didn't kick in, he turned the key a second time, then a third. After the fifth time, he knew they had a problem.

34

The motor wasn't kicking in on the huge 150hp Mercury outboard as Lou bent over it. "Need a little help there, cuz?" Jake asked.

"Hope it's just a bad contact," Lou whispered.

He checked the bulb on the fuel line. It was full. Then he pressed the side start button one more time. Finally, a plume of smoke rose into the air. Lou wasted no time burying the throttle full forward on the console knowing the sound of the engine would travel across the water.

Shouts from the dock faded into the background as the sturdy rubber inflatable came up on plane and raced out of the cove. Even if those on shore attempted a pursuit, Lou had a head start, his running lights were extinguished, and the moon had conveniently passed behind a cloud. The inflatable was light enough that with a 150hp kicker, Lou could stay ahead of anything in the cove that might give chase.

But what he couldn't outrun was a phone call.

Bad news travels fast and the man in the white linen suit wasn't too happy when his cell phone rang around four a.m.

The last thing The Chameleon ever wanted was for the cove, or his pirating scheme, to attract even the slightest notoriety. From the beginning, he had deliberately put a plan in place to dissuade tourists and divers from venturing to Bimini:

He was the one who had concocted and spread rumors of toxicity in the waters surrounding the island and who spread cartel money around the island which compromised every official, including the chamber of commerce.

He bribed the general manager at the airport to jack up gate fees to the point that commercial airlines no longer flew to the island.

He lobbied for excessive port fees that caused cruise ships to bypass the island. He planted stories that The Bimini Road was now off limits to divers due to ecological reasons.

He even went so far as to divert attention from Bimini by sending out anonymous letters about an ancient civilization being found elsewhere to unsuspecting high-profile oceanographers.

So early that morning, when word reached The Chameleon saying security at North Cat Cay had been breached, he acted quickly. Cartel goons went out from South Bimini with instructions to patrol the waters and sink any small craft coming north.

AS THE BOAT raced toward South Bimini, so did Lou's thoughts. He knew he couldn't outrun a marine radio or a phone call.

Chances are we're going to run into a reception committee.

When the lights on the small island just before South Bimini came into view, he turned the inflatable Zodiac toward shore and smiled.

There's gotta be someone who will gladly take this boat off my hands in exchange for a lift over to Nixon's Harbor.

Lou had a little difficulty convincing the first fisherman he met that he was willing to trade this great inflatable simply for a ride over to South Bimini. However, an hour after sunrise, the two cousins stood shoulder to shoulder on the starboard side of a local fishing trawler as it slowly made its way into Nixon's Harbor. They watched as a number of high-speed boats raced about, seemingly on patrol.

"Looks like we made the right decision changing boats, Lou."

As Lou reached up to touch the talisman around his neck, he nodded. "We still need to get off this next island and find our way back to where we belong."

As the trawler pulled into port, two more high-speed pencil boats left the harbor, their occupants armed with AK-47s.

"Looks like we may have poked a hornet's nest, Jake."

"Yeah, we oughta keep that in mind when we're over at the airport."

The trawler barely came to a stop when Lou and Jake leaped onto the pier and melted into the shadows. Once they reached the shore road directly behind the buildings, they stopped and hunkered down among the trash barrels. Jake took out his cell phone and clicked on an app.

"Let's see if we can raise an Uber this early in the day."

Cell coverage was generally spotty in the Caribbean, but the call went through, and within ten minutes they were on their way to the airport, in a faded blue slant six, Dodge Dart.

AFTER THE CHAMELEON had introduced Carlos to the man who would replace Sanchez, he had left North Cat Cay and spent the night in an upscale guest house on South Bimini. When word of the security breach at the cove reached him, he made two calls. The first call set the patrol boats in motion; the second was additional insurance that whoever penetrated his web would not escape.

When the cell phone belonging to the pilot who flew The Chameleon to Bimini first rang, he thought it was a dream.

After fumbling around in the dark to find his phone, the pilot managed to press the right button.

"Hello?"

"Get dressed and get over to the airport."

The man looked at the time on his phone, yawned, and ran his free hand across his eyes. "I thought you said you wanted to leave at nine?"

"There's been a change. I suspect another one of your rental planes is sitting at the airport. Keep an eye on it. Contact me immediately. if anyone goes near it."

At that point, the pilot shook his head, almost fully awake. "You want me to go over there now?"

"Yes, and if the guy you rented a plane to shows up, call me immediately."

With that, the call ended, and the pilot reached over to turn on the lamp on the nightstand. Cartel money definitely talked, no matter what time, day or night.

As the Uber pulled up to the airport, Lou looked at this cousin. "This place looks a little sleepy. Do we need to refuel?"

"Nah, we have enough to fly to Nassau. Miami might even be closer."

"You got much juice left in that phone of yours?"

"Some, yeah."

"I need to text Kate; let her know we're on our way."

"Include Koby on it. She'll wanna know."

After Lou sent the texts, he sent another one, this time to the coast guard in Barbados.

Jake was walking around the Beechcraft, preforming a preflight inspection, when a voice broke the silence from behind.

"Whatcha planning of doing there, fella?"

Jake hadn't noticed anyone else on the tarmac and was surprised by two things: first, that he wasn't alone; and secondly, someone was questioning him. He shrugged it off and replied, "Just getting ready to take off."

"Nope, I don't think that's going to happen. Not yet anyway."

As Jake turned around, he looked directly into the business end of a handgun. *This shit is really getting old,* he thought. A second later, he recognized the face of the man holding the pistol.

"Whoa, put that thing away. Nobody's trying to steal anything. I'm the guy that rented this bird, remember?"

A sly smile came to the man's face. "I do. Like I said, you're not going anywhere."

The man with the pistol was standing just far enough away that Jake knew he'd catch a bullet, if he tried to rush him. When he saw Lou emerging from the hangar, he immediately threw his hands high in the air, saying loudly, "Okay you got me. Just be careful with that thing!"

Jake's actions confused the man with the pistol. His mistake was dismissing it. "That's better. Now nice and easy, let me see you spread eagle on the ground."

Jake took his sweet time going down, stopping on one knee, buying time for Lou who was slowly working his way closer.

"Come on, let's go. Spread eagle, on the ground."

Jake made a big deal out of taking a deep breath and rolling his eyes. "This is crazy. I hope this isn't about my credit card. That's it, isn't it! That's gotta be it. It's that damn friggin' credit card!" Jake kept the man's attention on himself.

"Shut up and get down, asshole!"

Lou was about six feet behind the man with the pistol when Jake dropped to the tarmac. Lou sprang forward like he'd been shot out of a cannon, deliberately slamming into the man's lower back and right elbow. The impact knocked the man's elbow forward and the weapon fired harmlessly into the air.

In a heartbeat, Lou had his opponent on the ground, and his knife sticking a quarter inch into the man's neck. "Drop it, now, or you bleed out where you are." Lou had had enough adventure for one trip.

The man opened his fingers and released the weapon.

"Okay, now push it away, real gently." As soon as he did, Jake was on his feet and kicked the gun a little further away before picking it up.

"Who sent you?"

"I don't know his name, he's . . . he's with the cartels. Honest, that's all I know."

"Jake, get some wire. This guy's coming with us.

When the cartel's patrol boats failed to stop any suspicious boat that morning and the pilot wasn't responding to his phone calls, The Chameleon sent people over to the airport to check on things. It wasn't long before he heard that a small plane had taken off earlier, destination unknown.

The Chameleon smelled a rat, knowing his whole scheme

was suddenly at risk. The next call he made was to the cove on North Cat Cay.

"Move the *Marlin Sea*. Get her out of the cove, now!"

"She's not ready. We need a few days to prepare her."

"I said move her *now*."

There was a pause on the line. "Where would you like us to take her?"

"It doesn't matter, Miami, Fort Lauderdale, Havana, just get her out of the cove."

Before Jake took off, he walked over to a Cessna with pontoons affixed to the landing gear. When he reached the plane, he opened the door on the pilot's side and took out a blank flight plan and wrote "San Juan" as the destination airport and "Bimini" as the departure airport.

Next, he looked at his cell phone and wrote in the current date and time, then filled in the aircraft's registration number from the markings on the tail. He wrote the number "two" in the passenger field. Then he looked at the license he'd taken from the pilot's wallet and filled in the space reserved for the pilot's identity.

Finally, he drew a huge letter X on the form. Next, he separated the original from the duplicate and left the duplicate on the seat.

As soon as he returned to the Beechcraft he had rented, he started the engines, taxied over to the runway, and waited for tower clearance.

Although the coast guard on the island of Barbados no longer had an active search and rescue operation for the *Marlin Sea*, they issued an advisory that the boat had been seen in

Bimini. Among those monitoring the airwaves were MI6, Tom Mullin's wife, Kathie, and of course Inigo Montez, otherwise known as The Chameleon.

When Tom received a message from his wife that the *Marlin Sea* had been seen in Bimini, he called Nisbett's two former crew members into his office. "I just received word, Nisbett's boat is up in Bimini. So, here's the deal: you can go back on board if he ever gets here, or you can stay on with me, your choice."

The men looked at each other. Miguel was certain he had seen the *Marlin Sea* in San Juan harbor just weeks ago. The men were loyal to Nisbett, but loyalty was a two-way street. There had been no word from Nisbett in over a month and Mullin had been treating them well. Miguel nodded to the former first mate, who returned the nod.

"We work for you now. You good boss, mon."

With that settled, Tom gave the two men a thumbs up and went back to what he was doing. *Jim, you're a damn fool to give these two up. Either that, or you're in a watery grave somewhere. I hope it's not the latter,* he thought. *But either way, I guess they're staying with me.*

The next thing Tom Mullin did, was walk over to the coast guard station at San Juan Harbor and ask if there was any further word on the *Marlin Sea.*

When Jake set the Beechcraft down in San Juan, he taxied over to a tie-down area for transients. While they were taxiing, Lou moved from the co-pilot seat to the passenger section where he had tossed their captive.

"Hey, I've got something I'd like to show you."

With that, he unfolded a copy of the fake flight plan Jake had filled out. "We left the original in the plane you flew to Bimini. What do you think might happen when the cartels find this?"

The pilot's eyes scanned the document and were suddenly ablaze with anger. He knew exactly what would happen. The man in the white linen suit took no prisoners and would come for him. The man twisted his body as he struggled to free himself from his bonds.

Lou patted him on the shoulder. "Yeah, I know. I know what you're thinking. You're being set up. You and I both know you didn't pull a double cross, but how are they gonna see this?"

Again, the man struggled to free himself.

"You might want to think about creating a new life." As Lou leaned forward to duct tape the document to the man's chest he said, "We're gonna leave you right here where you are. I'll leave this bottle of water next to you. That way, when they come to collect the tie-down fee and find you, you can have a drink. Oh, and we'll leave the keys in the ignition. You can fly home and face the music, or you can say the right things to the DEA agents and maybe qualify for their witness protection program. It'll be your call."

After wiping their fingerprints from the inside of the plane, the two cousins passed through U.S. Customs with the passport MI6 had provided Lou and headed over to an annex the British Consulate General maintained in Puerto Rico.

As they walked, Jake looked at his cousin. "You sure know how to show a fella a good time, Lou."

35

When the United Kingdom's diplomatic representative learned that two Canadian citizens wanted to meet with her, she told her aide to refer them to the Canadian consul in San Juan. In short order, the aide returned to her superior's office.

"Ma'am, the Canadians are insisting upon seeing you. They're not ordinary tourists, by the way, they are members of the Royal Canadian Mounted Police."

"Is this an official matter?"

"I'm not certain, ma'am."

The diplomatic representative leaned back in her chair, looked up at the ceiling and thought for a moment. "All right, I'll allow it. Show them in."

"Thank you, ma'am."

WHEN LOU and Jake entered the representative's office, she came around from her desk with an outstretched hand. "Good day, gentlemen, it's not often I have the pleasure of meeting with fellow members of the commonwealth." Pointing to an arrangement of chairs near a window, she said, "Please, have a seat."

As soon as they were seated, the Crown's representative wasted no time with pleasantries. "My assistant said you were rather insistent upon seeing me. What's the purpose of your visit?"

Lou was just as succinct. "We have information that is of interest to MI6."

"I see. Now, if I may I be so bold, share just a tad more about the matter."

Lou looked at his cousin before speaking. "Ma'am, your government is currently conducting a clandestine operation in the Caribbean. We have information that will help them."

"I see, and you'd like me to connect you with MI6, is that it?"

"Precisely."

"Before I do that, would you tell me how it is that the Royal Canadian Mounted Police and MI6, both distinguished agencies, lack an official communication channel for such matters of importance?"

"Look, here's the deal: we're not officially representing Canada," Lou said. "We came to the Caribbean on our own and fell victim to the same people who stole a couple of boats belonging to your monarchy and who killed a couple of MI6 operatives along with their families." Lou's boldness captured the representative's attention.

"You're sure of that?"

"Positive. We believe we may have uncovered the backbone of their operation."

The representative took in a deep breath, stood up, returned to her desk, and picked up her phone. "Margret, please tell Cedric to come into my office."

As the representative walked back to the sitting area, she cleared her throat. "The person you wish to speak with will be with us shortly. He's part of MI6."

WHEN CEDRIC POTTER ARRIVED, Lou and Jake left nothing out when they relayed all they had pieced together from Carlos' words and their own personal experience.

"If what you say is true, you may have just given us the bloody map we needed."

"If you move quickly," Jake added, "you'll find a guy who may be able to tell you a lot more to save his own skin."

"Not that we won't corroborate your story ourselves, but who and where?"

Lou removed a driver's license from his pocket. "Here's his information. He's in the back seat of a Cessna over at the public tie down area at your airport. I doubt he's spoken to anyone about this since we left him a little earlier."

After several more questions, Cedric stood up. "Gentlemen, I'm not quite sure how to put this, other than to simply say, his majesty's service is deeply indebted to you."

As Cedric handed Lou one of his business cards, he added, "We should be able to take it from here, chaps."

AS SOON AS they stepped outside the consul's office, Jake elbowed his cousin. "We could hang around and watch this thing go down. You know none of this will make the evening news."

Lou had a faraway look in his eyes. After a few minutes he

said, "Nah, we have the talisman. I've got a whole season to start getting ready for. I would just as soon get over to the airport, get something to eat, and head home. Like Kate, I miss the twins."

Jake shrugged his shoulders, "I'm okay with that. Just remind me to stop at the duty-free store."

"I'm not sure the wives are looking for any mementos from this trip, Jake, but we should pick up some Cuban cigars for Angelo."

"He did mention that."

THERE WERE ONLY a few cars on the road heading over to the airport, but the situation inside the airport was completely opposite. People were backed up wall-to-wall, luggage strewn everywhere. Lou took one look and said, "Whoa, is it spring break already?"

Jake looked at the crowd. "Lou, I don't think these are the people who go on spring break. Something else is going on."

A crowd had gathered around one of the large flight information screens, their eyes glued to the monitor.

"Come on, let's go see what's going on."

Even from a distance, they could see the disgusted looks on people's faces. Every flight on the screen with a destination north of the Mason Dixon Line was either delayed or cancelled.

"Jake, pull up a weather app and see what's going on."

"Already on it . . . looks like there's a huge system hanging over most of the Midwest and Northeast. I don't think we're going anywhere soon."

"Give Travel by Tatten a call. Maybe Linda can get us home."

THIRTY MINUTES LATER, Jake got off the phone with the travel agent they always used. "Okay, here's the deal. This is a slow-moving storm; the commercial flights are all grounded."

"Can't they fly above it?"

"Nah, this one's way too big. Linda said there's a couple of seats on a private charter going to Quebec City. Other than that, we're gonna be here for a while."

Lou tilted his head back and looked up at the ceiling. Finally, he said aloud, "How much?"

"About five times what it would cost us to fly commercial."

"Each?"

"Yeah, Gulfstreams are expensive, remember?"

"And that plane can fly above it?"

"Hell no, they'll go around it."

"Lou thought for a moment. "Does it leave from here?"

"Yeah, within the hour."

"Frig it, I've been through enough. Tell Linda to book it. I just want to get the hell home and see my kids."

Forty-five minutes later, Lou and Jake were sitting opposite one another as the Gulfstream jet lifted off the runway, finally on their way home.

AS WINTER slowly began to release its hold on central New Brunswick, life for the year-round residents at the sporting lodge known as Havre de Poisson returned to normal. Kate had stepped back into her dual role as mother and leader of the Mounties Major Crime Unit. Koby returned to her dual routine as a working mom and staffing the clinic twice a week at the Village of Grey Elk. Jake was back flying the mail plane five days a week, and Lou was busy preparing for the upcoming fishing season.

In the evenings, Jake and Lou walked over to Chef Angelo's cottage and all three men enjoyed a Cuban cigar along with a glass of bourbon, while spinning yarns beside an open hearth.

Throughout the following spring and summer, Koby stayed in close contact with Dan Shively. As fall approached, they worked out details and reached an agreement on what it would take for her to come on board and be part of his exploration dive team.

BY LATE NOVEMBER, Shively's research vessel, the *Magnavox II*, was anchored off the coast of a small, volcanic island located in the Lesser Antilles. Shively's discovery had attracted worldwide attention. Archaeologists, oceanographers, treasure hunters, and the media were all waiting anxiously for him to start.

Many believed Shively had purposefully delayed his search until the hurricane season had passed. However, weather conditions had nothing to do with it. The delay was due to lawyers.

In the Caribbean, property rights to a sunken ship typically belong to the country whose territorial waters the ship was discovered in. Lawyers representing Bion, and the other descendants of the culture known as Ancient Ones, successfully argued before the Caribbean Court of Justice that the sunken city should be treated like a shipwreck. The court had finally agreed that ownership of the site be granted to Bion and his people.

To maintain the delicate balance of the ecosystem and preserve the underwater city, Bion's lawyers insisted upon stringent environmental impact clauses. It wasn't until lawyers on both sides agreed to those conditions that Dan Shively was able to give his team the green light.

Once Shively cleared the legal hurdles, he had another problem, namely logistics. The *Magnavox II* wasn't large enough to accommodate the complement of personnel and equipment needed to explore the site. Shively needed a land base. He then had no choice but to enter negotiations with Bion to establish a site on the sacred island.

Bion was shrewd and Shively ended up agreeing to create two villages and an elaborate wharf on the island. One village would house Shively's people, the second would provide permanent housing for Bion's people. Fortunately for Shively, National Geographic agreed to underwrite the entire cost of the construction, in exchange for exclusive coverage of the expedition.

As soon as the exploration began, artifacts from the city beneath the water were continuously brought to the surface and unloaded onto the deck of Shively's ship. After photographing and cataloging each item, Shively's team carefully packed them and sent them off to waiting curators.

SLEEPING accommodations aboard the *Magnavox II* were limited. However, as a personal favor to Koby Callahan, Dan Shively agreed to provide onboard lodging for her and three other Canadians. Koby's reason for being aboard was straight forward, she would lead the dive teams. Two of the other Canadians were her guests. The third Canadian tagged along merely because spending a little down time with his wife trumped delivering mail.

As Lou stretched out on the aft deck of the *Magnavox II*, soaking up the rays, Kate sat up and looked over at the island off which their ship was anchored.

"I still can't believe I actually agreed to come back down here."

"Kate, I don't think we had a choice once the twins found out they had a chance to see the island where we were marooned. Especially after Bion wrote us that the twins were welcome to stay with him in the village of the Ancient Ones."

"I just wish that whole vacation had turned out differently."

Lou smiled. "Be careful what you wish for Kate."

She ignored the platitude. As she stared at the inactive volcano pushing up from the lush tropical rain forest, her thoughts drifted.

Maybe someday, someone will write a book about our little adventure.

"Lou," she called to him, "Do you remember that Floridian who came up to fish last season? He writes books."

"McKeon?"

"That's him. We should call him," Kate said.

"What? So he can write about 'The Gaults Go On Vacation?'"

"No, the title should be 'Curse of the Caribbean.'"

Epilogue

Kate O'Grady-Gault arrived home without incident. After being reunited with her twins, she resumed her blended role of mother, wife, and head of the New Brunswick Major Crime Unit for the Royal Canadian Mounted Police.

Koby Callahan-Gault returned home and after reuniting with their young daughter, resumed her duties staffing the clinic in the Village of Grey Elk and serving on the New Brunswick Wetlands Protection Board. Throughout the summer she and Dan Shively discussed the terms and conditions necessary for her to be a part of his team.

Lou Gault returned to central New Brunswick with the scared talisman once again adorning his neck. Within a matter of days, he began preparations for the start of another season at the sportsman's lodge known as Havre de Poisson. Midway through the season, a letter with a return address of Number 10 Downing Street, London, arrived. Inside was a personal letter of appreciation along with an embossed open invitation to attend "high tea" with the Prime Minister of England.

Jake Gault traveled home with his cousin and two boxes of fine hand-rolled Cuban cigars. Two days after his return, he resumed his job with Canada Post, flying the mail plane. Jake received an identical letter from the Prime Minister.

Tom Mullin arranged for a Celebration of Life on the island of Josh van Dyke for his childhood friend, Jim Nisbett. Mullin's Dock continued to thrive, due in part to Nisbett's two former crew members, both of whom continue to work for Mullin.

Dan Shively spent the better part of ten months aboard Magnavox *II* exploring the underwater city. To date, the artifacts brought to the surface exceed the wealth Mel Fischer recovered from the Atocha, a Spanish galleon that sank in 1622 AD, by tenfold. The most intriguing discovery to date was an item made from a substance which metallurgists have yet been able to match to any properties on the periodic table of elements.

Bion and the remaining descendants of the ancient ones have all taken up permanent residence on the sacred island. Bion continues to serve as an advisor for the museum curators handling the artifacts Shively's team continue to bring to the surface.

Carlos Morales had no further interest in pirating after he avenged the death of his brother. At his request to the cartels, he was assigned to smuggling illegals across the Mexican border into the United States. Carlos had always been a planner. The funds in the account he had with the Central Bank of Mexico were transferred to the Bank of America shortly after he arrived in Mexico. His exact whereabouts are currently unknown.

The Chameleon - Once Inigo Montez knew his cover had been blown, he fled the island of Barbados. Authorities believe he is living somewhere in Honduras. Although his influence within the cartels has lessened, he still wears his hallmark white linen suit.

The *Marlin Sea* was scuttled in an attempt to avoid detection and rests on the seabed a few miles off the coast of Bimini. Seaworms and other marine life have already claimed ownership to the once pristine luxury yacht.

The pilot Lou and Jake left in San Juan's airport, bound hand, and foot, sang like a canary when the DEA authorities questioned him. In exchange for his agreement to testify against the cartels, they placed him in the witness protection program. Unfortunately, he died from stab wounds before he could testify.

The Lost City - In 2001, a symmetrical complex was actually discovered off the west coast of Cuba. The submerged site has all the markings of an urban center built over 6,000 years ago. The structures are located on a plateau which appear to be the bottom of a mud volcano, 700 meters beneath the ocean's surface. The megaliths are similar to those found at Stonehenge and Easter Island. Real evidence of advanced ancient cultures exists in the Caribbean and Central and South America.

In addition, ancient writings such as the *Drawn Stone of Inga* in Paraiba, Brazil, provide testimony of advanced cultures. The complexity of the stone has fostered various theories of hidden treasures and the possibility of extra-terrestrial beings.

This author took advantage of narrative license and transported the location of this actual, true site from Cuba to the Lesser Antilles for the purpose of this storyline.

Books by Dave McKeon

THE LOU GAULT THRILLER SERIES

Relentless Pursuit

War Chief

Howl of the Banshee

Sabotage

Curse of the Caribbean

Coming soon:

Eyes of the Assassin

SNEAK PEEK

EYES OF THE ASSASSIN

BOOK 6
IN THE
LOU GAULT THRILLER SERIES

COMING SOON

Chapter 1 - Washington, D.C.

A bdul Karim stood inches from the window, the rifle butt tight up against his shoulder. It was a 52mm Carcano Model 38 long-barrel, identical to the weapon Lee Harvey Oswald used to kill President John F. Kennedy, back in 1963.

The assassin usually preferred to work with a blade, but he had done his homework. Already in town for weeks, he had studied the man the Hashshashins had sent him to kill. He had taken his time and carefully selected the kill zone. He had practiced with the chosen weapon in fields behind the safehouse across the river in Virginia. He had used a different alias when registering at the hotel two days earlier and had willingly paid the ridiculous upcharge for a fifth-floor room facing the open plaza. Once he checked in, a "Do Not Disturb" sign permanently adorned the door of his room. He needed privacy while using a glass cutter to remove a large section of plate glass from the window.

When Trey Baldridge entered the plaza that day, he came

from the direction he always did, and Abdul Karim was not only ready . . . he was waiting.

The hollow point round burst from the muzzle and sped toward the newly-appointed U.S. Attorney General with a velocity exceeding a thousand feet per second.

Baldridge should have died that day, except for three things: the angle Abdul had was extreme; the shooter failed to sufficiently allow for the weapon's tendency to pull slightly to the left; and at the last minute, Baldridge swerved to avoid two oncoming joggers.

In a flash, the left shoulder of one jogger, and the left wrist of the other, disappeared in a cloud of blood and bone fragments.

Baldridge recognized the popping sound for what it was and instinctively dropped to the ground. A combat war veteran, he had been in many fire fights. Somewhere in his basement, in a forgotten box among the rubble, was a Purple Heart, adorned with four Oak Leaf Clusters.

Swiftly, the assassin chambered another bullet, moved closer to the window for a better angle, pressed his cheek against the stock, and squeezed off a second round. This time, the missile imbedded itself into porous cement inches from Baldridge's chest as he lay on the ground, sending a cloud of chalky debris into the air.

The plaza became deathly quiet. Baldridge and a few others were all lying face down and exposed without cover. Then he heard someone talking.

Was that a prayer? he thought. *It didn't sound like a prayer, but maybe it was.* He heard the word "Jesus" twice, but also heard the F-word and his thoughts raced.

He won't miss a third time.

Then Baldridge took what might have been his last breath and clenched his fists.

Come on, shoot, damn it! Get this over with!

Seconds passed. Except for the sound of a few sirens fading off in the distance, the plaza was completely still. Baldridge lay on the cold cement listening to his inner critic.

Okay, Trey, get your thoughts together. How do we play this one? Do you move, or do you just play dead and hope for the best? It's up to you. He's up there, high up; you know he's gotta have a scope, but you can do it.

More seconds passed.

Come on, shoot! Get this over with!

FIVE STORIES ABOVE, Abdul Karim stared at his weapon. He had never fired a Model 38 Carcano before arriving in the States. It was an older weapon, acquired illegally and untraceable. He had familiarized himself with the weapon, but wasn't used to a bolt action mechanism. In his haste to chamber a third round, the weapon had jammed.

Suddenly there was a knock on his hotel door. The chambermaid working the fifth floor had been in the room directly next to Abdul when both shots were fired and had heard the noise. She had come to investigate.

"Housekeeping," she called out and knocked lightly on the door.

The knock startled Abdul Karim. Instantly, he turned away from the window and stared at his only exit.

Why are they here? I told them . . . I told them I do not want housekeeping!

MARIA WAITED a moment before she knocked again. With the

second knock, she spoke a little louder. "Housekeeping . . . hello? Are you there?"

As she waited in the hallway, Maria's thoughts flashed back to the previous week. Her friend, a maid on the tenth floor, had used her pass key to enter a room with a "Do Not Disturb" sign on the door.

It's a good thing she went in, Maria thought, *the guest was unresponsive and lying in bed. My friend dialed 911 and the EMT's arrived in minutes. I wonder if she's heard yet what happened to the guest?*

Hotel policy was vague, maids were discouraged from entering any room displaying a Do Not Disturb sign, but they weren't prohibited. The handbook merely said they should knock first and advise management, if they entered any room with a sign on the door.

Maria glanced at her trolly only one room away where her cell phone lay on top of a stack of towels, and hesitated. Pockets in the uniforms of hotel housekeepers were shallow. Maria had gotten into the habit of leaving her cell phone on her trolly after she had picked it up off the floor enough times.

Maria knocked a third time, "Housekeeping, are you there?"

As she waited for a response, her eyes glanced over at her trolly. *Do I call down first to let them know?*

It was close to her break time. She closed her eyes, took a breath, and decided she would ask for forgiveness instead of permission should anyone complain or question her. So, she reached into her pocket for her passkey to enter room 512.

As soon as she held her key against the lock, two small green lights appeared, and she opened the door. Even though it was mid-morning, the room was dark.

The curtain is drawn, she thought. *They must not be awake yet. But how could they have slept through the noise I just heard?* As she made the sign of the cross, she whispered, *Jesus, Mary, and Joseph, please do not let me find any dead people!*

AFTER MARIA'S second knock on the door, Abdul had cleared the rifle jam and turned back toward the window intending to fire the killing shot. However, raising his rifle and looking down, he saw people talking on their phones and pointing up at him. His eyes scanned the plaza for Baldridge. But he was gone.

With Maria's third knock, Abdul had dropped his rifle and drawn the curtain over the opening in the window glass. Next, he walked over to the entryway, silently unhooked the security chain, and pressed his back against the wall.

The moment Maria entered the room, she tried leaving the door open, but somehow, the door closed. She tried turning, but something tugged at her hair and pulled her head back. She never felt the blade that came across the soft flesh of her neck. In a matter of seconds, she was bleeding out.

Abdul dragged the dying woman into a closet off the vestibule and walked over to the bathroom. He needed to wash the blood from his hands and the knife. When he saw his reflection in the mirror, the amount of blood on his shirt surprised him. This was supposed to be a clean kill. Now time was running out and he was losing patience. He cupped his hands and splashed water on his shirt, hoping at least to dilute the blood. But when he heard the sound of approaching sirens, he left everything and ran down the hallway, his wet shirt still clinging against his skin.

Slamming his body against the crash bar on the door leading to the stairway, his footsteps echoed as he hurried down the stairs, taking two at a time. Just last night, Abdul had practiced taking these stairs and exiting through the kitchen into the parking lot. This time, when he reached the ground floor, he bolted into the kitchen and grabbed a white apron before walking through. He was a mere thirty feet into the room when someone tapped him on the shoulder.

"Hey, you . . . don't go nowhere, I need you to put this stuff inside the cooler."

Abdul ignored the order and mumbled, "I'm on break."

"Hey, come back here!"

Abdul flipped the man off just before exiting the rear door.

ONCE OUTSIDE, he scanned the parking lot. To the right, someone just closed the side door of a panel truck and was walking around to the driver's side. Abdul moved fast and opened the passenger door as the driver slid behind the wheel.

"Hey whaddya think yer doing? Get the hell outta here, I ain't running no friggin' taxi."

Abdul responded quickly, "I only gotta go two blocks. My momma's sick."

"Out!" the driver motioned with his thumb. "Ain't nobody allowed in here, but me. So, get yer dumb ass outta here!"

Patting his pocket, Abdul continued with the ruse. "Come on man, I gotta get this medicine to her. I only got a short break. Help me out, will ya?"

THE DRIVER WAS NOT TOTALLY surprised. People had tried hitching a ride with him inside the beltway before. Giving Abdul the once over, his first thought was: *He's an Arab. Do I wanna take a chance? What the hell, he's clean shaven; he's wearing an apron, he obviously works here.*

After staring at Abdul, the driver finally said, "All right, ya found yourself a good Samaritan. Which way?"

Abdul anxiously checked the side view mirror. "Left. I need to go left."

TWO HOURS LATER, Abdul pulled out of a rest area just north of Baltimore. He had switched license plates with another white van and dragged the lifeless body of the good Samaritan into the nearby woods. Now, he would use the van to reach a safe house in Maine. As he drove along the interstate, he wondered what would happen next.

How long before they send another to do what I have failed to do? Who will it be? Maybe Jamal? They favor Jamal. His eyes tell him things no one else can see.

The more he thought about it, the more he was certain Jamal would be the one sent. But heaviest on his mind was whether Azra'il, the Angel of Death, would be sent . . . for him.

Chapter 2 - Trey Baldridge

When news of the attempt on Baldridge's life reached the oval office, the president immediately instructed the Secret Service to add his attorney general to the list of those they needed to protect.

In addition to being a philosophical misfit in a city of politicians, Baldridge was a country boy who detested city life. A real loner, there had never been anyone else in his life, and he had always been free to do whatever he wanted. Three times a year he disappeared into the wilds of New Brunswick, Canada, to commune with nature and do a little fishing.

Now, after stewing over the president's insistence that he be provided Secret Service protection, Trey Baldridge called his Commander and Chief.

"Office of the President," a man answered. "How may I direct your call?"

Baldridge recognized the voice on the other end of the line. "Harold, put me through to him."

"Who is this, please?"

"It's your damn Attorney General! Now cut the BS and put me through to him!"

Moments later, the president picked up the phone. "What's up, Trey?"

"Tell that damn secret service director of yours to keep his idiots away from me."

"Trey, I don't want anything to happen to you. Just go along with it."

With that, the line went dead.

TREY BALDRIDGE HAD BEEN in Washington for years but still had no friends. He had a style that alienated people, and his views were too controversial. He looked at life through a lens most did not. Besides being agnostic, he was a stubborn Connecticut Yankee. Throughout his life, all his beliefs and actions had been based purely on whether there was scientific evidence . . . and whether it could be proven. If logic or science could not confirm a point of view, it was false as far as he was concerned, and he refused to accept it, whatever it was.

Because of his dystopian views, many thought his political career would be short lived. However, through a quirk of fate, he ended up as ranking member of the powerful Senate Appropriations Committee.

Baldridge ruled with an iron fist. Nothing left his committee unless he was in favor of it. Also, it was well known that he vehemently railed against liberal ideas, and he abhorred socialism. Trey Baldridge was a firm believer that one lived one's life according to the cards dealt.

Not one piece of legislation containing even the slightest hint of fostering a nanny state, or contributing to a utopian society, ever left his committee. He expected people to stand on their own two feet, face problems of the world on their own, and accept their fate. That philosophy framed the way he had chaired the Senate Appropriations Committee for the past six years. Not a single bill contrary to his beliefs, had ever come to a vote on the senate floor.

Baldridge's myopic views even alienated the colleagues in his own party. They often verbally assaulted him and gave him the finger during meetings. Voters in both political parties came together to demonstrate against him. His tires had been slashed, his car antennas snapped off, his house egged, and he had received countless threatening letters. Yet, despite it all, he had never been physically accosted.

Nor did Baldridge share the same concern for his own life as the president did. He was an independent cuss and even lobbyists had been unable to reel him in. He saw the Secret Service and media as intrusions on the independent life he wanted to live.

The first time a secret service agent arrived at Baldridge's door intending to travel with him, he made it abundantly clear he had no intention of traveling with any extra baggage. Only after a series of back-and-forth arguments, did Baldridge and the director of the Secret Service settle on an approach. They agreed to limit Baldridge's protection to those times when the attorney general was physically in Washington, D.C.

Unlike the president and the vice president, Baldridge had a legal right to refuse Secret Service protection. Having worn down his adversary and forced a compromise, Baldridge headed to Washington's airport intent upon traveling north to a remote, fly-in sportsman's lodge in New Brunswick, Canada, to do a little fishing. He was on his own again, just the way he liked it.

COMING SOON

EYES OF THE ASSASSIN

Book 6
in the
Lou Gault Thriller Series

Dave McKeon

Acknowledgments

A special thank you to my early readers: Alan Adler, Barry Colvin, Carl Johnson, Tom Mullin, Dan Shively and Kathy Zimmer. Your willingness to carve out time to review my early draft, and offer your unabashed critique, opened my eyes to what I was unable to see.

Again, a shout out to Paula Howard, my editor and publisher, who continues to put up with me. Paula, thank you for all you do. You are a joy to partner with.

Lastly, a tip of the hat to Bob Hurley, the talented graphic artist who turns my ideas into exciting covers.

About the Author

Dave McKeon is an award-winning author of short stories and creator of *The Lou Gault Thriller Series* of which the first book, *Relentless Pursuit,* became an Amazon Bestselling Action Thriller.

Dave's stories reflect his own diverse background, life experiences, sense of humor, and unquenchable love affair with the outdoors.

A native New Englander, he has hunted, fished, hiked, camped, skied, and traveled in the eastern United States and throughout New Brunswick and Quebec, Canada, his entire life. He has visited over sixty foreign countries and distant lands around the world.

A Vietnam-era veteran, Dave has formerly held both a Top-Secret Clearance and the Department of Energy's "Q" Clearance. His stories are influenced by his experiences working with the NSA, EPA, and Department of the Navy.

To Learn more about Dave McKeon
Visit www.avillagewriter.com